DIAMOND JO

DIAMOND JO

DAPHNE ROOKE

REYNAL & CO. New York, 1965

R

40278

DIAMOND JO

PART
1

1

I shall write two books. One, the memoirs of Sir Emmanuel Bernstein, is for my wife and all the world to read. This other is for myself alone, for Mannie Bernstein the kopje walloper who used to trudge from claim to claim buying diamonds; for an earlier Mannie who was a pedlar travelling to the diamond diggings of the Vaal.

March 1868 . . . It is easy to recall the goods in my pack . . . I have a note in my journal: trinkets, stuff for dresses, and blankets and the pair of cashmere stockings that had red roses on them. I can remember my little donkey Archibald who was light grey when we set out but slowly turned dun in colour as the dust settled into his hide; and the frail cart like a box on wheels that miraculously held together through the long journey. But what do I remember of Mannie the pedlar? In fact, what do I remember of youth?

There is Jo of course whom afterwards we called Diamond Jo. She is in the yellowing pages of the secret diary-ledger that I kept from 1868 onwards: To 1 Pair Printed Cashmere Stockings . . . To 1 Satin Pelisse . . . To I Diamond £300 (50 Carats Orange) . . . and later, in an entry made in Paris: To setting of 1 Diamond Pin 40 Matched Cape Whites in all 400 Carats £729 (Diamonds valued £1000) . . .

I was a millionaire then and she Madame Halden, tall and elegant in the rich clothes. She was not received in the best society or by respectable people, it is true; but she had a certain vogue for half a year or so among the sporting aristocracy and a few men of business. She was to be seen at the races and at casinos; the recklessness of her betting was a point for discussion. At a card table she was ready to match herself against any man: she would strip the rings off her fingers to cover a bet.

She favoured blue as a colour because she thought it lucky. Something to see was Jo in blue velvet with diamonds being touched off by her every move.

She had reddish hair but on her arms and legs, even on the insides of her thighs, there were white downy hairs.

2

I cannot always conjure up Jo's face and her shape but the essence of her remains with me . . . that vitality, a yeastiness that seemed impervious to disaster or age. She was like a field of lilies to run wild in.

I sit in this room with its Adam fireplace and silken Chinese carpets; a multi-millionaire. The room has a scent of roses, somewhere in the house a piano is being played. I sit here alone through the long English twilight for the family believes that I am studying. There are hundreds of books here and some are bound in fine leather with pages like satin and some are shabby but only because they are rare and old. I like to put my hands on my wealth, I like to compare these days with the days of my poverty.

Once all I possessed in the way of books were those given to me by Reb Gamsay for study; and a copy of Shakespeare traded to me by a farmer for six pairs of hose. I learned to recite sonnets as I walked beside my donkey over the monotonous plains beyond the Drakensberg . . . Shall I compare thee to a summer's day? was one I knew. I would want the words to roll out grandly but my voice was puny in that vast dome of light roofing the plain.

I have a title and honour, I am an honourable man, I am an honoured Jew. And sweet like a fragrance through my days is Leah my wife; and the three children. I have two sons and a daughter.

Why then must I sum up my life with what happened between Jo and me?

I have loved Leah. I love my daughter, in fear and wonder.

But Jo had the best of me.

3

I first saw her on the journey to the Drakensberg which we had to cross to make the Free State and the Vaal. She was with a troupe of performers rushing to the diamond diggings from Durban. They travelled in a waggonette drawn by two horses that had red, white and blue ribbons plaited into the manes: all the girls were dressed in gauzy stuff and wore veils that floated behind them as the horses dashed along.

Such an equipage could not last of course nor could the cattle stand up to the furious pace for long. A wheel came off and rolled down a krantz, the horses were so knocked up that they had to be left behind on a farm. The party separated. Two or three of the girls were given lifts by officers rushing to try their luck on the diggings while on furlough. Jo I saw holding on desperately to the back of a gig which was carrying as well four stalwart officers and the driver. The gig came to grief in the foothills of the Berg and thereafter I saw Jo riding in a post cart. She was a jolly girl. As they swept past me plodding next to Archibald, she blew a long blast on the horn.

By then we were in the light of the Free State plains. Fifty miles on, I came up with her: she was riding a dying mule.

"You can have a ride in my cart, miss," I said.

She got down from the mule at once.

"I was thinking of giving him a rest."

The mule stood with his nose almost touching the ground, his legs splayed. We watched him. The ribs, etched against his hide, worked in and out hard like bellows to keep him alive for a few minutes longer.

"Poor mule," said Jo and suddenly began to cry loudly, like a child would.

The mule fell. I put a bullet through his ear.

We went on. She would not get into the cart but strode along beside me. I was disappointed in her. For weeks I had noticed her from afar and she had seemed to be beautiful. But now I thought her plain. She had a big mouth and a nose that turned up. Her steps were light but like a man she wore a bowie knife in a sheath on her belt.

"Oh God, there was nothing for him in the end but a bullet," she said. "The vultures tear their eyes out. Poor mule . . . I didn't think he was so bad or I would have got down long before. Captain Halden gave him to me as a present while we were still in Natal. He was so fat and shiny. Animals die quickly here." She turned her head slowly and looked at the far encircling horizon. "I suppose people die quickly too. Some of the girls are frightened all the time . . . we have heard lions and we saw a hyena. It puts the girls off. But I am not afraid. Sometimes I feel that I could walk out among the animals, I trust them. It's on a moonlight night that the fancy takes me to go wandering among them." She turned her face towards me and that was the first time I saw the momentary blending of

13

flesh and spirit that I came to look for in her. I was her lover before I ever touched her.

She was wearing clumsy velschoens which she must have bought from some Boer cobbler on the way; the hem of her dress was in tatters and was stained with mud. Of all the finery in which I had first seen her decked out, she retained only a chiffon scarf, still pure white, floating out behind her. I touched it for its softness.

Jo swung round on me, with the bowie knife in her hand.

"None of that, Ikey Mo," she said. "I'll stick you like a pig if you put a hand on me."

"You can't stick me like a pig, you've got to respect my religion," I said but that did not draw a smile. "I didn't mean anything," I added hastily. "It was just that the scarf looked so soft and rich, I couldn't stop myself from touching it."

"Here, have it then," she said, good-natured again but a little contemptuous. She sent the scarf floating over to me. I caught it and trailed it behind me, looking back on its lightness.

Jo laughed. "What a baby. Yet to look at you a person would think you were manly."

"I can box and run and jump. I was the best athlete at Mr. Graham's Gymnasium in Durban . . ."

"My, what an honour to know you . . ."

". . . but I like the pretty things girls wear . . ."

"The prettiest is a diamond. I mean to have my share. Oh, when I think of that river . . . It's like a great big piece of black velvet rolled out over the grass and sprinkled all over with diamonds."

"You wish it," I said. "I've heard one has to move boulders a ton weight, and dig and sieve. You're thinking of a jeweller's shop."

"Never mind. Even if I don't pick one up, I expect there will be quite a few wanting to give a girl a diamond. Chap told me in Durban that girls on the diggings are as scarce as hens' teeth. Plenty of diamonds to go round, he said, but not enough girls. That will suit me. I get sick of girls. That's why I came on alone."

"You'll get killed by a Kaffir or eaten up by a lion."

"I've got Biddy here." She patted the bowie knife. "Captain Halden gave it to me. He brought it all the way from America."

"This Halden seems to give you a number of things."

"He gave me that scarf," she said. "It was bought in Paris."

"Were you in Paris with Halden?"

"Captain Halden to you, you pipsqueak. He was an officer on the *Alabama* while you were still playing with the punchball at Mr. Whatsaname's Academy."

"Well, were you in Paris with Captain Halden?"

"No, but I've been in Paris. I've been all over the place with Uzzell's Entertainers. We're supposed to be on a world tour now . . . we were going to India where the maharajahs and rubies are . . . only Uzzell got wind of the diamond rush. So here we are in the middle of bloody Africa." The swearword brought a laugh from me; suddenly I wanted her and I felt no awe of her, no preliminary shyness.

"Hey, what's your name?" she said.

"Mannie."

"Mine is Josephine."

"Call me Napoleon."

We marched on. When I glanced at the girl, I saw that

her skin was reddening although she wore a wide-brimmed hat to keep off the sun.

"Take your scarf back. You'll get burned."

"Thanks." She covered her face with the scarf. "I'll bet you've got sisters, Mannie."

"Wrong. Mind you, I've got a sort of a sister . . . she's an orphan, the daughter of Reb Gamsay . . . my father looks after her . . . Leah."

"Leah, Leah . . . What a pretty name." She began to sing: "Leah, Leah . . ." Her voice was robust despite the immensity of the sky and the plain.

"And you? Have you sisters and brothers?" I asked her.

"None. Not even a father and mother. I was farmed out. But there was some money set aside for me and I was sent to school when I was twelve. I can read and write and play the piano . . . I was supposed to be a governess." Jo put on a severe expression and scraped her hair back. "Fancy me. When I was fourteen I ran off with Uzzell's Christy Minstrels. He dressed me up as a boy and they never found me. I played in Ipswich right under their noses.

"You are from London, I can hear it. Did you come to Africa after diamonds?"

"No. My father and I have been trading with the Zulus . . ."

"Oooooh, would you now?" She danced along, stamping and grunting. "And did you find yourself some Zulu wives? I've heard they'll make you a chief if you'll take a hundred wives, Ikey."

"I know who you are," I cried, suddenly remembering a poster I had seen in Durban. "You're the Nightingale of the South . . . Jo Carrari."

"Jo Carr really. Carrari is my stage name."

"Leah and I wanted to go and hear the concert but my father was against it."

"Never mind, you can listen now . . ." She sang to me as we walked along; *Doodah Doodah Day* and *The Valley of Diamonds*.

A trap packed with girls, an old woman and some poodles was scurrying down the road towards us. It came to a halt in eddying dust.

"Climb on, Jo," a dazzling blonde girl cried. "Man, was that your poor old mule lying back there?"

"Yes, he died," said Jo.

"Oh shame."

"Have you some water, mister?" one of the girls asked.

I ran to the cart and pulled out the demijohn. I was mad about the fair girl. I gave the first mug of water to her.

"This is Bonnie," said Jo, and derisively: "If you can take your eyes off her for a minute I'll introduce you to the others. Madame Olpresci . . ." The powdered old woman holding a poodle bowed regally. "Fifi, French . . . Sweet Jasmine Riley . . . Horseface Sixpence, she's our comedienne . . . Maria, and Baby Doll . . . And this is . . . I've forgotten his name . . . Ikey, that's it." She sprang onto the trap and sent the scarf sailing down to me. The girls shrieked for I did not catch it until it had almost fallen onto a thorn bush.

"Goodbye, Ikey Mo," Jo said to me. "Thanks for the company."

"I told you to call me Napoleon," I shouted.

The girls laughed and blew kisses. Presently the trap vanished behind a kopje. Loneliness brought a lump to my throat: the plain went on and on into nothingness. When the trap reappeared it was small on the veldt. I watched it greedily.

"Bonnie, Fifi, Sweet Jasmine, Baby Doll, Jo Jo Joso," I said aloud again and again: their very names were company.

The trap faded into the pale horizon. I forgot the other girls now and remembered only Jo. I went over every word of the conversation we had had: she was a wraith beside me.

4

From a long way off I saw a house on the plain. The veldt here was dreary, an expanse of dry dark grass relieved only by the shimmer of white rocks and salt pans: it was good to see a habitation. I wondered if the people would give me shelter that night; it could be cold on the high veldt. But the Dutch farmers were not always anxious to have a Jew in the house, or any sort of Englishman for that matter.

The blonde girl . . . I thought of her again. She was Dutch, you could hear it in her voice. She had cheeks like pale pink roses and shiny hair and a pink slack mouth. She was prettier than my girl. I felt uneasy like a person does who has shopped too hastily. Perhaps if I met the girls again I would pay attention to the blonde one. Fancy kissing a girl like that, I said aloud.

There was a fat woman in the garden in front of the Boer house. She was making a pattern with white-washed stones, perhaps marking out flowerbeds. I watched her as

I travelled on slowly. Would she be one of the arrogant Boer women? . . . their isolation gave them a great opinion of themselves. Some were so suspicious that they would slam the door in your face or meet you with a cold, uncomprehending look even when you spoke to them in their own patois.

Perhaps this woman would be simple and kind, ready to welcome the stranger at her gate. Once or twice on the journey I had been overwhelmed by hospitality but in general the Boer women were to be feared. I wished my father were here, I wished for his dignity. No rebuff could shatter him.

I wished I had a beard. If I were older, with a beard, at least I would command respect or even hate . . . but I was nineteen, there was just the beginning of a moustache and the most I could expect from the narrow farmers was a good-humoured contempt for my youth; and my Jewishness.

The woman trotted about, setting out the stones and once I saw her spread her legs wide. I smiled and told myself to remember to look for the damp patch at the gate. Seeing her do that made me feel more confident. Are we not all alike then? What's a Jew, what's a Gentile? I said.

The woman sat down on the stoep and took onto her lap a blue monkey which was tied by a long chain to the single gum tree next to the house. She must have seen me then for she shaded her eyes with her hand and stared across the veldt towards me.

There had been clouds in the sky all during the afternoon, thick clouds tinged with yellow from the dust. Now the clouds were turning green, there was a smell of hail in the air. The veldt was still, there was not so much as a blade of grass moving: the quietness encompassed the sky too.

My donkey Archibald jerked about and stood with lowered head. His behaviour was another indication of the storm about to break. I threw a sack over him.

I sheltered under the cart. Looking out, I saw thin strokes of lightning in the sky, like rivers inked in on a map. Simultaneous with each flash was the sharp crack of thunder. I shivered. It was the sort of lightning to strike and burn a man to a blackened shell. It would find the metal on my cart. I was afraid and crept out and unharnessed Archibald, then hurried away from him and the cart, to sit on a bare patch of veldt.

The woman had gone into her house and the monkey was flinging himself against the door, begging to be let in. I caught something of his terror. I stood up and cried: "Loosen him, loosen him . . ." and took a few steps forward, puny and squeaking beneath the sky.

Lightning struck, so close that I was flung to the ground. I looked up fearfully, thinking to see the farmhouse ablaze or my cart in smithereens. My cart was not touched, Archibald was safe and I could see nothing amiss at the farmhouse. Even the tall gumtree was untouched.

Presently the storm clouds rolled away to the south. The woman came into the garden again. She met me at the gate as I climbed from my cart.

"Our ape is gone," she said in the Taal.

"He got loose then?"

"Look." She pointed to the chain which was welded now into a solid piece of metal and lay in a deep furrow in the earth. "And the ape is gone," she whispered.

We searched the garden but we found nothing of the monkey, not so much as a tooth or a hair.

"Fatherland, to vanish so completely." The woman stood with her hands clasped beneath her apron, made solemn by the monkey's fate yet with a glint of merriment in her eyes. I found this merriment within myself and had to turn away to hide a grin that came as suddenly as a yawn. She looked down, smiling openly now, and fingered a corner of her white starched apron.

"He knew he was going to be struck," I said. "He was flinging himself against the door."

"Poor thing. Mind you, oxen know what is going to happen before the lightning runs along the chain. I've seen a span of oxen struck . . . Perhaps if Apie had been loose . . ."

"On the Drakensberg I found the body of a duiker that had been struck."

"It just shows you. When your time has come, your time has come. The Lord lays His finger on you. It was Apie's time to die. He would have been killed even if he was loose. I don't reproach myself. But I can't believe that there is absolute nothing . . ." She scanned the air to find some wisp of the monkey. "Nothing." She sighed. "He was my companion. I have no children. But come inside, mijnheer, we'll drink coffee." She extended her hand suddenly. "Mevrouw van der Spuyt."

"Bernstein," I responded.

We shook hands. I followed her into the house. She was a clean woman. The house smelt of harsh soap and wax and camphor. We went into the front room.

"Sit here," said the woman, pointing to a big chair covered with red plush. The chair had wings to keep off the draught. "It is as big as a bed, that chair," she said.

She went out and came back with coffee and rusks and

a bottle of preserved oranges. We made a meal of it. The woman left the table several times to get more food.

"The Kaffir maid went to her sister's place for the afternoon. Good thing. I don't want her to know I ate in here. I've never eaten in here before," she said, gasping as she finished off a cup of coffee. "But it just came to me all of a sudden . . . do as you like, you might be struck dead tomorrow. Not so?"

"It's true."

"Fancy the ape," she said, leaning on big dimpled arms and staring at me.

To avoid her eyes, I looked around the room. It was not often used, I guessed that. The windows were shut fast, with lace curtains looped back. These curtains were the only dainty things in the room: it was not a woman's room. The furniture was old heavy stuff. There were such things as the foot of a rhinoceros which had been used as an ashtray by a pipe smoker. There were buffaloes' heads glaring from the wall, and zebra and lion skins on the floor. When I had looked at everything, I found that the Dutch woman was still staring at me. I looked determinedly at the rhinoceros foot.

"I see you have taken a fancy to the rhinoceros foot," said my hostess: I thought the thing hideous but I nodded. "My late husband shot the animal. This house is mine and the land and the sheep, everything you see was left to me by my late husband."

"So Mevrouw is a widow?" I said politely: I felt dizzy in the airless room after eating so much.

"My husband was an invalid, mijnheer, so thin and frail I could lift him in my two arms like this." She picked up an imaginary body and nursed it tenderly. "He died years ago . . . I looked after him to the last. Everything was done for him but it was hopeless . . ." The storm clouds had shifted again and the room was filled with green light. Suddenly hail came down. I would have liked to run out and collect hailstones: Leah and I had always done that as children. I was pierced by a sudden longing to see Leah.

I could not hear what the Dutch woman said but I could see her lips moving valiantly. She lit a candle and I noticed for the first time that her features were beautiful. She had a straight nose and firm curly lips such as one sees on a statue. I had not noticed this beauty in her before. Now in the candlelight her face was tinged with gold.

She leaned close to me and kissed me.

"You're only a little boy," she said, stroking my cheek. Again she kissed me. She drew away from me, went to the door and stood there listening intently. Then she returned and caught my head in her big, hard hands and looked at me.

"Does Mevrouw want me to?" I stammered.

She nodded solemnly. I clutched her, guided by her voice grown suddenly sweet like the trill of a bird.

5

I fell asleep in the stuffy room, squeezed against her in the red plush chair. She left me while I was asleep. When I awoke, I saw at once that every vestige of our feast had been cleared away. The storm was over. There was the sound of crickets.

The girl Jo stood in the doorway, holding a candle. In

its light her hair cut a glittering swathe for now she was wearing it in loose curls on her shoulders.

"Hey, Ikey Mo," she said. "What do you mean by it, sleeping in the front room?"

"Where did you spring from, schickser?"

"Two of us had to come back here to sleep. There is an inn about five miles further on but it's full. People are sleeping even on the tables. The skoff here is ready. You're invited to come." She entered the room and changed her voice to sound like the Dutch woman's voice. "I don't know what has happened to our monkey. Everybody knows that Jews can do clever things. How do we know he hasn't spirited our monkey away?"

"You're lying, she can't even speak English."

"She can. She was at an English school in Port Elizabeth. She has just told us so."

"Do you mean she is saying things about me? We were so friendly . . ."

"Aha, but her husband is home now."

"Her husband . . . She is supposed to be a widow," I said, aghast.

"I've caught you, Ikey. I knew it, I knew you were a lady-killer. You've been flirting . . ."

"We were just friends, on account of the monkey, you know."

"Don't be upset," said Jo, suddenly tender. "I've only been rocking you. Come on." She caught my hand and drew me from the room.

6

Van der Spuyt was at the table waiting to begin supper. He was a big horny man . . . it must have been some disease that had turned even his lips hard. The black hair on his chest was so long that it curled up from under his shirt strong as wire. What had his wife thought of my smooth chest? I felt shy; and mortally afraid of van der Spuyt.

"Good night," he said, shaking my hand until he saw me wince. Words came from him in a bellow.

He had a broad face with a beard that he kept close cut; it was as square and black as the beard of an ancient Assyrian. He stood well over six feet and he was wide of shoulder, thick-boned at wrists and ankles. What had that wicked woman meant with her talk of invalids? She was mad, I had been in the clutches of a mad woman. But to look at her now, one would not have thought her different from any other housewife dishing up the supper . . .

Madame Olpresci, the old woman I had seen in the cart, had also sought shelter here.

"You have seen my act, Monsieur Bernstein?" she said as I seated myself on the bench next to her. I shook my head. "I do an act with my six poodles. We are on a railway station . . . one poodle is busy buying tickets, another is the porter . . ."

"The lady said she would let the dogs show us some tricks," Mevrouw van der Spuyt murmured to her husband.

"Dogs in here? Never."

"You deny your wife this simple pleasure?" asked Madame in High Dutch.

"No dogs in here," van der Spuyt growled but he was a shade more respectful to Madame: "Madame is Hollands?"

"Swiss. But I speak Dutch . . . not your patois though I understand that well enough."

Food and tobacco mellowed him somewhat. When the table was cleared, he leaned back and from behind a fug of pipe smoke muttered that if the women wanted to make fools of themselves looking at dogs, let the dogs come in.

Jo waltzed round the room with a poodle, singing: "My name it is Toto de Fropps and for lunch I have mutton chops . . ."

"It is not in nature," grumbled van der Spuyt as Madame marshalled the dogs into line and got them walking on their hind legs, left right left right . . .

"Salute!"

The dogs saluted as one. I clapped and so did Mevrouw. Van der Spuyt nodded grudgingly and suddenly pulled at one of the hairs on his chest, drawing Madame's attention to it: so help me, it was nine inches long.

"That's a trick dogs can't do," he said.

Affronted, Madame called the dogs and put them away in their boxes.

"We're to see the Jew's pack," said Mevrouw with a nervous glance at her husband.

"Women people are always interested in rubbish. Be still."

Mevrouw nodded meekly and then stole a look at me. No doubt she was remembering what had happened in the red chair: was that done to revenge herself on this big bully? I quaked at the thought. She was an unpredictable woman. Her resentment might carry her far enough to tell him what we had done.

I stood up. "I'll go now. I see there is no room for me. Thank you for your hospitality . . ."

"If you've taken offence . . ." grumbled van der Spuyt. "Ach, don't be childish but bring your pack, Bernstein."

His wife threw a cloth over the table.

"Put the things there," she said disdainfully.

There were combs and ribbons, a bolt of calico, a bolt of print. "And here are a few trinkets," I said, laying out glass bangles, coral necklaces and a bead brooch.

"Is that all?" Jo asked.

"Some trousers and blankets. Interested? And these, the only pair I have in stock."

I laid down a pair of cashmere stockings, black printed over with red roses.

"Ah," said all three women.

Mevrouw was the first to touch the stockings. Her husband's hand dropped on to her wrist. A quick look passed between them.

"I don't agree with stuff like this," said van der Spuyt. "They are the temptations of the devil."

Madame Olpresci smiled bitterly. "Your wife likes the stockings."

"My wife agrees with me," he said.

"Not so," shouted Madame. "What woman would agree to be shut up here, and in such clothes? Women like change and beautiful things. This place . . . this is a man's house . . . Look." She pointed to the hasp on the door, placed high where Mevrouw would have to stretch on tip-toe to reach it.

"She is right," Mevrouw murmured.

I regretted showing the stockings: van der Spuyt was looking at his wife threateningly.

Jo said: "I like the stockings."

"You can have them for a present," I whispered.

Immediately she snatched them up and went out of the room. When she returned she was wearing the stockings. She sat with her skirt slightly lifted and Mevrouw van der Spuyt could see them. The Dutch woman flushed, not only in the face but all the way down her neck and arms. She hung her head, it was an agony to her, that bright flush. Jo dropped her skirt over her ankles.

Van der Spuyt sulked behind a cloud of smoke.

"I may buy your wife a present?" Madame asked.

"What?" he said.

"A coral necklace?" said Madame, looking at the Dutch woman.

"Do you want it?" van der Spuyt said harshly.

Mevrouw said Yes but she did not put the necklace on; she sat all through the evening swinging it on her finger.

The maid came in with a basin of water to wash our feet. She knelt down and pulled off van der Spuyt's shoes; and washed his feet carefully, even between the toes.

When his feet were dried, he sat with them placed on a small rough stool. It was his wife's turn now. After that, the maid, at a gesture from van der Spuyt, crept round to Madame Olpresci.

"Faugh," said Madame. "My feet are clean."

But Jo allowed the maid to wash her feet. She had taken off the stockings and laid them one on top of the other on her lap. I saw that she had delicate white high-arched feet but van der Spuyt had eyes only for the stockings.

"Are they not the same ones?" he said in a loud whisper to his wife.

"Yes. The Jew gave them to her."

"There will be no fornication in this house," van der Spuyt announced.

He now sent his wife to fetch the Bible. It was a family Bible, brass-bound, with tough crackling pages.

"Bernstein, go out," van der Spuyt ordered. "We are going to have prayers."

I prayed on the veldt beyond the yard where the sound of my voice would not reach them. I would have gone on that night but I could not find Archibald. And van der Spuyt himself came to the door and called me: "Bernstein, there's a bed here for you. Van der Spuyt never turned so much as a dog from his door yet."

7

The van der Spuyts slept in a double bed. Madame Olpresci was given a narrow bed in a corner of the same room and Jo was on a mattress on the floor. My place was on the floor of the kitchen. My bed had been made up on a new sheepskin that crackled even when I breathed. Each time the sheepskin crackled, van der Spuyt coughed. There was no door between the two rooms and I could hear every sigh from the others.

I was on the point of dozing off when van der Spuyt appeared in the kitchen. He carried a candle. The gigantic figure terrified me . . . I thought that his wife, infuriated over the stockings, had told him everything and here he was to make a reckoning with me. He wore a day shirt as sleeping attire so that I had a good view of the pillars of his legs and the huge feet that might trample life out of an ordinary man like myself. But he stepped over me and proceeded to a bin.

The fellow had gone to get a basinful of sugar which he now sprinkled onto the floor between my pallet and the bedroom. Then he went back to bed and with an uncouth blast blew out the candle.

"There will be no fornication in this house," he said, his voice impressive in the darkness.

"You are so wasteful of the sugar, beloved," his wife lamented.

"Just let one of them try and move without me hearing," said van der Spuyt. "That's all. Let them try."

For a long time I lay still. When at last I eased myself round, van der Spuyt gave a braying cough.

I said: "Excuse me, mijnheer, but is this a sheepskin I am lying on?"

He pretended to be asleep. It was his wife who answered me.

"Yes, it is a sheepskin."

"It is against my religion to lie on a sheepskin."

"So?" she said. "I was always of the opinion that it was pigs you Jews were against."

"Also sheepskins," I said firmly.

"Ach now fancy," said Mevrouw in a tender voice.

Van der Spuyt rasped: "What are you two at?"

"The Jew says he cannot sleep on a sheepskin, it is against his religion."

"Bernstein?"

"Yes, mijnheer?"

"Hold your mouth and go to sleep."

"Yes, mijnheer."

"But if it is against a person's religion . . ." Mevrouw began.

"Be still."

A smell of brandy came suddenly. There was the sound of somebody drinking stealthily from a bottle.

"Brandy," cried van der Spuyt, rising from his bed. "What have I in my house, Lord? Who of you Outlanders is drinking brandy?"

Nobody answered and presently he got back into bed and there was quiet in the house.

8

I slept that night by fits and starts. My waking thoughts were of Jo and these thoughts merged into dreams. I thought of Jo wearing the stockings and catching up her dress to show them to me. But when I dreamed, Jo became Leah: we were walking in some far-off place with blue rocks under our feet. We were children . . . but it was a vile dream of lust. I forced myself to wake up from it. Now I imagined dancing with Jo. Her skirt would fly out and the stockings would be seen. We would dance away somewhere out of sight . . . these imaginings whirled into a dream of vultures. One of the vultures was encrusted with jewels. It turned into Leah . . .

Madame Olpresci's low cry of anguish awakened us all. "Günther . . . Günther . . . Günthie . . ."

A candle was lit. Mevrouw ran for red lavender but was ordered back to bed by van der Spuyt for it was obvious that Madame was drunk.

"So now we know who has been drinking brandy," van der Spuyt said. "She leaves here at once. I'll have no drunken women in this house."

"Please, don't put her out," cried Jo. "I'll keep her quiet."

"See you do it then."

Jo muffled the cries for Günther by placing a pillow over Madame's head. Madame was determined. When Jo lifted the pillow so that she could breathe, Madame was ready. "Günt . . ." Down came the pillow. But Jo must have fallen asleep for later that night Madame was again calling for Günther. It was a desolate sound from some uncharted landscape where she wandered in search of a lover or husband or son. I never did find out which he was though afterwards I often heard her call for Günther when she was drunk.

In my dreams that night her cry for Günther changed to a cry for Leah.

I wished that I had not been tricked into touching van der Spuyt's wife. Was I guilty of adultery? Is it the act or the intention that makes a sin? I asked. That was a question for a learned man.

I felt afraid. What if Leah were seduced? The laws of retribution governing mankind would be invoked against me. I would kill the man who touched Leah and kill her too. You shall not kill . . . You shall not commit adultery . . . I felt the weight of my sins.

I sat up, parched and aching. The room was dark. Ma-

32

dame Olpresci made no sound. Inch by inch I moved my-self along the sheepskin, with the intention of getting up and leaving the house. The sheepskin crackled. Van der Spuyt coughed, delicately. There was nothing for it but to lie still and pretend to sleep.

I will do sums, I thought; and began to reckon up what profits I might make on this expedition. Profits we needed badly. My father was making nothing . . . well, he was more of a Talmudic scholar than a trader. So much depended on me and I had given away valuable stockings to the schickser.

She owed me something. Seeing her tonight, I had changed my opinion of her looks again. It was a beautiful face, surely. The skin was not fair, it was golden but there was some pinkness in it too . . . the skin was the colour of ripe apricots and like fruit was marked by freckles, little round freckles that might have been put in with the point of a fine nib. That big mouth, you got used to it and were fascinated by it. She had blue eyes but not light eyes; dark blue irises were set in blue-tinted eyeballs. She was slender. To ride the mule she had dispensed with a crinoline and now in the night I remembered how her skirts were blown against her thighs in sculptured folds.

9

With the first light I was out of the house. I found my donkey and while I was harnessing him, Jo brought a cup of coffee to me. I had thought of her too much during the night and I felt an aversion to her now. I noticed the down on her arms and it seemed to me a disfigurement then though afterwards I took a delight in it.

"Uppish today," she said and left me to myself.

All I wanted now was to be away from the goyim. But it was not my luck to escape so easily. Van der Spuyt himself came out to talk to me. He stood invincibly on wide feet with one great hand caressing Archibald's neck.

"They call me the Zastron Giant . . . I come from Zastron. Look at this." He held out his arm and flexed the muscles. "Feel that," he said. His biceps were like rock.

I began to fear that his wife had talked in her sleep for now he made me exhibit my muscles.

"Muscles are funny things. Yours are not as big as mine, Bernstein, but they are of a different kind," he said generously. "Long muscles like yours, it doesn't mean you're a weakling, old mate."

His sudden friendliness made me glow. "I can box all right," I admitted.

"That's for namby pambies. Have you tried the pinching match?"

"No."

34

"You catch here." He rolled up his trouser leg and caught the flesh of his inner thigh. "Pinch as hard as you like, nobody ever made me give in yet. We'll see what you are made of, Bernie."

This alarming conversation got no further for at that moment a man came into sight, marching along the narrow path that led past the yard. His clothes were ragged and he carried a bundle.

"From the diggings?" called van der Spuyt.

"Yes."

"You didn't find any diamonds by the look of you."

The stranger cursed. "They're dying like flies there, of fever . . . I've had more than one go of it. Diamonds? I never found one. And there are hundreds can say the same. It's a fraud, it's a swindle. If there are any diamonds on the river banks, the ostriches brought them there from somewhere else and left them in their droppings. As for me, I'm off home and be damned to the lot of it."

He continued on his way, still cursing. Silently van der Spuyt pointed to his footprints. The stranger had been wearing shoes but now we saw that he had only the uppers to his feet; the imprints he left on the path were made by his bare toes.

"Almighty," said van der Spuyt.

He went after the stranger and caught him by the arm.

"Come back to the house. It's breakfast time now. Bernstein, you too."

The other man turned back willingly but I demurred.

"Everything is ready for me to go."

"Nonsense," roared van der Spuyt with terrifying goodwill. He unharnessed Archibald himself and sent him off into the veldt with a smack on the rump. I went back with some misgivings; you can't be sure of a Dutchman. When he seems most friendly, that's when he is laying a trap for you.

The newcomer's name was Caston. He walked carefully as though holding his fragile body and threadbare clothes together. He was yellow in the face and there came from him a harsh, strange smell; this was the rankness of fever which I got to know afterwards. Mevrouw van der Spuyt could have lifted him and nursed him as she had claimed to do with her husband.

"Foei tog," she muttered when she saw him: she gave him a double helping of mealie meal and meat.

The poor devil must have been starving. He ate until his eyes glazed over and afterwards was seized with colic. Van der Spuyt had to roll him to help him get rid of the wind.

10

I set off to look for Archibald again. He circled away from me through the weeds of old mealie lands, right back to the yard. But before I could catch him there was a commotion of singing and shouting as a crowd of bluejackets came into sight, swinging along under the command of a red-bearded man nearly as big as van der Spuyt himself.

"Is it an army?" cried van der Spuyt.

"They are sailors on their way to the diggings," I said. "God."

"See here, we don't understand your lingo, Dutchie,"

the red-bearded sailorman said. "But we want breakfast. Savvy? Look lively now. We've got money to pay." He flung a half-sovereign to van der Spuyt.

"This house isn't an inn," said van der Spuyt; but he picked up the money and stowed it in his pocket. A Kaffir girl was set to catching some fowls.

Hearing their squawks, the sailor grinned. He and his companions seated themselves on the ground and pulled off their boots.

"Must have marched a thousand miles," one of the men grumbled, "but it was worth it, I must say." He leered at Jo who had come out of the house, ready to leave. She stood chatting to Mevrouw.

Van der Spuyt was sitting on a chair on the stoep with Caston beside him. He beckoned me.

"What do you think? Are there diamonds on the Vaal, Bernstein? These Jews are clever," he confided to Caston.

I said: "I am hoping there are diamonds. The whole country will prosper . . ."

"Excuse me, that's the last thing I hope for," said van der Spuyt: his early morning good-humour had vanished. "Is it going to be like this all the time, with people tramping over a man's land? If it is, I'm trekking on. I know a place in the Transvaal . . . Alidasrust . . . my father lived there for a while . . ."

Caston had been rubbing at a pebble embedded in the wall. Now he asked Jo to lend him her knife. With the point of the knife he prised out a shiny stone from the mud brick wall.

"It's a diamond," he said, not raising his voice. "By Jesus, I rocked a cradle on the diggings for six months and never found a stone . . ."

"Give me my knife," said Jo fiercely and set to work on

the wall. Within a few seconds she had a diamond glittering on her palm.

A sailor bounded to his feet. He drew from its sheath a villainous-looking knife and prized out another diamond. His howl of delight brought even the Kaffir servants clustering round him. His mates left him to rush the wall. They stabbed and hacked at the mud brick. I found myself there too, kicking loose a hard clod of earth. One of the Kaffirs was clawing at the wall with his bare hands: Madame Olpresci was prodding with the point of an umbrella and the poodles were joyfully digging in the loosened earth.

Several holes gaped in the wall. Van der Spuyt got his shotgun while Mevrouw wrung her hands and wept. It was the outside of the sitting room wall which was under attack; already one had a good view of the rhinoceros foot.

Van der Spuyt blazed away, peppering the wall above our heads, but the digging went on unabated.

"Move or I'll fire lower," he yelled.

A sailor screamed as he was shot in the calf of his leg but that did not stop him from digging at the wall; blood was running from his leg onto the stoep.

This was too much for van der Spuyt. He charged, laying about him with the butt of the gun. The wall fell. For the first time that sitting-room was exposed to the air; and there was the red armchair for everybody to see.

"We need a sieve," Caston said authoritatively. "This whole lot needs sieving and sorting."

From the spluttering crowd, some men now dashed forward to attack the clods with bare hands or the heels of their boots. Madame was crying in a rage: "Behave yourselves, mind the dogs . . ." The van der Spuyts stood side by side, staring open-mouthed at the havoc, in the midst of the struggling people.

"Fatherland," van der Spuyt said to his wife. "But no, I'm dreaming."

I eased myself out of the throng. Archibald allowed me to catch him and I harnessed him quickly. Instinct told me to get away from that farm at once. When van der Spuyt recovered his wits, he would probably call in the magistrate and demand damages.

Even yet I was not to be allowed to go in peace. Mevrouw had given chase. I went on resolutely although she called out to me. When I looked back, I saw her up on an antheap. She lifted her skirts and with one leg extended showed me a cashmere stocking with red roses printed on it.

I puzzled over the stockings but I had to shelve the question: I could think of no reason why Jo had given my present away . . . she had truly admired the stockings.

In the lonely hours of my journeying I remembered Jo. She sat beside me on the narrow seat of the cart or walked through the veldt with me. At night she lay with me, more beautiful than any woman I was ever to know.

Some days later, the trap shot past me with its load. The girls waved gaily and that fair girl cried "Good luck" and lifted her skirts.

I looked for Jo. She stood up perilously and blew kisses to me until she was carried from my sight.

A Coloured man walking to the diggings told me that a minor rush had taken place at van der Spuyt's farm. Van der Spuyt was selling, and trekking on.

"But whoever buys is a fool. There is nothing on the farm except this one handful of diamonds they have found, brought there by the ostriches. Everybody knows you don't find diamonds in dry ground."

11

"Why did you give the stockings to Mevrouw van der Spuyt?" I asked Jo.

"She told me you meant them for her but you were afraid of her husband so you had given them to me and I could hand them on . . ."

"You didn't believe that."

"No. But I was sorry for her. She wanted the stockings. I was going to tease her with them when I first put them on. But I was sorry to see her go red like that . . ."

We were at a river waiting for the water to go down. Here where we had encamped there was bright sunshine but up country rain was falling, causing a flood. Most of Uzzell's girls had gone back to the nearest inn. Jo, Bonnie and Madame Olpresci had elected to stay in a waggon on the river bank.

I had hoped that Jo was staying because she wanted to be near me but it soon became obvious that the attraction was the poker game that was played every evening. Madame Olpresci and Jo sat in on the game but the fair girl Bonnie did not play; nor did I. My father had invested heavily in my pack and I did not dare risk losing any money or goods.

I was afraid of Uzzell. I knew I would be no match for him at the card table. He was a conjuror, and his hands were long and beautiful. The supple, arching fingers could open out a pack of cards in mid-air; and I had no doubt he could deal any hand he chose. He had a quirk to his nature. He took a delight in driving his opponents to the limit, as though he were testing their courage. At that time he was out for Madame Olpresci's blood. The game was played in Uzzell's tent at a rough table with a rug thrown over it. Madame sat opposite Uzzell and on a stool beside her was her most gifted poodle Toto de Fropps. One night Uzzell hinted that Madame should stake the poodle.

"Nevair!"

Her hands, worn and roughened by care of the dogs, held the cards clumsily; in the evenings she used to powder her hands. The powder flew up in tiny bursts that made her sneeze, and she would drop her cards to grope distractedly for a handkerchief. In contrast, Uzzell did not make an unnecessary movement. His face, still and guarded, was so fine that you could see the shape of the bones. I had noticed women looking at his mouth; the lower lip jutted sensually. Bonnie stayed up so late to moon over him. Nobody else had a chance with her.

I happened to be standing behind Madame and saw that she had been dealt ace, queen, jack, ten and seven of diamonds. She discarded the seven and bought the king of clubs to a straight. Jo threw in her hand, muttering, "Rats and mice." The others dropped out too, except for Uzzell who bought three cards. He staked ten pounds.

"La, I haven't money like that to bet with," cried Madame.

"You've got Toto. Wager her," said Uzzell softly. His face glowed, it was tender as he regarded Madame. She held the cards so tightly that they bent in her fingers: she was sweating.

There was silence in the tent. Then Madame said: "But you dislike dogs."

"I'm willing to take the bet."

It was a disgrace to continue to watch Madame. The sweat was rolling down her face now and splashing the cards, her breathing could be heard.

"Very well, I see you, monsieur."

"For Toto?"

She nodded. Uzzell laid his cards on the table one after the other: a king, a queen, a ten and two nines. She stared at the cards.

"But you had nothing," she whispered and began to cry. Toto sprang up and licked her face. Uzzell contemplated Madame's tears benignly while he cut a cigar. Madame gathered up the money and with Toto under her arm, stumbled from the tent.

"Women," said Uzzell, smoking peacefully.

The poker game started each night at eight and finished at dawn. A hurricane lantern was placed in the centre of the table and to augment its dim light there were a few candles fixed onto saucers or stuck in bottles. We sat on kegs and boxes, as many as fifteen of us crowding into the close little tent. Jo always sat on with the last players. Uzzell would cut a cigar and push it between her teeth. She was remote from me then but at midday she would come yawning to my campfire, and whine for coffee; somewhat yellow of complexion from the cigar-smoking, but wearing lovely gowns. The waggon containing the trunks of the company had caught up with them and Jo whiled away the time by dressing herself up.

"You saw what Uzzell did to Madame Olpresci?" she asked me.

"Does he do that sort of thing on purpose?"

She nodded. "He gets a thrill out of it . . . you understand?"

"The old brute."

"I wonder, would you stand up to him?"

That day she wore a magenta silk gown with stiff piqué trimmings. She had on a pair of satin boots exactly matching her gown; and pale grey silk stockings. Her hair, in ringlets, was copper in the sunlight.

She leaned towards me. "Uzzell would break you, I think. Look how frightened you were of van der Spuyt."

"His wife had lied to me. I thought she was a widow . . ."

"I suppose you make love to all the farm women."

"No. I'm in love with you," I said desperately.

She was laughing. "I'm not a stupid Boeress to be taken in by you."

I said: "Shall I compare thee to a summer's day? Thou art more lovely . . ."

"I am too old for you."

"Aren't you twenty?"

"Yes."

"I'm twenty-five."

"Liar. But I am too old. I've been with Uzzell since I was fourteen and that makes me old."

"Did he give you all these clothes?"

"Halden gave them to me."

"Do you love Halden?" She hesitated before she said No. "You love Uzzell then."

"No," she said flatly. "But I belong to him, as if we were related. It doesn't pay to get fond of people. I thought I could trust Madame Olpresci . . . But look at her. She risked Toto de Fropps. She would have handed him over to Uzzell."

"Love me," I cried. "Jo, you can trust me. I'd do anything in the world for you."

Cautiously she put her hand on my cheek.

"I want to love somebody," she said.

12

Jo had thought of a new name for herself. She was painting it on to gaudy posters . . . Diamond Jo the Nightingale of the Diggings.

She had a gingham apron tied about her and wore a white frilled cap. I had lost her; she had no time to spend with me for Uzzell had set his troupe to working. Madame was rehearsing her dogs, Jo learning a new song and painting these posters; the Minstrels were polishing up their routine. Uzzell was training Bonnie to become his assistant.

The water level was falling and in a few days the company would make the final dash to the Vaal.

"You never come and have coffee with me anymore, Jo," I complained.

She touched my nose with the brush, then rapidly painted a little curly moustache on her upper lip. She was showing off in front of two Kaffir girls, servants of a trekking Boer family; the girls laughed and screamed and stamped.

44

"I'll go for a walk with you when I finish this poster," Jo said.

It was sunset before she threw down her brush. She wiped the paint off our faces with a turpentiny cloth. She had taken off the apron and cap; her hair was springing in the wind, it crackled like silk does when there is lightning about. An edge of cold touched the air as the sun disappeared. We sat behind a grassy knoll out of the wind, like sweethearts with our fingers interlaced. She leaned her head against my shoulder.

"I dodged you because of Uzzell. But he is too busy to worry about you now. You saw what he did to Madame Olpresci. He will do that to you. He'll try to show you up for a coward."

"I'm not a weakling, I can look after myself."

She said sadly: "But how would you feel if I started making bets on you? I bet Uzzell that Madame wouldn't stake Toto de Fropps. He bet that she would."

"You needn't be afraid to bet on me. I'm strong."

She crushed my biceps in a hard grip and then kneaded my body, from throat to hips and down the thighs.

"I want to love somebody," she said.

It was dark. There was a bitter smell of some herbs bruised in the grass beneath us, I remember.

13

The next day the river subsided and the trek westwards began again. Jo and I travelled together once more and then I was left far behind in the race to the Vaal. Plodding through the veldt with Archibald, I followed tracks made by vehicles passing to and from the diggings. On each side of the tracks the grass flowed like a sea to the horizon. And if one looked for them there were flowers to be seen growing close to the soil. Herds of springbok bounded through the grass; birds rose beneath Archibald's hooves . . . partridge, plover, quail. And there were stretches of veldt unrelieved by flower, animal or bird. Then I would look up at the sky, and the ache of my loneliness was almost more than I could bear.

I came through miles of barren lands and salt pans to a kopje where a transport rider had his camp. The man's name was Tungay.

Tungay comes to me in my dreams. For weeks on end, night after night, I am haunted by him. He stands before me as though he were alive; a brute of a man, thick-armed, with hair hanging on to his forehead in a Newgate fringe. There was a chubbiness to his face that did nothing to disguise the menace of him.

He made me welcome in his own fashion.

"You can put your gear on the last waggon," he said

as we sat smoking by the campfire after supper. "I'm riding transport for one of your kind, a Jew named Solly Reuben, and I don't expect he would mind me helping a fellow Israelite." He leered and winked as though we were about to enter into some shady transaction.

I travelled with Tungay for a week.

A Boer's waggon was following us and the two Kaffir servant girls were often to be seen on the veldt, gathering firewood or fetching water. Tungay suggested that we waylay the girls. His talk stirred me to watching them and there came to me a longing I had never known before: I grew lustful in my bed under the waggon.

I thought I had kept my feelings hidden from Tungay but he with his peasant's shrewdness had summed me up: he used to tease me with gross descriptions of the girls.

"Bah, you don't find me a-courting of any female," he boasted. "That's why I like the black ones the best . . . no fancy goings on like the white girls want . . ." His voice was usually grating but when he spoke about women it changed to a smooth, mocking tone.

One evening he went away from the camp to shoot guinea fowl. He was gone for such a long time that I began to think that he might have had an accident on the veldt or had got lost; I kept firing my rifle to give him the location of the camp. It was nearly midnight when he strolled in unconcernedly with a brace of guinea fowl. I had left some venison stew in the pot for him and he ate it with his hands, even scooping up the gravy.

"I not only got the brace but I caught another sort of chicken as well," he said, wiping his greasy hands on his trousers.

I felt a prickling in my groin. "What do you mean?"

"I caught one of them Kaffir girls. They usually hunts

47

in couples but today she was out alone, picking up sticks. Her mate was sick. She didn't fancy me," he added.

"Did you force her?"

Tungay nodded. He was grinning with wet lips. For the first time I noticed that his lips were freckled: he had a light skin that was scattered over with orange-coloured freckles.

"Aren't you scared she will tell? You could be arrested."

"Who will believe her? It's my word against hers."

He had the oxen inspanned at once and we trekked at a shuffling run that before dawn had put miles between us and the Dutch family.

Looking back at dawn, I saw vultures in the sky.

"They're after my girl," said Tungay.

"Is she dead?" I whispered.

"As a doornail." I stared at him. He was sitting close to me on the waggon box. He touched his hunting knife and jabbed his thumb stiffly sideways in the air as much as to say that he had cut the girl's throat.

My first thought was: They will blame the Jew. I saw myself seized and beaten, hanged . . . "Father, Leah," I said as I dropped down from the waggon. Archibald trotted in the rear, pulling the empty cart. I brought him up alongside Tungay who had remained on the waggon.

"I'll travel alone," I said. "Give me my gear."

"You're getting excited like. There ain't nothing to be excited about."

"I'm going on alone. I want my pack."

"Now now, matey. You got the wind up? Blimey, I did one in in London and they ain't got me yet. How the hell are they going to catch me in a God forsaken hole like this?"

"You're nothing but a murderer."

48

Tungay halted the oxen. He swung himself down from the waggon.

"Now you wait a bit. The Dutchman may be catching us up in a short while. I been expecting him. You go running off and what will he think? He'll think you done it. You and me was together last night, sport. I'll speak for you and you speak for me. Understand?"

An hour later, the Dutchman came galloping up to us on his sturdy pony. Tungay was waiting for him with his thumbs hooked in his belt, his round freckled face creased into an enquiring grin.

"Morning," said the Dutchman, slipping from the saddle. "I'm Schoeman."

"Tungay."

"Bernstein," I muttered.

The Dutchman hesitated and then shook hands with us.

"You speak the Language?" We both nodded. "You people trekked early."

"Yes," said Tungay. The freckles stood out dark as tea on his face; he was wary and taut.

"One of our Kaffir girls is missing. She didn't run off with a boy of yours?" He looked round deliberately.

"You can ask my boys but I'm sure she didn't come with us. Look round. Search the waggons."

The Dutchman pulled at his beard, uncertain but suspicious, while Tungay had the canvas taken off the loads. One he left covered up.

"It is only the Jew's stuff," he said carelessly.

Schoeman pulled so hard at his beard that he showed his lower teeth and gums. I shook with rage and nervousness for I could see that he was convinced that the girl was hidden under the canvas: he suspected me of hiding her, no doubt.

"Well, we must get on," said Tungay. "It's a long time from outspan."

"I'll ride along with you for part of the way," said Schoeman. "My waggon is following. I had them inspan before I rode off this morning."

"You're welcome," said Tungay.

The Dutchman questioned the Kaffirs desultorily as he rode along; but his eyes, little shiny buttons in the dense curling growth of his beard, kept turning towards the waggon carrying my gear. He had a sjambok with him and as he rode past the waggon brought it down with a tremendous crack.

"He thinks he will flush the girl out," said Tungay to me and bellowed with laughter. I sweated for I was afraid that the girl's body was hidden under the canvas and that I would be blamed for putting it there.

We outspanned at midday. The Dutchman drank coffee with us, two cups. He refused a third and rose portentously to his feet.

"I'm going back. But first I want to look among the Jew's belongings. It's been worrying me all the time. She is there," he shouted suddenly. "I am certain of it. Otherwise, why show me what's under the canvas on every waggon except that one?"

"Show him, Bernstein," said Tungay.

"No, I'm not responsible for anything," I said.

Tungay got the boys to pull back the canvas. There was nothing under it except my goods and a plough. The Dutchman burst into a roar of laughter and hit me between the shoulder blades.

"Well, that was a good joke," he said. "All morning I've been riding along, convinced she was there. At one time I was thinking of forcing you to open up at the point of my gun . . . Well, old mates, I can see it has nothing to do with anyone here. She must have run off on foot with some Kaffir. Until I see you." He kicked his pony and rode away.

I loaded my stuff back onto the cart. Tungay took no notice of me. He had climbed into his waggon and lay half asleep.

I drove a mile or two along the road and then turned off. I outspanned behind a kopje. There I waited for the Dutchman. Late in the afternoon I saw Tungay's waggons pass. The Dutchman did not come that way until sunset. He outspanned within walking distance of the kopje and I set off at once to see him.

"You again," he said.

"I've been waiting for you."

"So?"

"I waited to tell you that your servant was murdered."

"You joking again?" he said coldly.

"No, it's true. The man I was travelling with is mad. He murdered the girl last night after raping her. He told me so himself."

"Then why on earth did you say nothing to me this morning?"

It was impossible to tell him that I had been afraid. I said: "I was thinking of the delay. But then I decided to do my duty. Tungay told me he did it once before, in London."

"If you're serious, we'll have to make a report to the magistrate. That means going back fifty miles. You'll have to do it. I've got my sick father in that waggon there. I can't leave him for long."

"I can't go back. My donkey will just last out the journey to the Vaal but no more."

The Dutchman looked at me suspiciously. "Is this a trick to get a horse out of me perhaps? You don't catch an old bird with chaff, lad. That's it, you want me to lend you a horse."

"There's my cart and goods I'd leave as security, damn you . . . But I'm anxious to get to the Vaal. I've got my living to earn. There will be endless delay if I make a report."

"True. And it won't bring the girl to life . . . but you may be joking. I can't take you seriously altogether."

The Dutchman and I smoked in silence and watched the oxen grazing out across the veldt.

"Nice beasts," I said.

He said: "I've been thinking things over. What difference will it make if a report is handed in by a runner? Let me send one of my Kaffirs back."

"That will be best and no delay for either of us," I said eagerly.

"We will have done our duty." The Dutchman spat: he annihilated a struggling beetle.

"Yes, a written report is the thing," I said.

Heading the report Klipdrift on the Vaal, I wrote down all that Tungay had said to me. Both Schoeman and I signed the paper which was then placed in a cleft stick for the runner to take.

Early the next morning I watched him speed away under the stars. Schoeman shook my hand and climbed onto his waggon. He had a fast span, magnificent beasts that drew the waggon out of sight within the hour.

I did not see him again but a few months later at Klipdrift I had a letter from the magistrate, Naude. He wrote to say that there was no case to be taken up for though a thorough search had been made, the girl's body had not been found.

14

It was May when I came at last to the Vaal. I stood on the bank, still grasping Archibald's reins, and watched the scene. Great trees fringed the banks of the river and underneath the trees stood the tents of the diggers. Their camps gave to the whole business of digging the air of a grand picnic. Craters had been dug out of the gravelly soil and in these and around them hundreds of men were working. Kaffirs, Coloureds and some white men dug with picks and then shovelled the soil into buckets or levered with crowbars great boulders that stood on the claims. Others were rocking the gravel in cradles or combing through the final sieving. Occasionally, when a diamond was picked out, there were shouts of congratulation that thrilled me: I felt a longing to start digging for myself.

A digger, looking up from sorting, called out to me: "Hey, what you got to sell?"

"Blankets, shirts . . ."

"Got trousers?" he asked, indicating his ragged corduroys. Patches of flour bags had been sewn on the knees and had been patched again with squares of red flannel.

"I've got the very trousers to fit you," I said, overjoyed at finding a ready customer.

He left his claim and sat on a rock while I opened up my pack.

"Solly and the other traders have been out of stock for the past month. Let me see." He measured a pair of mole-skin trousers against his legs. "These will do. How much?"

There was no time to answer. The cart was being rushed by the diggers. A ragged Coloured boy who had been standing idle flung himself into the fray to help me. He demanded prices that I would have been too frightened to ask for and at the end of an hour or so when my entire stock of clothing and blankets had been sold, I was in possession of two hundred pounds.

The Capie stood with folded arms watching me count the money.

"Well, I saved you," he said: he spoke English with a heavy Cape accent and would switch to the Taal without warning. "I could see at once basie didn't know anything about the trading here. On the Fields you can get any price for blankets and clothes, flour too . . . you can make a fortune here if you have only got the goods to sell."

"Here's a pound for your help."

"How about making this permanent, basie?"

"I don't really need anyone. I've come all the way from Natal without a servant."

"You can't manage here without me. I know the ways of the place. Just my food and a pound a month. I broke my leg. I don't walk properly yet so I can't dig."

I saw that he was thin.

"All right. I'll take you on. What's your name?"

"Stokkies Truter."

I outspanned Archibald and left him with Stokkies while I went to the bank to deposit my money, all except ten sovereigns. As I strolled through the little town, I saw one of the posters that Jo had daubed. It was displayed outside the hotel on the corrugated iron wall. I went inside to spruce myself up and to enquire where Jo lived.

The publican directed me to a big stone house at the end of the main street. Many of the girls of Uzzell's company were seated on the front stoep watching the passersby and yawning, or eating candied fruit from a big bowl. Jo looked out of a window. "You got here, Mannie." She threw kisses to me. "I thought the lions had eaten you, ducks."

"Jo," I said: I had to tell somebody. "Jo, I sold my whole pack in one hit."

The girls cried out, greedy as birds: "Then you are rich? Stand us champagne . . ."

"I am yours," shrieked Fifi, a sallow French girl. She made as if to tear her clothes off. Bonnie danced away to get some champagne. Jo had come on to the stoep, dressed for walking with her skirt in a holder, to show ankle boots and scarlet stockings; she was wearing a hat of blue feathers the colour of her eyes.

"No poaching," she cried, pushing the other girls away from me. She kissed me on the mouth. "I never thought I'd see my darling Ike again. And rich . . ."

"Here's the champagne," screamed Bonnie. A houseboy followed her, carrying a dozen bottles.

Corks began to fly: the dozen bottles were emptied at great speed and more were sent for.

"They're drinking it like water," I whispered anxiously to Jo.

"Only they never drink water so fast."

"Isn't our champagne wonderfully cool, Mr. Bernstein?" said Sweet Jasmine. "It's due to a charcoal cooler we had built at the back. We're quite civilized as you can see, Mr.

Bernstein." Jasmine had cultivated a refined accent but sometimes her voice played tricks on her and *a* came out as *i*. Whenever this happened, her eyes would open wider and she would put her hand to her lips with a murmured "Pardon me," as though she had belched. She had had lessons in elocution from Uzzell. I was afraid of Sweet Jasmine: she was respectable and determined to get married.

Jo rescued me from her.

"Push off, Jas," she said. She took me firmly by the arm and marched me out along the dusty road. "I was going for a walk down to the river, Mannie, and a bit of a row across . . ."

"By yourself?"

"Captain Halden has a claim at Pniel. I go over there and sit and talk to him sometimes. We won't go there today, though. Let's go to Sanger's for tea. Did Archibald get through?"

"Yes, there he is under the trees."

"I see him," said Jo. She went through the grass to him and stroked him. "Artsibald . . ."

She came back to me with that lovely look of hers illumining her.

Tungay saw her for the first time. He had been at Reuben's store and was now standing outside with his thumbs hooked into his belt, watching Jo. The freckled, slick lips parted in a smile of wonder at Jo in her blue hat coming through the grass from among the trees.

15

I was sitting in my tent one afternoon before going to meet Jo and I began figuring out how much money I had left. There were six pounds in my pocket and one hundred and ten pounds in the bank.

Immediately I suspected the Coloured boy Stokkies of having robbed me but further working out revealed that the money had been spent on Jo. We had been to the races several times, we had had meals at Sanger's nearly every night. I had bought some lengths of silk from an Indian pedlar for gowns for Jo and paid a dressmaker to have them made up. Champagne at Uzzell's, the hire of two horses, five pounds lost on a boxing match, Stokkies's clothes and food . . . it is all written down in my secret ledger. During the three weeks I had been on the diggings I had plundered our small capital.

I called Stokkies. He entered, dazzling in a white drill suit.

"You're sacked," I said. "Here's your money. You can keep the suit."

"But my baas, what I have done?"

"I'm cutting down expenses," I said. "Here, take a message to Miss Jo. Tell her I will be late today because I have business to attend to."

"Yes, my baas."

I had made an effort to follow up my luck, by ordering

more goods from the coast, but the advices showed delivery would not be made for six months owing to shortage of transport. I had cancelled the order.

I sat there and pondered. The sensible thing to do was to get back to Durban and bring more goods myself for sale on the diggings. But that meant I would have to leave Jo. I thought of ways of investing money on the diggings. Diamonds? I knew nothing about them and I would ruin myself learning the value and quality of stones. As for digging, I had tried that for a few days and all I got was blisters. A partnership in a store, that was the thing. Solly Reuben was always struggling to make ends meet. He would welcome capital and help in his store.

I was friendly with the Reubens. They were Polish and spoke unpredictable English which they insisted on practicing at all times except emergencies. Twice I had spent the Sabbath with them. They lived in a room at the back of the store. Here with the candles lit Mrs. Reuben had made a home in the wilderness.

The place was always crowded with Jews that Solly invited in the goodness of his heart; he would invite first and regret later. We did not go there simply for the taste of home cooking though Becky Reuben was a great cook: there was also the attraction of her round face and three chins, her pudgy hands, her lively censorious dark eyes, her orthodoxy and her dominion over Solly. In our hearts did we not all wish for such a woman? It was good to be mothered . . . scolded, pitied, interfered with as to the manner in which one's food was cooked. That woman was an anchor in the shifting life of the diggings.

I snatched up my hat and went round to Solly's place straightaway. I thought it would take perhaps half an hour to settle my business with him and there would still be time to see Jo before the evening concert.

The store was built of iron so new that it flashed in the sunlight. A few dusty fowls scratched furiously, a span of donkeys dropped in the shade of a straggling thorn tree, Kaffirs squatted about. Solly came outside to supervise the stowing away of bags of mealie meal and a keg of butter that had been standing under the lean-to. A Kaffir in a new striped shirt trotted beside Solly while he rolled the keg away: Solly was doing the hard work, he didn't seem to mind.

He was a big, stooped man ready always to smile but clever enough and shrewd enough to make money at anything he turned his hand to.

"Come inside, Mannie," he said. "We're just closing up."

Mrs. Reuben gave me a welcome. "Sit, sit," she cried and made a place for me on a pile of new saddles. Opposite me were two little girls so like their mother as to be droll.

"Say good-evenink," Mrs. Reuben said.

"Good-evenink."

I gave up hope of seeing Jo that evening. Mrs. Reuben insisted that I eat and then I had to play oranges-and-lemons with the little girls. Only when they were in bed did Solly encourage me to talk business.

"This is the problem," I said. "I'm looking for a partnership or a share in a business. I've got money and nothing to invest it in unless I go down to the coast for more goods. There's nothing here I can deal in . . ."

"Except diamonds," said Solly. "Vot, he is jokink for sure." He winked at Mrs. Reuben. "Lookink for somethink to invest in? My poy. Look arundt you . . ."

"Not diamonds," I said.

"Vy not? Vot you got against diamonds?"

"I was thinking of going in shares with you . . ."

Solly shook his head. "No, Mannie. My wibe and me make a libbing. Bring in a partner, bring in trouble."

"I know nothing about diamonds. And my capital is not so big. If I bought even one dud I would be ruined."

"But of course you must go in partners with somebody," Solly advised, turning his hands out, palms up. "I know the very poisson for you . . ."

"It's Abie?" said Mrs. Reuben, her face glowing. "Vell, and he's got a sister . . . you might do vorse . . ."

"She means Abie Moskowicz, her cousin. That is who I was thinking of for you."

"Just the one," cried Mrs. Reuben. She was so excited by the prospect that she clapped her hands. "They will love it, the Moskowiczes. Everypoddy is knowink your father is a wunnerful man . . ."

I had the impulse to bolt.

"You've taken me by surprise," I said. "Please don't rush anything." I edged towards the door. Mrs. Reuben followed me.

"You be a goot poy, Mannie," she said, patting my shoulder. "Oh, it shouldn't be . . . going off into the darkness to a tent, to food cooked by a half-caste . . . vot's that for a life?" She looked despairingly into the starlit night. "So fine outside but only listen . . ." She shook her head accusingly at me.

From across the way we could hear Jo singing to the men congregated on the stoep at Uzzell's place:

> ". . . Give me a bright diamond as big as a star,
> Valley of diamonds, valley so far . . ."

Other voices joined in, and the time was beaten out by

a stamping of feet; but the chorus was obliterated by a fusillade of shots from a rifle, never to be explained. Mrs. Reuben sadly closed the door on me.

16

"Basie?" Stokkies fell into step beside me. "Who's this Abie Mosk What's his-name?"

"You hell, you've been listening at the door." I aimed a kick at him but he dodged. He marched on beside me, just out of reach.

"Do you want to marry this Abie's sister and get tied up, a stud animal? Ach man, time to marry when you got to. Listen, basie, what would you say if I told you I know diamonds better than this Abie ever will? And I haven't got a sister you must marry."

"Stokkies, for the last time . . . stop your insolence."

"Basie, I can spot a schlenter simply by the feel of it."

"You're a liar."

"It's a gift, basie, I was born with it. Some men have an eye for a girl, for a horse or a dog. But, my basie, Stokkies has an eye for a diamond. You ask Mr. Nairn the diamond buyer. He said to me: Stokkies Truter, you're a thief, a robber, you're nothing but a crook, but you know a diamond when you see one. Mr. Nairn, I said, you give me a reference, my old one, write all that down . . ." He followed me into the tent and went on inexorably: "Now to become a diamond buyer you must get a license, then

61

you buy a scale to weigh the diamonds on. That's all you need, plus Stokkies. You pay by the carat, basie, so much extra for the colour . . . it's white ones that fetch the most. You've got to keep up with the prices. Mr. Nairn used to say the Kaiser gets up on the wrong side of the bed and down goes the price of diamonds, Lord Muck-on-Toast quarrels with his fancy woman and down goes the price . . . you got to watch all that. On top of it all you got to watch for shape. You got four shapes. There's a true diamond shape, that's an octohedron . . . you see I know even the big words . . . then there is a square, a round diamond and a three-sided stone. Octohedron is the best." He squatted down and drew the shapes on the earth. "There must be no flaw and the market must be just right when you sell . . . Now listen, basie, you listen to me when you are buying a stone. When I cough . . . careful, hear? You leave that diamond alone. But if I sit there quiet, you buy the diamond. We'll work out a code for the prices you must pay. Stokkies will make you the richest man in the district."

"Where did you learn about diamonds?" I asked grudgingly.

"All us children played with diamonds when I was small, basie. I could tell you even then what was a good stone though I didn't know you could get money for them. I would separate the pretty stones I found in the river; the bantoms on one side, all sorts of colours, and on the other side the shining pebbles. We lived on a farm near here. Mr. Nairn was a trader then, he used to buy ostrich feathers and skins. He took the shining pebbles . . ."

"Where's Mr. Nairn now?"

Stokkies looked up with a smile. "In jail, my baas, for stealing a parcel of diamonds out of the Post Office.

"He could have been a millionaire. Long before any diggers came to the Vaal, Mr. Nairn sold diamonds secretly. Basie, do you know what he was going to do? He was going to keep all the diamonds of the Vaal for himself. And I was so simple, basie, that I was happy to get a few pence from Mr. Nairn for bringing him the right stones and not a kick for bringing him the wrong ones. He kicked like a mule if you gave him a piece of crystal."

There was a silence. I was getting ready to visit Uzzell's.

"Did you see Miss Jo?"

"Yes. She had plenty of attention, she didn't miss you, basie.

"What about it? Yes or no?"

"Buying diamonds? All right, I'll risk fifty pounds."

"That's my baas."

17

I set out with Stokkies next day on a tour of the claims at Pniel. I had my license and my scale in my pocket; and fifty sovereigns in my money belt. I rode a cream coloured mare while Stokkies tagged along on Archibald. In white britches, glossy black boots and a white helmet with a scarlet puggaree and a blue ostrich feather, I reckoned I cut a fine enough figure to inspire confidence in the diggers. Stokkies had in his pocket a soft red duster which he would whisk out when we stopped; with it he rubbed up my boots.

By luck we stopped at a claim owned by a Russian, Prozesky, and watched him washing gravel.

"I'm in the market for any stones you might want to sell," I said.

"You come wrong place," he growled. "I not see a stone for month." Then he laughed: a diamond had been turned up in the gravel. Prozesky tossed it to me. "You bring me luck. Weigh."

My hand began to shake. I glanced at Stokkies. His eyes were a blaze of encouragement.. He coughed. I put the diamond on the scale.

"One carat."

"Nice if the baas could find thirty like that," commented Stokkies: this meant that I was to offer twenty-five pounds and not go above thirty-five.

"Twenty-five pounds," I said to Prozesky.

"Thirty."

I counted the sovereigns into his hand and slipped the diamond into a matchbox. I remember the little shock of surprise . . . I was thinking: So diamond-buying is a business after all.

"There is big find," Prozesky said. "A man Korsten has diamond, he asks ninety pounds for it."

"I'll buy that," I said to Stokkies as we rode away.

"You are getting the taste for it now," Stokkies crowed. "But what about money?"

"I'll give him a cheque."

"You can try it. But remember, the rule is cash."

"Well then, I'll value the diamond and take an option on it for ten pounds."

"The baas knows business," said Stokkies, fluffing up the fur on Archibald's neck.

Korsten's claim proved difficult to find. Stokkies rode

one way and I another. We were to meet again under an acacia tree on the ridge. My way took me past Captain Halden's claim. He messed with a young Englishman named Britt Tyzack. As I rode up the two of them were strolling across the claim to their tent: it was the midday break. Both of them knew me. Halden and I had sparred together at the boxing academy in Klipdrift and I had seen Britt there too though always as a spectator.

"I'm in the diamond-buying business," I announced, "and I'm looking for a fellow named Korsten. I hear he has a diamond for sale valued at ninety pounds."

Halden folded his arms and looked at me with an interested air. "Is it the guy whose tent was washed away in the floods?"

"I don't know."

"He is six feet, thinnish, going bald," said Britt urbanely.

The other goy said: "I know, he's got a white-handled pocket knife."

"Oh, bloody funny," I said.

I left those two jokers and hailed a digger on the next claim. He turned to face me: he had been sitting with his back to me, sorting gravel . . . It was Tungay.

I had seen him once or twice in Klipdrift, at Uzzell's concerts. I always ignored him.

Now I walked on. Damn Halden and Tyzack, I thought, it's me being dressed up like this that makes them wild . . . they are jealous of my clothes . . . and Halden is jealous because Jo and I are true-loving . . .

Tungay had caught up with me. "Where are you off to, Bernie?" He linked his arm familiarly in mine. I tried to throw him off but he had me in a good grip.

"I'm looking for a chap named Korsten."

"You're going in the wrong direction," he said, and swung me round. "I'll show you the way. It's only a step if you know the short cut."

We set off briskly. Tungay went straight across the pocked land, heedless of bushes or water, into a wilderness of worked-out claims. I managed to free myself from him and took time to skirt the bad patches.

"You'll have to be a bit quicker," he said. "I've got to be back to start my boys."

He took hold of me again with a policeman's grip. We plunged in a minor landslide to the bottom of a hundred-foot hole, and his grip was broken, yet though we stood in mud to our thighs he got hold of me again, dragging me to the top of the crater.

There he let go of me. He looked round with a puzzled air.

"I've clean forgot where that claim is."

"You've gone mad. Put up your fists. I'll teach you a lesson."

He hooked his thumbs into his belt. The pale eyes were menacing.

"I'm going to do for you, Bernstein."

He was on me. I stood no chance against him. He stopped me with a boot and slammed his fist into my mouth even as I shaped up. It was over in seconds. He had a hold on me that I had never even heard of. He whirled me suddenly, crashed a fist on the side of my head and sent me hurtling down the slope into the hole. He meant me to drown there or break my neck in falling.

I like to remember now that I remained cool, with a fine edge to my thinking. The hole was terraced by four ledges, outcroppings of reef that had been bared during the mining. I was aware of these ledges and I rolled and twisted so that I landed on hands and knees each time. Only on the last one as I was growing weaker I smashed my face on a rock.

I was still conscious as I hit the water though I came up blinded by mud. Above me Tungay had gone berserk. I heard boulders from the top squelch in the mud and when I got some sight back, saw that he had balanced a row of boulders on the lip of the crater and was systematically heaving them over. Perhaps he would have killed me if Stokkies had not come seeking me and distracted him long enough for me to creep under the shelter of an over-hanging ledge where there was a small cave. I fitted in there neatly.

"Where are you, Bernstein?" Tungay roared. "I'm coming for you."

I heard him on the slope and then I heard his careful edging along the rock. I shivered. I could not tell exactly where he was. His voice echoed round the crater: "I'm coming for you, Bernstein." Then there was a silence. He may have grown afraid in this shadowed place and thought I was stalking him. I heard him returning to the top.

Now he began to hurl boulders at random. Some of them fell into the mud near me and others far across the crater: I was safe enough from a chance hit.

I was in pain. My face had been injured during my fall. I could see the bulge of my swollen cheeks when I glanced down. Somebody told us once when we were children that in a rock at the heart of the earth sits Lilith with Satan's child. I remembered this now and I was afraid again as I had been as a child . . . I could stand it no more in the cave where I was bound hand and foot by the rock.

I moved out cautiously, along the ledge towards the side of the crater opposite Tungay, thinking I might climb out before he reached me. Like a wild thing he stood there against the sunset. He gave a howl of joy at seeing me and with his madman's strength launched the rock far out across the crater. Then he ran to the side where I was climbing.

Stokkies arrived with Halden and Tyzack. It took the three of them to lay Tungay out.

"Fatherland, your face," Stokkies said as he helped me out of the crater. "Did he get our diamond, basie?"

I felt in my pocket. The matchbox was still there.

"It's all right, I've got the diamond."

Halden and Tyzack bore me off to their tent. Stokkies was sent to get Doctor Vollantyne who had been confining a Boer woman at a nearby camp. The doctor hurried over to stitch the gashes on my face; and prescribed whiskey. Stokkies then took him to Tungay who had been left unconscious at the crater.

I washed in the river and Tyzack gave me some of his clothes to wear. These were good quality. Everything I could see about me was of first-class quality; there was silver and fine linen here in the wilderness. The tent had an awning and was lined with baize.

I fingered the matchbox, wishing it contained a bigger diamond.

"We'll all have some of Bernstein's prescription," said Britt, pouring whiskey into silver mugs.

Lucky Tyzack they called him on the diggings. He was no athlete but he was admired: he read Plato. People admired him for that and for his breeding and good looks but it was his luck that really attracted them. Luck was what made you a great man here. A fortune might slide away from a lord, to be picked up by a Kaffir. Britt was little more than twenty years old yet he was said to be worth ten thousand pounds which he had made since his arrival on the diggings a few months before. And this was his second attempt at digging. His first venture had yielded two diamonds worth eight thousand pounds and on the proceeds he had gone to Cambridge to study law.

Halden was the older man, he was past thirty. He had a face seamed and marked by a life of adventure; a tragic clown's face. Experience had blunted him. Next to him, Britt shone.

"Have you been reading much lately?" I asked Britt. He looked at me in surprise. I was pleased. He knew me only as an athlete.

"Reading, Bernstein?"

"You know . . . Plato and so on."

"Well yes. I've only a few books with me of course."

"I read a lot. I'm always reading. Shakespeare."

"I see."

"I learn a piece out of Shakespeare every day," I said recklessly.

"Do you mean you're an amateur actor as well as a boxer?"

"No, of course not. Only I like to get off some of the stuff by heart."

"Don," Britt said solemnly to Halden who had been glancing through an old paper. He looked up. "Bernstein can recite Shakespeare."

"I heard. How about something from *The Merchant of Venice*, Bernstein?"

Britt said quickly: "Some more whiskey, just what the doctor ordered . . ." and the doctor's appearance at that moment raised a laugh which broke up the hostility between Halden and me.

The doctor was followed by six bull terriers that accompanied him wherever he went. He sprawled in a chair with two of them on top of him, one on his knees and the other on his chest.

"How's Tungay?" I asked.

The doctor laughed, stretching his neck to look round the bull terrier. "Fast asleep, like a baby and in an odd way looking like a baby."

"Have you certified him?"

He met this with a guffaw that fairly unsettled the dogs. "Bernstein, you can bring a case of assault against him if you like . . ."

"But he is mad."

"Not in the legal sense. I had a long talk with him." The doctor dribbled out a little whiskey for each of the dogs. "I gave Tungay some opium, he'll have nice dreams. He'll be right as rain tomorrow." He laughed again. "What have you been up to, Bernstein? Do you know what the trouble is? He is jealous of you. This girl Jo Carr . . ." He turned a bright, malicious glance on Halden. "Wasn't she your girl, Don?"

"She quit."

"Lucky for you," Vollantyne said. "Otherwise it would have been you getting bombarded by rocks. Tungay is in love with Jo."

We all laughed at that.

"If he is sane, you ought to challenge him to a fair fight," Britt said to me. "I'll second you."

"Now you're talking," said the doctor. "Damme if I don't second Tungay. But make it a month from now, Bernstein. You don't want those cuts opened up again too soon."

Even with the whiskey in me I felt a flicker of anxiety at the thought of having to face Tungay in the ring: the man would go berserk and kill me before anybody could intervene. I determined to tell the doctor later about Tungay and the Kaffir girl but at that moment I was enjoying the popularity peculiarly reserved for the principal in a fight. The monitor within me warned me that if I queried Tungay's sanity now, these others would put it down to my being a Jew and a coward; and here I was being invited by the doctor to bat for the Diamondfields Cricket Club against Colesberg.

We sat under the awning. The sunset had faded except for shafts of purple in the west. Diggers on their way from the claims stopped to hear the tale of my adventure. I was drinking whiskey out of a silver mug. And the betting on me was six to four.

From my enchantment I said to Halden: "I was in Cape Town when the *Alabama* came in, both times . . ."

"Was your mother holding you up to see the pretty ship come in?" he snarled.

"Have you been long in Africa?" Britt asked me.

"Since I was fourteen . . . um . . . ten years," I lied. "We've been trading with the Zulus."

"You hear that?" Britt cried. "Bernstein knows the Zulus. What about them, Bernstein? They say there's a chief among them likely to cause trouble."

"Cetewayo. He was friendly to us."

"I want to know more about the Zulus. They're a force to be reckoned with. You're an Englishman of course?"

"Oh yes."

"You must have thought about politics here on the diggings," he said eagerly. I nodded though the truth was that in the three weeks I had been there politics had not once crossed my mind. Britt went on: "We've got to get into the game. Listen. If the supply of diamonds on the

Vaal is inexhaustible . . . I mean, if it's true that the diamonds are washed down the river from some source that is constantly replenished . . . then this country has a future. Agreed? What's that future going to be, I mean who is going to be the deciding factor in it? This Zulu chief? The Boer Presidents? The Kaiser?

"Or is it going to be Great Britain? America won't want to be dealt in . . . But there's a great game waiting to be played here."

"I wonder if you would like to be dealt in, Bernstein?" Vollantyne murmured.

"As a first step, join the Vaal Mounted Rifles," said Britt. "We drill on Wednesday afternoons . . ."

"Easy on the guy," Halden protested but Britt had already brought a paper for me to sign.

The hour lost its edge. I spilled whiskey over the borrowed clothes.

"Bitches eat the placenta, why don't women do it, they'd be healthier," the doctor was roaring.

I was sick.

I remember being propelled by Britt to a cart. It must have been the doctor's vehicle: a bull terrier flung himself on me and snored as though he were on a mat. A dozen men crowded on, tumbling one on top of the other.

Perhaps the doctor gave me some opium . . . I had strange, violent dreams of women and the stars flamed through the sky like comets and burst and there was golden rain falling.

The men with me were out to make a night of it at Uzzell's. I don't remember getting there. At some time I was put to bed in the passage outside the girls' dormitory.

I regained consciousness in the clear light of the afternoon. I could hear a Kaffir girl singing two notes over and over again, a sound to haunt you forever. She was sitting near me, a young woman. In that light I saw purple tones in her skin which had the smoothness of grapes.

Seeing me awake, she cried out shrilly and Jo came yawning from the dormitory. She chased the Kaffir girl away.

"Are you better, Mannie?"

"I must get up."

"Stokkies has brought your clothes."

"I got drunk. Tungay . . . I've challenged him to a fight."

"He certainly gave you a pasting."

"It will be different in the ring."

"I wouldn't trust him anywhere."

Stokkies glided in with my clothes which he had brushed and cleaned.

"Have you still got our diamond?" he whispered: Jo had left me to get dressed. "I wanted to sleep here last night in the passage but they wouldn't let me. Has anybody stolen it?"

I drew out the matchbox and reassured him with a sight of the diamond.

"Let's get away from here," he said. "I'm getting a headache from the smell of scent."

But I was not allowed to leave then. Madame Olpresci, who acted as housekeeper to the company, insisted that I stay to supper.

"There will be no pig," she said earnestly. "Mock duck is on the menu, it is true. But though the recipe calls for pig, I always use sheep."

18

Supper was to be served at a long table in the front room. A stage had been rigged up at the end of the room for it was here that the company gave a concert every second night of the week. Dances were held here too.

The house had been built on a grand scale by a rich German trader who had died of apoplexy. Jo could describe to you his death agonies. An old Griqua woman, a servant of his, who still hung about the house told all who would listen how that rich and powerful man had succumbed.

There were still elegant gilt and crystal chandeliers left over from the German's time, and some flowered wallpaper, but for the rest the furniture consisted of deal benches and tables.

The lamps were lit. Madame walked round the table, counting places.

"I'll see that Jo sits next to you," she said. "My poor boy . . . when I saw you last night, I thought you were finished. I've been talking to Mrs. Reuben about you today . . ."

Uzzell strode in, accompanied by Britt and Halden.

"The man's himself again," Uzzell cried, slapping me on the back. "Your friends came to enquire after you and I've invited them to take pot luck."

Madame glanced anxiously at the table, whispered to

74

the servant and began to rearrange the places. The company was drifting into the room. The girls were painted, ready for the concert. The Minstrels were in costume but had not yet blackened their faces. Madame's poodles, in caps and ruffs, were sitting in a row on the stage, except for Toto de Fropps who occupied a small high chair near Madame's place at the end of the table; that evening Toto wore a sailor top and cap. Madame herself was all pearly powder and velvet and jet.

Jo came in after we were all seated and slid into the chair next to me.

She whispered: "I saw Tungay. He won't fight. He is clearing out, riding transport . . . All I had to do was . . ." She made a sound of kissing. "Ugh. Never again . . ."

"No sweet nothings at the table," cried Jasmine.

"What have we here?" said Uzzell as the Kaffir maid placed his supper before him.

"It's mock duck," said Madame Olpresci.

Uzzell tried some. He set down his fork and looked at Madame.

"Madame," he said solemnly, "this is one time that you have carried your mockery too far."

"Never satisfied," Madame flared.

"But it is delicious," said Britt gallantly.

"Haw haw," said Bonnie, in imitation of Britt's accent.

"Now then, Bonnie, get on with your mock duck," said Uzzell.

Bonnie picked at her food. She was thinner but still the most beautiful girl of the troupe. I noticed Britt glance at her, attracted by the rose petal skin and golden hair. She ignored him after the jeer at his accent. But Fifi, the French girl, set out to entice him: she undid the hooks of her bodice and jerked her head sideways as much as to invite Britt to go to bed with her at once. Madame, jowls quivering, made signs in the air to persuade Fifi to cover herself. Fifi was a whore, tolerated by the other girls only because her motives were high: she was earning a *dot* so that she could go home to her village and be married.

"You'll have to go and tell your swain to fight," I said to Jo.

"But he'll kill you."

I felt a stab of dislike of her.

"Are you trying to make a fool of me?" I said.

Now she turned her back on me and began to play up to Halden. I sank into misery.

"Oh do eat, monsieur," cried Madame. "You will never get your strength back otherwise. I swear to you it is not pig."

"It must be. The receipt says pork," said Jasmine. "I know how to cook."

"Bah. I use sheep. Rest assured, a man does not want to marry a cook," said Madame venomously. "Feed him, Jo, like you would a child, spoon by spoon . . ."

"I know what I'd like to feed him."

"Little birdies in their nests agree," said Jasmine.

"I don't want to be in his nest," spat Jo.

When the concert started, she arranged with the Minstrels to lead off on *Here Comes the Alabama,* and herself sang it. I left the place.

Stokkies was waiting for me.

"Diamond all right, basie? I fossicked a bit today and found out exactly where Korsten has his claim. He hasn't sold his diamond yet."

I lay on my bed. I thought of Jo kissing Tungay.

Presently Britt Tyzack strolled into the tent. Stokkies made some coffee for us.

"Been playing poker," Britt said.

"You don't want to play with Uzzell."

"I won."

"Winning is not important, not with Uzzell. He tests a person's courage at the card table. He likes to find a man's limit."

"Hell. I don't begin to understand people. You know, Bernstein, I made a bit of a fool of myself tonight, over that fair girl Bonnie."

"She's mad about Uzzell."

He got up and moved about restlessly. "I thought she was a prostitute. I thought they were all prostitutes. I tried to give her a pound . . . You should have heard her."

"Only Fifi is one. The others are on the make but you have to be careful."

"I see." He sat down and looked dolefully at me. "The truth is, I don't get on with people in the ordinary sense. Now and again I seem to hit the right note . . . There's Halden and yourself. But I never know how to take Vollantyne though we see eye to eye in politics, and he is active in the Society."

"The Society?"

"Actually, that's what I came here to talk to you about. I want you to join us. You've taken the first step by joining the V.M.R."

"The V.M.R.?"

"The Vaal Mounted Rifles. You signed last night," he said impatiently.

"I remember signing something."

"You're to come and train on Wednesday. And afterwards there is a meeting of the Society at my camp. Before I go any further, do you want to join?"

"What are you trying to do?"

"The aim ultimately is to unite the whole world in a commonwealth of nations . . . that's the grand plan . . . we'll let you in on the details when you join."

He began to talk to me. At times he was excruciatingly dull then just as the bitterness of ennui crept over me he would touch on an idea so wonderful that my whole being was captivated: he was giving me glimpses of the visions he had, of power and glory and goodness on a vast scale.

Suddenly he paused. "I'm telling you all this. But are you going to join us?"

"Yes."

"Good. I think you'll go a long way if you are sensible and keep your eye on the main chance . . . you could easily get into politics.

"There's a great deal to be done here. We have to establish the diamond fields as a British possession which means international ownership in the long run. What we've got to do is keep the Boers out.

"By the way, Halden is going north in a few weeks' time, he is going to prospect for gold . . . he is friendly with a Dutch geologist who has some influence with the President.

"But what we are planning immediately is to attack the next Boer magistrate who rides in to collect taxes. We must show them we mean business . . ."

"Won't we get into trouble?"

"Of course we will. But we've got to get the Government to act."

"I've got a family to think of," I muttered.

"A family?"

"My father and a sort of sister . . . she's an orphan and I have to help support her."

"You gave me quite a fright," said Britt. "For one awful

78

moment I thought you meant you were married. A father and a sister to think of . . . that's bad enough, but a wife! I would have had to ask you to withdraw, Bernstein. It's goodbye if you get a wife. You might as well go and live in the suburbs in London.

"What you want to do now is think of education. I'm going back to Cambridge in September. What about you coming with me? . . ."

He had talked the night away. We went outside. Diggers were already astir. The rattle of a cradle could be heard, sharp as gunfire on the morning air.

Britt said: "See you Wednesday," and slouched off down the road.

"Gids, that one can talk," said Stokkies as soon as Britt was out of earshot. "He'll land himself in jail. Now that he has gone . . . Hurry, basie. We must get to Korsten today."

I returned to the tent and sat on the edge of my stretcher and stared at the ground.

"What's the matter?" Stokkies asked.

"Those two chaps . . . Tyzack is going overseas to study. Halden is going north to find gold."

"And you're jealous. Which would you rather do, my baas?"

"Go to Cambridge to study, I think."

"But you won't go, hey?" he asked anxiously.

"How can I? I've got my family to look after."

Stokkies sighed. "I'd go to the north . . . Man, I would like to find some gold. When is baas Halden leaving?"

"Ask him, if you want to go," I said shortly.

"I can't go, basie."

"Why not?"

"I got no feeling for Halden." There was silence between us. "It's bitter bread you eat if you take wages and

79

kicks from somebody who means nothing to you," he said forlornly. "I got to have feeling for the person I work for. I had feeling for you the minute I saw you on the river bank."

"That's just a Capie's flattery."

He went away to saddle the mare while I dressed. A shadow darkened the entrance of the tent. Jo was there, pale and guilty as she often was in the morning.

"I came to see how you are."

"I'm better, thank you."

"I did come last night but that Tyzack was here jawing. I saw Tungay again. The fight is on. But you do realize that he has at least a stone in hand?"

"Don't worry, I'll make mincemeat of him."

She laughed and came close to me. The sour smell of the night was on her.

Sergeant McCallaghan undertook to train me for the fight. He had done garrison duty at Durban and had seen me fight as a schoolboy. "I'll make ye fit, Mannie," he said with a grim smile. "I'll make ye that fit ye'll never get over it . . ." He had me crawling to my tent from the gymnasium but he kept his word and when I entered the ring against Tungay, I was on my toes.

I had bought a pair of dark green silk britches and matching boots to fight in. Uzzell's girls cheered me when they saw me. We fought outside the boxing academy. Tungay was favourite, I was six to four against. I could see why when Tungay stripped. He was like a gorilla.

The crowd roared . . . "Get measured for a wooden suit, Bernstein!" "Hammer him, Mannie, just keep away from him!"

A precise thought formed in my mind: You damn fool,

you had a chance to get out of it . . . and then the bell had rung and the referee was bawling: "Come out fighting . . ."

Only once did I let Tungay get hold of me and that was in the fourth round. He threw me out of the ring into the willing arms of the spectators; they soon enough helped me back.

"Stay in there, Mannie," Jo was yelling, and I could hear the sergeant's admonishing voice: "Box him, Mannie, just box him nice and easy . . ."

"Kill the Jew!"

Tungay came in, too confident. I let him have it on the side of the head with my right and straightened him up with a left. Then I got away from him. I boxed him, right round the ring; and there was fear in his eyes. He was getting winded.

The big ape went down to a left hook in the fourteenth round. And so help me, I would not have blown a candle out, my breath was so steady.

19

It was something to be Mannie Bernstein after that fight. A fancier who had backed me gave me a diamond ring for my little finger, people I didn't know would come up to me and ask advice about boxing; somebody was forever slapping me on the back. I remember sauntering along with Jo one afternoon near the diamond market under the envious eyes of the diggers who were coming up from their claims.

Somebody hailed me. It was Uzzell. He slapped me on the back.

"You're game, Bernstein. That was a damn good fight and I won quite a few pound on you. Look here, I've got a parcel of stones I want you to see."

"I didn't know you had a claim."

"These are diamonds I won playing cards. Come round to my place and have a look at them now." He was in a lively mood, there was a flush on the thin cheeks, I noticed. He said suddenly: "What would you say the weight of that stone is?" pointing to a green stone in the road.

"About a pound," I said.

"I'd put it closer to half-a-pound. Bet you five bob it's half-a-pound. Come on, let's get Bloody Dan to weigh it."

Bloody Dan's butchery was conveniently near. It was just a few rough planks and a scale, set up on the side of the road. As we approached, he drove a chopper into a plank and extended a blood-stained hairy paw to each of us in turn.

"Nice to see you gentlemen. Now if it's kosher you want, Mr. Bernstein . . ."

"Matter of fact, we've come to you to settle a bet," said Uzzell.

"Gratified to do it."

"Weigh this stone. We've got a bet on it."

The stone weighed just over a pound. Uzzell paid me and I went with him to his place to view the diamonds. He possessed six fancy stones that were beyond my means but I agreed to negotiate the sale for him. In the end I failed to pull the deal off for he would not accept the highest price I could get.

Whenever we met over this transaction, he would make a bet on some absurdity; on the speed of two birds flying overhead, on the number of times a donkey would bray. Soon all Klipdrift was talking about these bets.

It seemed to me that he was having a harmless game with me: I sensed no danger. I was concentrating on plans for the future. My father had written from Durban to tell me that he and Leah were coming to the Vaal some time during September. I owed this to Mrs. Reuben who had written to him about the irregularities in my life.

Well, let them come, I thought, but they will spoil things for me. My father, I knew, would want to separate me from Jo. He would stop me from mixing in politics, even from playing cricket. According to him, time that was not spent in business must be given to study.

There were innumerable problems. It was unthinkable that Leah should stay in Klipdrift. Thousands of men were now digging along the banks of the Vaal and there were only a few girls; some men like Tungay were dangerous brutes. I had decided to buy a farm and had taken an option on one about ten miles from the diggings. I hoped that with my family safely out of the way on the farm, I need not give up Jo and Britt Tyzack . . .

"You watch out for that Uzzell," said Stokkies. "Everybody in Klipdrift is only waiting for him to get you."

"As long as I don't play cards with him."

We were on our way back from the claims, somewhat later than usual. A crowd of diggers had collected in the road near the diamond market.

"They're waiting there for you," said Stokkies. "They want to see what you and Uzzell are going to bet on tonight. Listen, basie. I've put a big black and white stone nicely on the side of the road and the one next to it is reddish, hear . . . then there is a real dark green stone. I weighed all those stones. The big black and white one is four pounds, the reddish one is half-a-pound and the green one is just on five pounds."

"You go to hell, Stokkies. I don't cheat."

"I just thought I'd let you know that they were there. You may need them . . . It's two to one on that the other baas will himself weigh such likely-looking stones, just to be on the safe side."

A cheer went up from the crowd. "Here's Bernstein . . ." "What's the bet today, Uzzell?"

Jo and Bonnie were there, and Madame Olpresci in black like a duenna. The girls were turned out as if for the races, in high-heeled boots and silk gowns.

"Afternoon, Mannie." Uzzell was every inch the show-man. He beamed on our audience while he was greeting me. I would not have been surprised if he had brought his Mr. Bones with him to engage in a little cross-talk. "How's business today?"

The presence of the crowd at once exhilarated and embarrassed me. I wanted to stand there casually, wink at the girls and hold my lapels between forefingers and thumbs; instead, I eagerly took out the box containing the diamonds I had bought that day and nearly dropped it while I was showing my purchases to Uzzell.

"Bet you ten bob the lot weighs three carats," said Uzzell promptly.

"You lose . . . three-and-a-half carats."

Uzzell paid up while Jo clapped her mittened hands and Bonnie cried "Shame!" Stokkies said: "Hoera for my baas. It's his turn now. You name something, basie."

I was tempted to call the weight of the stones he had

planted on the roadside but instead we put our money on the length of time it would take a grasshopper to climb to the top of a stalk of grass. This time Uzzell won. Then he laid a bet on the green stone, giving its weight as five pounds.

"It's no bet," I said. "That's my guess too. I'll lay you the black and white stone. Four pounds . . ."

"My guess too," said Uzzell while a howl of derision went up from the crowd. "We're getting too expert for this game. How about a game of cards instead, Mannie?"

He had slipped the challenge in before I had a chance to sidestep it.

20

Bookies laid the odds on the card game: two to one on Uzzell and three to one on me. The game was fixed for Saturday night from ten to twelve at Uzzell's place. We were to play poker, no limit.

I had for my business three hundred sovereigns which I kept in my money belt. Besides there was four hundred in the bank. One hundred of the money in the bank was earmarked for buying the farm I had on option. And I had ten diamonds which I was holding against rising prices, at present valued at five hundred pounds.

In the uninvaded territory of my mind was the monitor that advised me to go sick or find some excuse to leave the diggings for a while, anything so long as I did not risk the money. But I knew that to dodge the game with Uzzell would mean the end of me on the diggings; it would be the same as welshing.

Still I might have done it if it had not been for Jo. Since my fight with Tungay she regarded me as unbeatable in any line and she was backing me to win.

Stokkies had backed me too. He was delirious with excitement. He ran a book at the Malay camp and stood to win fifty pounds on me, all square if Uzzell won.

Ten o'clock that Saturday night found me at Uzzell's in my best clothes. The gambling room was crammed with spectators. Even Halden and Britt had come.

Uzzell and I sat down. A new deck of cards was solemnly opened. From somewhere in the house came Madame's dolorous cry: "Günther!"

The game proceeded without incident for an hour or more. Then I was dealt four kings. Uzzell drew one. I thought I saw a shadow cross his face. That slight change might have meant anything from disappointment to elation.

I sweated. I was in for it, I knew I was in for it. Uzzell looked up at me with a smile of anticipation: he knew I held four.

The place was quiet except for Madame's voice.

"Somebody gag that old tart," said Uzzell; but Madame was not silenced.

Uzzell placed chips carefully in front of him, building them into five piles of similar height.

"Raise you fifty," he said.

Ten pounds of my money lay on the table. I added fifty. "Raise you ten."

Even as I laid down the bet, I was tempted to throw in my hand and lose everything. I felt depressed. Uzzell was

86

a skilful player: he would master me. Why be a fool for the sake of the schickser? I thought. Jo was sitting quietly at the far end of the table: she was bright-eyed and pale.

Uzzell sat and watched me, enthralled by the struggle he had created in me.

"Günther!"

He raised me another fifty pounds. I put up fifty.

"One hundred," he said. I met that too.

"That's my basie," cried Stokkies from the edge of the crowd; he had been trying to force his way to the table, no doubt with the hope of being able to signal from behind Uzzell's back, but he was not allowed to approach.

Now a feeling of confidence swept through me. Uzzell was bluffing. I met raise for raise until the money in my belt was gone. I shook out my diamonds onto the table.

"Hotnot!" howled Stokkies; somebody must have clapped a hand over his mouth for I heard him no more during the game. But Madame Olpresci went on crying for Günther.

I staked my diamonds in groups of three. Still Uzzell raised me.

"I'm cleaned out," I said.

"I'll take an I.O.U."

Uzzell tossed a double handful of sovereigns onto the table. "Make the limit another four hundred," he said with a smile: he knew to a penny what I had in the bank. Some clerk must have told him.

A tremor shook me as I signed an I.O.U. for a hundred and fifty pounds.

"Raise you two hundred," said Uzzell inexorably.

I forced myself to be still. Look at this thing, said my monitor: where's your logic? . . . The money in the bank is for your family . . . You are still safe . . . Throw in and take the loss.

Ruin would mean that Leah and my father must be thrown into the hurly burly of the diggings: it was too late to stop them from leaving Durban. At least I would have the hundred pounds to pay for the farm if I quit now.

I signed another I.O.U. for one hundred and forty pounds.

"I'll see you."

"What is it?" "What did he say?" The crowd pressed closer.

"Bernstein sees Uzzell," bawled the scorer.

Uzzell laid down his cards one by one.

"Three queens," the scorer announced. "And Bernstein has four kings."

Stokkies roared: "Good my basie. Now I can go arrow straight to the Malay camp to collect."

There was time for a few more hands but I was undoubtedly the winner from then onwards. As the game ended, the girls were kissing me . . . it was congratulations all round except from Jo. But I did not notice that.

"Here, Jo," I said and scooped up the diamonds and put them into her cupped hands. I had ordered champagne and I was whirled away among the crowd. When I got back to Jo, I found her throwing dice with a Yankee digger.

"Roll 'em, Diamond Jo," he shouted, mad with grog and excitement: she had lost my diamonds to him.

21

I was drunk. I remember trying to fight that Yank. I remember wandering through the house seeking Jo, to the mournful accompaniment of Madame Olpresci's voice. Then I was stumbling on the road and cursing Jo. Other roysterers ignored me, yelling out their own obscenities or staggering silently past. I tripped over a prone figure and went sprawling.

A man, lumbering to his feet, threw his shape on to the luminous sky.

"Thieves and whores the lot," he declaimed. "Got a light, buster?"

It was Jo's Yankee digger. I tried to raise myself to hit him but all I was capable of was a clawing action that stirred the dust.

"You took Jo," I said.

"I ain't got her now." He had found a box of matches and after many false starts got a match alight. He took my diamonds from his pocket and counted them. One or two fell and he dropped to his knees and scrabbled in the dust. "Gone," he said. Then with boozy cunning he spread-eagled himself on the road. "Find them in the morning," he whispered. "There ain't nobody gonna find them but me."

I slept and awoke to the sharp bite of the dew. The dew brought out the smell of the dust. All around the camps were silent; it must have been four o'clock in the morning. My tent was not far off. I tiptoed past the sleeping Yank.

A solitary fire was burning. It was at my camp.

Jo was there, sitting on a three-legged stool with her hands to the blaze. She had some coffee boiling.

"You've been with somebody else."

"No, I've been looking for you." I said: "Uzzell knew to a penny how much I was worth."

"Yes, he found that out. You lost your nerve, Mannie."

"You whore."

"Cast-iron Jew, you bloody coward," she screamed at me. I caught her by the hair and slapped her face. "Coward, I'll knife you."

"Oh no, you don't," I said, twisting her arm to make her drop her bowie knife. "Take back what you said."

"What? That you're a cast-iron Jew. Jew, Jew . . . In our church we pray for the Turks, the Jews and the infidels . . ."

"They wouldn't let you in a church. Take back that I'm a coward."

She turned her head and spat in my face. "You are a coward. You let Uzzell beat you. I had a side bet with Uzzell." I let her go and stood with my foot on the knife. "You damn fool," she said. "Uzzell and I often bet . . . You remember my bet with him on Madame Olpresci. And didn't Halden tell you? I bet Uzzell that you would go all the way to the last penny. He put up a hundred pounds."

"And you?"

"I put up myself."

She sat down and poured out some coffee: her hands were trembling. We said no more but sat and watched the stars in paths and rivers of light above us.

90

22

I came on Friday nights to the candles of home. Our dining room was small, no more than six by six, with a low ceiling; the floor was of earth. But Leah made of it a bright place, shut off from the wilderness.

We did not allow Leah to go to Klipdrift but invited a few decent people to the house so that she might be seen. Becky Reuben had undertaken to make a match for her with one of the men who had struck it rich but nobody mentioned pleased my father.

It was not enough that the man have riches, he must be a scholar too, and a healthy man and a man of wit; he must be good-humoured and brave. What a man he wanted for Leah . . . A prince, Mrs. Reuben grumbled.

"She is young yet," said my father but he was anxious as he said it, and gnawed the back of his hand. The truth was that he was afraid now that the time had come to decide Leah's future. He feared the wild and desolate country and would have seen her living safely in some great city; he feared the sudden wealth that made rich men out of beggars. Hard-bitten men came as guests to the farm . . . he disliked them. But then he despised the supple jewel-lovers from the ghettoes who had come flocking to the Vaal after diamonds.

He feared Leah's beauty. Seeing her now at seventeen, I too feared her beauty.

From her Russian grandmother she had inherited a skin that was white and shining, it was like a piece of satin. Her hair was black and her eyes black, slanting above high cheekbones. I remember her on that farm, in the orchard when the peach trees bloomed; her lips were the colour of the peach blossoms.

She sat in a chair beneath the trees and embroidered scarlet roses onto a black cushion. Her skirt was of a light material but her bodice was dark and you saw the purity of her flesh; her flesh was a miracle of whiteness beyond the power of the sun to tarnish.

I had been telling her about the poker game with Uzzell.

". . . then he showed his hand and he held three queens, Leah."

She leaned back with a sigh, dropping her work onto her knee. A sparkle of sweat showed above her upper lip. It was a hot day and I was conscious of her body in the soft clothes, like a flower that had been slightly rained on.

I said: "There was a girl who had been watching us play . . ."

"Painted," she said adroitly.

"Well, she is a singer . . ."

"Lucky thing to watch a game like that," said Leah: she liked playing cards.

"What I was trying to tell you was that she thought me a coward because I would not raise Uzzell to the extent of my last penny."

"Only a fool would expect that," Leah said.

She picked up her work again, laughing suddenly. I felt ashamed of myself for having mentioned Jo to her.

In the tree shading her there were two green birds dipping for honey. Leah looked up at them. The beautiful lines of her face held me.

She said crossly: "What are you staring at?"

"You're good-looking."

"And your singer?"

"I shouldn't have spoken to you about her. But she isn't good-looking."

"She has a better time than me," said Leah, stitching away. "I get so tired of it here, Mannie. You have a good time."

"Trudging about the diggings? Try it for just one day."

"I'm a prisoner. Even getting dressed in the morning . . . think what I have to do. Skirts and hoops and stays and tight boots to keep my ankles small . . . An Oriental puts his womenfolk in a harem but at least they wear comfortable clothes. I have nobody to talk to here, nobody to visit since I can't go to Klipdrift. Klipdrift . . . what a place."

"It's nothing but grumbling," I said.

Later that day I heard her singing in the house. She sang Jo's song *The Valley of Diamonds*.

"Where did you learn that?" I asked her.

"Everybody is singing it, so Miri says."

"And who is Miri?"

"A Coloured girl who does the ironing. The song is called Jo's Song."

"Did Miri tell you that? I'll thrash her."

"She didn't tell me. I saw a poster in Klipdrift. It had written on it: Diamond Jo Speciality, The Valley of Diamonds or Jo's Song."

"And when were you in Klipdrift, miss, to see such a poster?" I said, catching hold of her arm.

She was afraid. "Only once . . ."

"Papa didn't tell me he was taking you to Klipdrift."

"I didn't go with him. He was on the Pniel diggings. I went with Miri. I get so lonely here that I could stand and yell."

"Does Papa know you went to Klipdrift?"

"No."

"I'm going to tell him."

"And I'll tell him about your painted girls."

I called my father.

"She has been in Klipdrift with the Coloured girl."

"What!"

"Perhaps she wants to marry a goy," I said.

"And he that thing who paints herself up," said Leah.

My father scolded her; Miri he threatened to beat with a sjambok until she bled.

23

I sat alone in the orchard. I could hear Leah crying, inconsolable hours after she had been scolded. My father was bribing her with sugar candy.

"Come, darling, there . . . Nu, stop crying . . . eat it, will you eat it?" There was a mumbling and a fresh outburst of tears. "For Miri too . . . yes, yes . . . A sweetie . . . there. . . ."

Later my father came into the orchard and sat in the chair that Leah had been using. His frail hands trembled as he folded them against his breast.

"Quiet at last," he said.

"You went to Pniel, Papa. You didn't tell me about it."

"Yes, I was there, watching the diggers. Such a thing I never saw. But now I shall stay here all the time. Leah on the diggings alone! Do you realize, she did not even go to visit Rebecca Reuben."

"Rebecca is boring, no doubt."

"Well, Leah is used to good company in Durban. Here she sits and does her embroidery and there is no culture. She must marry, the quicker the better."

"I agree. Speak to Mrs. Reuben tomorrow. There's a man named Lipmann made twenty thousand pounds . . ."

"An ignoramus."

"There it goes again. She must marry but nobody is good enough."

"It appears that she knows all about you and the schickser. For shame."

"She gossips with the Coloured girl," I said. "Get rid of the Coloured girl."

"More like it, you get rid of the schickser. Do you want to die a slow, rotting death from syphilis?"

"Don't say that. Besides I see nothing of her these days."

"Good. Good. I want that you should marry Leah."

"Papa!"

"You must marry. You caused all the trouble, otherwise we could have stayed in Durban where Leah was happy and satisfied . . . plenty of friends, not just a Coloured girl. You brought us here with your carrying-on. And tell me where is there a Jewish girl in this place for you to marry?"

"I think of Leah as my sister," I said, mumbling.

"My sister, my bride . . . You are fortunate, she is not your sister. And she has a dowry of two hundred pounds . . ."

One evening I rode home and found Leah waiting for me at the gate.

"I heard you coming from a long way off," she said. "It

95

is so still here, you can hear the hoofbeats of a horse when it is an hour away."

She opened the gate. The evening sounds were momentarily stilled nor was there any sound from her feet on the hard earth. I bent down and lifted her onto the horse. She put her arms round my neck. The horse walked forward slowly, in blue shadows.

She had on an organdie gown with hard blobs of paint on it; little flowers of different colours these blobs were, I saw that when we went inside afterwards. No wonder she was quiet walking; she wore satin boots, I felt them as I stroked her from her head to her toes.

I turned the horse back to the gate and got down and lifted her off. I held her for a while. It was a wonder to me that I would know her body, that even now it was ready for me beneath the crisp dress.

"I thought you would refuse," I said.

"I've known since I was thirteen."

"And it came as a surprise to me. Can we be married soon, Leah?"

"Next month?"

I met Jo near the diamond market soon afterwards and when I had sold my diamonds, we went to Sanger's for tea. Then we walked by the Vaal in the afterglow.

I said: "I'm to be married," and quick and fierce as though she held her knife in her hand, she said: "Who is it?" I told her: Leah.

"You can't be in love with her. You've known her all your life, haven't you? Isn't she your adopted sister?"

"Not exactly."

"I suppose it is because she is a Jewess."

The anger had drained from her and she was languid. She stood with her back against a tree, her reflection in the

96

river broken by gold and purple crests; there was a wind blowing.

"We will still be friends, Jo," I said.

"Oh yes. And perhaps one day I'll get married too and your wife will call on me. How do you do, Mrs. Bernstein? I'll say . . . have you ever noticed how smooth your husband's body is . . . he's not what you would call a hairy man, is he, my dear?"

"Stop it, Jo."

"Sorry. Yes, we will still be friends, Mannie."

I had to tell Britt Tyzack. He took the news as though I were informing him of a fatal illness that would lead to my early demise. For weeks he persisted in this attitude but when I continued to attend his meetings and the V.M.R. training, his gloom dispersed and I was once more allowed to listen to his discourse on the future of the world.

24

Once we were married I had expected that my lot henceforth would be quiet nights spent in study and dissertation, with Leah at her embroidery or waiting for me in the new fourposter; such had been the pattern of our home life in my mother's day.

But an astonishing change had taken place in my father. The truth was that he had diamond fever. He bought a claim at Pniel. He who had never sullied his hands with work would sometimes take a pick and break up the ground; he would spend from dawn to dark sieving and sorting. And when he picked out a diamond . . . oi yoi yoi . . . His hands shook, his body writhed, it was like an orgasm. This was a terrible thing for me to see in him, as though in his old age he had lost all sense of decency and had exposed himself in public.

In that first phase on the Vaal, diamond digging was an adventure, not a business. It was a game for young men, not men of my father's age. I felt ashamed of him, a scholar so nakedly greedy and without dignity. Always my father had been poor but he was honoured as a philosopher, a man who had to a certain extent detached himself from the business of making money. Now it was diamonds, diamonds that he talked about; like any of the thousands of diggers on the Vaal. And he made something less of me. I should have been the one on the claim, bullying the Kaffirs, seizing a pick in my frenzy . . . I should have been the one at the sorting table, looking for a whopper, like the other young men were. Let him buy the diamonds, I complained to Leah.

I blamed him for the streak of caution in me that Jo had said was cowardice. If I had not felt that everything depended on my efforts, then I would have taken more risks . . . I felt cheated but I hid my feelings from him; not from Leah.

There was no peace in our home. I did my best. Jo to me now was a friend I met in the street, I was faithful to Leah. But she wanted to be away from the Vaal and nagged us to leave. Who could blame her? Nearly always she was alone for my father was on the diggings while I was out buying. We came home at night to talk of diamonds.

25

My mother had a diamond ring which she wore on the middle finger of her right hand. She had had it from her mother and in our poorest days my father held it in trust for my wife. Now Leah wore it. The diamond came from Brazil and had been mined long before diamonds were found in Africa. I used to watch the sparkle of it on my mother's hand. To please me, she would move her hand so that I could see the stone catch fire from the light. This was in Whitechapel, that time when we were so poor that there was no furniture in our room. Our food came in parcels: charity food. My boots hurt for they had been handed on to me by somebody else.

And in Africa the diamonds were waiting for me, the poor Jewish boy. They were strewn on the banks of the rivers and hidden in pipes beneath the ground: the glorious Cape whites, the yellows, that great orange gem that I gave Halden for Jo . . .

We came as poor people to Africa. Poverty in Africa though was different from poverty in England. Here we were not so greatly despised for men were judged not only by wealth and breeding but also according to colour; poor Jews we might be but we were Europeans and beneath us were the Indians, the Coloured people and the Kaffirs.

My father went into partnership with Reb Gamsay a few months after our arrival in the country. The two men had this in common: both were poor at business but good at discussion. I went on several journeys with them through the Karroo, trading in ostrich feathers. Young though I was I had more of an idea of business than either of them had.

It was on one of these journeys that Reb Gamsay became ill. At first he lay quietly in the back of the cart while we were travelling and got down at the outspans but afterwards he lay on the cart all the time with my father attending him.

He was dying of cancer. We got him to Cape Town three weeks before he died. Leah was twelve years old then.

Reb Gamsay owned a house at Plettenberg Bay where Leah lived with an old servant. Her father . . . peace to him! . . . died without seeing her again for he did not want her to remember him as he looked in the grip of the cancer. It was heroic, his death; but his sacrifice was in vain for the servant Naomi who had seen him day by day described his dissolution to Leah. Naomi returned to Poland and Leah came to live with us. She was a daughter to my mother, a sweetness in our house when my mother died a year later.

The country in those days was nearly bankrupt. I've seen two hundredweight of potatoes rotting on the market square: the price offered the infuriated grower was a shilling. Although we returned loaded from our trading expeditions, there was little profit to be made.

Then my father heard that the market in Durban was livelier owing to trade with Mauritius and Madagascar. We came to Natal but we lost heavily on the move. It was not only that my father was unlucky in business though he was that; there was the essential poverty of the country to contend with.

Men began leaving Durban to try their luck on the diamond fields. One would notice a clerk missing from a store, a carpenter gone, even a doctor; at first there were only a few young men leaving but month by month the numbers grew until it was a rare thing to see men under middle age in the town.

Economists and geologists believed that the diamonds had been planted as a ruse to lure capital to South Africa; yet men were arriving from all over the world to dig the Vaal banks.

I wanted to go but my father opposed me. I can recall him sitting on the stoep in Durban on a summer's afternoon. It was hot. He wore a black broadcloth suit, skull cap, starched linen and elastic-side boots. The only concession he had made to the heat was to have Leah fan him with a palm leaf.

He had been sleeping, the newspaper slack in his hands but his silver-rimmed glasses firmly held by the arch of his nose although his head was sunk on his chest. His face still had the look of obstinacy with which he had met my demand to go to the diamond fields to sell a pack of goods. I stood there and watched him and there was a burning rage in me for I knew myself to be shrewder and stronger than he was.

"If he doesn't consent to me going, I'll be off anyway," I said roughly to Leah.

She gave a derisive smile. "Will you go like a tramp then?"

"I'll borrow money from one of the traders . . ."

He was no longer asleep though he pretended to be; I saw his eyeballs move behind his eyelids. Within the week he had consented to the venture and I left after all with his blessing.

"But I don't believe in this diamond madness," he said. "Crooks or ostriches, I don't know who is responsible for the diamonds but I want no part in it. Better to settle down quietly now and save up to go back to England. I'm tired of all this."

Now only look at him, after a month on the diggings. I rode past his claim one afternoon and he called out to me in the high, cracked voice of excitement.

"You have a big diamond for sale, mister?" I said with false jocularity.

He nodded and with trembling hands drew out a Vesta matchbox from his waistcoat pocket. There was a diamond of about four carats in the box. He shook it out on to my palm.

"It's flawed," I said, holding it up to the light.

He snatched the diamond from me. "Show me where."

"It's cracked inside, Papa. See, it makes a pattern like a feather . . ."

"You lie. You lie."

In his frenzy he dropped the diamond. It rolled into a fissure in a rock. With a howl he flung himself down and began to scrabble at the rock. I laughed. The sound halted him. He looked up.

"You laughed at your father, Mannie?" he said.

"I didn't mean to."

Stokkies had run his finger along the crack and had found the diamond. With the point of his knife he flipped it out and picking it up, looked at it.

"Flawed, baas," he said, giving it back to my father.

I felt sorry for my father, standing there in a frayed

black suit with his white beard straggling unkempt onto his chest; he was looking at the diamond with tears in his eyes.

"Worth nothing then?"

"Not much."

"Take it."

He forced the diamond into my hand and lowered his thin shanks onto a rock, moving so stiffly that I heard the creaking of his joints. His long fingers, with blackened and broken nails, stroked the ragged ends of his beard. I put my arm round his shoulders. He threw me off impatiently.

"Take the diamond to one of the bigger dealers for his opinion," he mumbled, breaking into Yiddish.

"What do you want his ideas for? Isn't my word good enough then? I earn our living but I'm a fool."

"Worms chew up your . . ." He stopped himself in time. "Give me back the diamond. I will take it to a proper dealer."

"Let them laugh at you. But what do you care?"

"May the marrow in your bones . . . give me the diamond."

I thrust it at him and he returned it carefully to the box which he put away in a waistcoat pocket. I was anxious to go on but I was unwilling to leave him there by himself. He had again sat down on the rock, staring into the hole that had been dug on his claim.

"Aren't you going home?" I said.

"It is early yet."

In the end I left him there alone. It was hard to see him like that. In business he had been a failure. It is certain that my mother was not happy; he did not provide well for her. She went short all the days of her life and was brought to Africa to face the hardships of a savage land. She had forgiven him his failure and so had I. We had said: This is the manner of man he is.

Peace to him. We had not known him.

26

Britt Tyzack had got me nominated to the Diggers' Committee. A general meeting was held towards the end of November. Stokkies had been out sounding people on my chances of election.

"One thing about it, basie, they know who you are when a person talks about you," he said while I was getting ready that evening. "There's some call you that young turkey-cock of a Jew and there's some call you that robbing swine of a Jew. But they all know you."

"Tell me who called me names and I'll slam the words down their throats."

Stokkies clucked with admiration. "Now now, my baas. Wait a minute." He adjusted my scarlet silk cummerbund. "My, that looks swanky. Now don't you go and fight. You must give them the sweet side of your tongue, doesn't matter what they say." He posed, with one hand in his pocket and the other playing with an imaginary chain. "Missa Chairman, gennelmen one and all . . . I've come before you to stand behind you . . . Last night in the middle of the day . . ."

Leah brought a clean handkerchief to me and a rosette to pin on my lapel.

"I wish I could come to the meeting, just to hear you talk."

"It will be rough."

"Oh, I know I can't go. I was only wishing."

My father came to wish me good luck although he did not approve of this venture into politics. He and Leah waved me out of sight from the gate.

I had ridden in early but people were already making their way to the top of the rise where a tent had been erected to hold the meeting. Stokkies had hired a little Kaffir to run beside me with a placard: "Mannie Bernstein the Diggers' Friend: British Rule."

"Nonna Leah did the writing," Stokkies told me.

I walked the mare sedately to the meeting place. At once the little Kaffir had the placard torn from his hands and was sent flying with a kick. I sprang from the mare and shaped up.

"Come on," I roared. "I'm ready for you all."

"Give him a ducking!"

Tungay was there, leading a Republican faction, but before he could get at me some of my supporters rallied to my side. They set me up on a soapbox and stood in a solid phalanx between me and Tungay: he was jerking backwards and forwards in his longing to get his hands on me.

Stokkies had arrived with a new placard.

"I knew they would tear the first one so I got nonnie Jo to write one as well," he said complacently. He smacked his fist into the palm of his hand. "Hoera for the Boers," he yelled. "Vote for the Jew!"

I was supposed to be making a speech and my supporters

gazed at me with admiration though no word of mine reached them in the bedlam of hucksters' cries and the booing of Tungay's faction.

Six black mules drawing a waggonette came dashing up. Jo and Fifi held aloft a white banner lettered in blue: A kiss a vote—Mannie Bernstein. Bonnie, dressed like a baby, was being rocked in a miner's cradle by Sweet Jasmine. Madame Olpresci played a mandoline while two poodles danced on a special platform. The driver brought the vehicle to a standstill near me and I was hauled on by the girls.

Tungay catapulted on to the waggonette and made a grab at me.

"Fair play!" Jo yelled. "British fair play! A kiss a vote!" She plucked at Tungay and he left me alone after that for Jo kept her arm hooked through his.

An Irishman was braying like a donkey in derision of my attempts to make a speech: it was a fine exhibition even to the lips pulled back over the teeth.

"Talking about donkeys, ever see a Flying Mare?" said a burly British Ruler, and he sent the Irishman hurtling over the heads of the crowd.

An iron clanged. It was the signal that the meeting was about to begin. There was a concerted rush into the tent. The candidates were to sit on a rough platform and I got to my seat after much jostling and pulling from my opponents. An American, the Mr. Babe who had invented the cradle used by all the miners, had come in with his friend Stafford Parker. "There he is, the only Babe who ever rocked his own cradle!" a barracker yelled and the chant was taken up. The chairman's hand was on the bell but so great was the noise that we heard no sound of ringing. At

106

last somebody lent the chairman a whistle. He blew several shrill blasts.

The crowd quietened. The outgoing chairman was a Yorkshireman, slow-speaking and with heavily hooded, suspicious eyes. Not everybody could understand what he was saying but interruptions did not deter him. He outlined the history of the diamond fields and then to the accompaniment of stamping and catcalls grudgingly gave way to the next speaker, the American Stafford Parker who was the chief advocate for a Diggers' Republic. He was an imposing man, solidly supported not only by his own countrymen but by many of the English and Irish.

"Who better to run the diamond fields than those who do the work?" he cried, to thunderous applause. "Are we to hand over to the Cape and be taxed out of existence? Are we to let nomads like the Griquas govern us? Or farmers like the Dutchmen? Is it Whitehall you want? But we're fit to govern ourselves, sirs, and I say . . ."

"British rule!"

"Shut up!" "To hell with it!"

Parker concluded his speech in an uproar. Then I was up. I had rehearsed my speech with Britt and Vollantyne that morning: I was to stir the diggers up against the Boer magistrate van der Hefer who had been trying to collect taxes for the past month.

"Gentlemen, the name of van der Hefer is familiar to us all. He wants taxes from us. . . ."

"We'll give him taxes!"

"You know he has moved his camp from Pniel. He is camped on this side of the river, well outside Transvaal or Free State territory. He says he is only here to collect taxes but can we believe that?" There was a sudden silence. I had the crowd with me except for a few of the Dutch and

Irish: Republicans and British rule supporters presented a common front to the farmers across the border. My voice rang out: "Diggers, here's our chance to show we mean business . . ."

Pandemonium broke out. Van der Hefer and his clerks had been treated as a joke when they demanded taxes but now a snarl of hatred could be heard in the yelling of the diggers.

"Let's tell them Dutchmen to get the hell out of it . . ." "Do you want action now, Bernstein? . . ." "Call up the V.M.R. . . ."

Two Dutchmen jumped me and were themselves downed by my supporters. In the ensuing brawl I was carried out of the tent on a wave of men and thrown against the trunk of a tree. I clung to this, thankful enough to have been extricated from the punching, gouging mob.

It was a cloudy, dark night and a few torches had been lit from bundles of grass tied to sticks. I saw Jo on the waggonette, inciting men to further violence. A column was forming under Halden's leadership, with Britt and Doctor Vollantyne rounding up the stragglers.

"Fall in," Jo cried. "Go on, you miserable looking things, call yourselves Englishmen. Hey, there's Mannie . . ." Bad luck, she had spotted me. "Here's another for you, doc, only too anxious to serve his country . . ."

Doctor Vollantyne, with several dogs following, bore down on me . . . Stokkies, drunk and still chanting "Hoera for the Boers, vote for the Jew," had brought my mare to me . . . I was mounted and in the vanguard with Britt and Halden as the column made for the river at the gallop. Our few opponents from the meeting were already skirmishing with the column. Halden dispersed them in a determined charge.

The Boer magistrate and his party were encamped about a mile away. They had been warned and were ready for us. Our force was greeted with "Halt! Who goes there?" and a volley of shots that sent the horses plunging. Doctor Vollantyne was thrown and took no further part in the proceedings. He lay unconscious with a boulder for a pillow and his dogs on guard until his wife had him carried home.

We surrounded the camp. Britt sent a messenger in, calling on the magistrate to parley. This brought forth van der Hefer who could speak English of a sort. Britt chose Halden and me to accompany him.

"Your names?" the Dutchman asked.

"Britten Tyzack." "Emmanuel Bernstein." "Donald Halden."

"And you are the leader," the Dutchman said, looking with contempt at Britt's lanky, immature frame.

"I'm acting for him. He got knocked out."

"And how old is he? Fourteen also?"

"I'm twenty," snapped Britt.

"And what's the matter with him? He looks old enough to talk sense." Van der Hefer jerked a thumb at Halden.

"He's an American," cried Britt. "I'm here as a representative of Queen Victoria and the British Empire."

"And I'm here for President Preotrius and the Transvaal Republic."

"Then you'll deal with me."

The Boer shook his head stubbornly. "I've come as a magistrate, with my clerks, to collect the taxes due to the Republic from the diamond diggers who are working on land we claim. And I'm not dealing with anybody who has no authority, much less young chickens just out of the egg . . ."

"Then take the consequences," said Britt, grandly.

We captured van der Hefer. We rowed him across the river and ducked him.

"Sure has a vocabulary," commented Halden.

Knee deep in the water, van der Hefer stood plucking at the air in his rage and cursing us. "Tyzack, Halden, Bernstein . . . I'll remember," he howled.

We rowed back blithely.

"Bit of luck them arriving when they did," said Britt. "We'll hold another meeting tonight. Every man jack will vote for the British Rule candidates after the show we put up . . ."

"Hold it. I'm a Republican," said Halden.

"It was V.M.R. organization," cried Britt hotly.

"I'm still a Republican . . ."

Stokkies was on the bank, signalling us. We mounted and rode over to him.

"Basies, they're after you. The police are out for the whole town, every digger that rioted. They are going to throw the lot of you in the jail."

"We'll have to get hold of Vollantyne. He's in with the police," Britt said.

"No use, it's at the doctor's place that they got police waiting to arrest people. The best thing for the time being is over the border. Wait by the big old camelthorn behind the kopje on the road to Christiana. I'll bring a message from the doctor."

While we hesitated, several members of the Vaal Mounted Rifles galloped past, urging us to leave at once.

"Ride, I tell you," admonished Stokkies.

Britt tossed him a sovereign. "Lay my boys off . . . you know the claim . . ."

So we rode across the border. We spent the day with about twenty others sleeping in the shelter of the kopje. After dark Doctor Vollantyne and Stokkies appeared.

"They think I'm in bed," said Vollantyne. "They've got soldiers waiting in the front garden but the mutts have left the back unwatched and that's how I am here. Warrants are out for Bernstein, Halden and Tyzack. The rest of you are in the clear. They are not going to make mass arrests. It's van der Hefer who put you three away. Listen, boys, if you want to duck a man, what the hell give him your names for?

"It looks bad for you at the moment. The latest is that a contingent of soldiers is on the way from Colesberg. I think you three will have to ride for it. In the meantime I'll work for you here. Get out for a few months and by that time it will have blown over. I'll send you reports."

"We'll make for Alidasrust district," said Halden. "There's only one farmer within a radius of a hundred miles and he is a friend of mine. I've been up there prospecting."

"Right. I'll send a runner as soon as you're in the clear."

"What about our claim?" Britt demanded.

"Damme, you'll have to let it go."

"Sell it then. But don't take a penny less than three hundred pounds."

"My father and my wife," I cried. "I must see them. And I must have money. I left my money belt at home."

"Here's money. I've brought each of you fifty pounds. Write your family a letter, Bernstein. I'll see that it is delivered."

Vollantyne had brought provisions and blankets and with these on a packhorse, we rode northwards. Halden was unquestionably our leader because of his knowledge of the terrain.

He took us across barren country close to the desert. It was country that I was to learn to know well and my recollection of that first sight of it is vague now. What comes back to me clearly is the remembrance of our insubstantiality as we faded into the horizons behind yellow-tinted mountains; and the shimmering globe of the sky that night and day remained cloudless.

PART 2

1

This I remember: We had camped near a water hole. It was a place of grey, twisted trees on a plateau. That day the sun had come up out of a white sky and the heat was fierce yet the water hole did not look inviting when we came upon it in the afternoon. A thousand hooves had trampled the mud at its edges, there were broken boughs rotting in the slime.

We set the boys to gathering great heaps of fuel for the place was infested with lions, Halden said, and we would need fires. At sunset a troop of zebras came to drink at the pool, their heads nod nodding, their hooves placed neatly, as girls walk. The clear light held their reflections in the pool to the last moment of the day; night came out of the folds of a dark blue sky.

There were soft blue shadows in the night, and stars. Stars upon stars, in thousands, glittered and flashed from the vast dome and spread light over the veldt. It was light like mist, blurring the shapes of things. The boys lit the fires.

They were arguing and laughing but we three white men sat quiet. An indefinable barrier had grown up between us. We seldom spoke to each other and Halden in particular was withdrawn and often trekked on alone, a stage ahead of us.

Out on the veldt there was at first the thundering of herds pursued, the terrible sounds of the lions and one other awful questioning voice that paralyzed thought. Then came silence.

The Kaffirs slept but we three sat on by the fire. And there was a sudden yell from the darkness.

"Basie! I'm here, it's Stokkies Truter." He pounded into the circle of firelight and threw down a carpet bag at my feet. "Your things, and I got letters too. Christ man, I was in a tree for a couple of hours. I could see the fires."

"Did Doctor Vollantyne send a message?" Britt asked.

"It's all in the letter to my baas. The doctor went to see basie's pa."

Stokkies took two letters from an oilskin pouch which he had been wearing under his shirt. One was from my father and the other from Leah. I skimmed through my father's letter to find Vollantyne's message, for Britt and Halden were waiting impatiently.

"What's Vollantyne say?" "Hurry up, can't you? . . ."

"Here it is. The doctor came to see me . . . There's no difference. We are to stay away for six months or so, he's getting at the right people to have the summons withdrawn."

Stokkies had taken himself off to the Kaffirs' fire where he sat swilling coffee while he recounted his adventures. The boys were lively again but at our fireside there was utter silence.

I opened the carpet bag. Inside were my phylacteries, a shawl, cap and prayer book, all tightly bound up in linen. There were also in the bag a bottle of old cognac and some rusks of Leah's making.

"We're in luck," I said.

I called Stokkies over and gave him a drink of brandy. He took it with smacking lips but as soon as the mug was empty, keeled over and went to sleep.

We three drank in silence while I read my letters. My father wrote dolefully that Leah was not pregnant but she herself was cheerful and did not mention any disappointment.

I folded the letters and put them away. The brandy was taking effect. Speech burst from me. I told those other two the story of my life, even to such a detail as my parting with my father and Leah before setting out on the journey to the Vaal.

When I stopped talking and looked at them, I saw that the brandy had made no difference; they were as taciturn as ever. I thought: What's the matter with them, are they ashamed of their families?

"Do you come from a big family?" I said to Halden. He nodded. I turned to Britt to include him in the question but he did not notice because he was drawing complicated patterns on the ground.

Well, if a person won't speak about his family, try him with sport.

"Have you always been keen on hunting?" I said.

"Hell yes." Again there was no response from Britt.

117

"Have you hunted the grizzly bear?" I asked Halden.
"What would I do that for?"

From sport to women is the rule in conversation but I decided instead to try politics, knowing Britt's weakness. Politics made these two sick, if you were to judge from their expressions.

So I said: "What did you think of her?" Now there was a flicker of interest. They both looked at me enquiringly.

"The Boer girl at that last farmhouse we passed. She was standing on the stoep."

"Oh yes, I remember," said Halden. He outlined a pair of big breasts with his hands.

"Dry up," said Britt.

Halden winked at me. "She's somebody's sister, you know." He reached for the cognac bottle, poured out an unfair drink and downed it in one gulp. Then he leaned back with his hands clasped behind his head.

"You want to talk about women? I know a girl, she's as pure as the driven snow . . . I don't think. And she's got hair when she gets in the sun it's bright, a reddish colour, and she's got blue eyes . . . angel's eyes. And all over her, she's got a down, a white silk down, even on the insides of her legs up here . . ."

"That's Jo Carr," I said.

He got up. I did too. I knew him to be a good boxer yet that night he fought primitively as Tungay did and I rolled about helplessly in his grips. Then by luck I got his thumb between my teeth and that brought him to his senses.

He sprang away from me. Britt got between us. Still in the circle of firelight, Halden stood with his hands hanging loosely at his sides, the tragic mask of his face offered to us. One of the Kaffirs was sitting up watching but the others slept on.

"For God's sake," said Britt. "Here, let's finish this." He measured out three equal shares of the brandy. "Shake hands, you two."

"Won't be shaking hands with anybody for a while," said Halden, lifting his bloodied thumb. "Bit of a cannibal, aren't you, Bernstein?" But he made the motion of giving his hand to me.

"Forget girls," said Britt.

"Sure, forget girls," cried Halden. "Like a eunuch does."

"I haven't been thinking of girls, you fool, because I've been working our plans." I saw now that in the rough gravel he had drawn a map of Africa with a system of railways and had marked in great ports and a maize belt. He said: "It can be done. We'll establish the pax Britannica throughout the continent. And the best way to accomplish peace here is to use Britain to annex the Transvaal. From there we go on to defeat the Zulus. We'll make them bring ten thousand redcoats to fight the wars. The defeat of the Zulus will give us a reservoir of labour for the diamond fields. And with the Boers under control we can prospect the whole of the Transvaal for gold.

"We'll make a dent in eternity . . ."

Halden clapped a hand over Britt's mouth. The two of them wrestled but it was in sport, pretty to watch.

"Pax," cried Britt.

"Pax Britannica," Halden jeered; but he left Britt alone.

After that Britt was silent but Halden was garrulous and this made Britt sleepy. Presently he turned in. When he was asleep, Halden started talking about Jo again. This time we did not fight.

He was saying: "I saw her first in Capetown after we had captured the *Sea Bride*. She was in a white dress and she had that Madame Olpresci with her . . . laugh, Bernstein. I thought she was a young lady and that Madame was a relative or chaperone. They had quite a lot of fun with me that day. And then I found out it didn't make any difference that she wasn't a lady.

"That's a hell of a thing to happen to a man, isn't it? I wanted to marry her real bad.

"With my prize money I bought a schooner in Capetown and I called her the *Josephine*. I took Uzzell and his company from the Cape to Durban as passengers.

"And one night we played a game of poker, Uzzell and I, and I lost the *Josephine* to him. But I got Jo. They had a side bet, she and Uzzell.

"I nearly killed her when I found this out. Sometimes even now I'm sorry I didn't. I kicked her out. She went back to Uzzell. And sometimes I'm sorry I kicked her out. You understand."

"Yes."

"She hasn't found a man to match her," he said with sudden tenderness. "Closest she has come to loving is with Uzzell. You'll find she will always go back to him. And she will gamble with him as if she was mad just to prove to him she has guts. I had the guts she wants in a man but she never loved me." He bowed his head on his knees. "A woman like her . . . She isn't one to come crying to you, Marry me before you touch me. She is reckless with herself, she's game. And her sort of honesty is to stand by her friends . . . she expects that honesty from her friends. Hell, I've said to her, what do you think human beings are? I've said, Don't you know that the farmer's wife who hand feeds a calf will sell it later on to a butcher? . . ."

I took out Leah's letter and read it again. Suddenly I

had the longing to tell Halden about Leah's tight, smooth body; but it was too late, he had gone to sleep.

I too slept. I awoke before the others and bound on my phylacteries and put on my shawl and cap. The soft cadence of my prayers awoke the Kaffirs. They sat still, watching me. The oxen stamped on the velvety quietness. And far away a jackal cried on a single note.

2

Halden trekked out before us. Our rendezvous was at Beneke's farm Goudklip in the Alidasrust district where Halden had met with friendliness on his previous expedition.

Britt and I were partners now. We had bought hides and skins from the farmers and Kaffirs. And now that Stokkies was with us, we had the freedom of ranging forward on horseback while he brought on the waggon and mules we had acquired.

In the middle of December we came to a Boer's house that had been built on top of a slight rise. We were met at the door by a young man. He was handsome, with side levers and a black moustache.

"Hans Niman," he said, shaking hands.

He stood aside for us to enter. I saw the red armchair, the rhinoceros foot and the looped curtains of the van der Spuyts' front room. Mevrouw came in.

"You, mijnheer Bernstein," she exclaimed. Her face

glowed; evidently the woman thought I had pursued her here.

"How is your husband?" I asked at once.

"He is to the north hunting lions." I smiled in disbelief. "See this," she said. With small steps she trampled underfoot a lionskin which lay on the floor. "See the size of the brute, people . . . One day a lion will get Theuns." She looked pensively at the lionskin, then bending, put the tip of her finger into a bullet hole. She straightened. "But excuse. Mevrouw van der Spuyt." She shook Britt's hand.

Coffee was brought in. The Dutch boy handed us steaming cups of coffee, each with a rusk tucked between cup and saucer.

"Hans is related by marriage to us by my mother's side," said Mevrouw. "We have adopted him as he is an orphan." Then she said to me: "Mijnheer Bernstein, you're not comfortable there. Come, we're old friends, you sit in the big chair." She took my cup from me and placed it on the rhinoceros foot. With a firm grip she guided me to the accursed red chair. I sat on the edge of it, ready to spring up the moment van der Spuyt entered the room.

But this time Mevrouw was not lying. Van der Spuyt was indeed away on a shooting expedition.

"My uncle is taking me with him next time," said the boy.

"Am I to stay alone then?"

The boy looked wary. No doubt of it, he was Mevrouw's lover.

"Where is the Benekes' farm?" I asked.

"Twenty miles from here," said the boy. "Is it you who must meet the American there?"

"He was here," said Mevrouw. "Lucky for him Theuns

wasn't at home. He is looking for gold. Hans caught him panning down by the river."

"My uncle will shoot him," said Hans.

"We got chased off our farm by those diamond-diggers, mijnheer Bernstein. Everything went . . . fences, Kaffir huts, fowl pens . . . there was nothing left." Mevrouw smirked. "Mijnheer Bernstein was the Jew who arrived that day Apie was struck by lightning, Hans."

"I saw the sitting room wall come down," I said.

"Afterwards you couldn't walk in the yard without nearly breaking your neck," said Hans. "So my uncle sold out, loaded up his waggons and trekked for the horizon, man. Five hundred miles he counted off before he built here at Alidasrust."

"And now the American comes looking for gold." Mevrouw leaned back and laughed.

3

When we were leaving, Hans slipped a note into my hand. "Give that to Beneke's daughter, please. Her name is Poppie." He had been careful not to let Mevrouw see him give the note to me.

Beneke's farmhouse stood among trees on a grassy plain. In a bed of pansies and mignonette a girl was kneeling to pull out weeds. She was fair. Her thick, coarse hair was bound in plaits on top of her head; I saw at once that she was not pretty.

123

She blushed and sprang to her feet.

"We're Mr. Halden's friends," I said reassuringly. "And I have a letter for you . . . Poppie."

She shook her head and went into the house. Tow-headed boys had left their play on the banks of a spruit and stood watching us as though we were invaders. A voice called from within. "Who's there?" This was followed by the appearance of a tall man, neatly dressed and with steel rimmed glasses on the end of his nose.

"Beneke," he said heartily, extending his hand. We introduced ourselves. "I've been expecting you. Halden is in the north . . . Coffee, treasure," he called: he spoke English but with such a strange accent that it was difficult to follow him.

In the front room every chair was covered with specimens of rocks.

"I'm a bit of a student as you can see," said Beneke. "A geologist, in fact. All this I'll bring to Pretoria some day and put in a museum." He cleared some chairs and invited us to sit down. His wife brought in coffee. She was a spare woman, quiet except for a sudden high laugh. Poppie was dragged into the room, with pleas of "Little treasure, come now . . ." The young span was not allowed in but had to content themselves with skirmishing at the windows and yelling.

"Excuse my wife and daughter, they have no English," said Beneke. "My English I learned from books. I have practiced with Mr. Halden. You must go on to Baster's Pan to meet him. He is up on my boundary there, shooting out lions. For the last few years the lions have been a pest but we have a Nimrod in our midst now . . . van der Spuyt. He is shooting elephant in the Sabie district or we could have called on him to deal with the lions."

Poppie hung her head and looked at us from beneath a fringe of hair. She was so shy that she plaited her fingers and shifted one foot onto the top of the other incessantly. Such a parade of shyness irritated me and I was astonished to see that Britt was taken with her.

"It's too sweet," he said when her parents had gone into another room to search for a specimen of gold-bearing rock that Beneke wanted us to see. "Ask how old it is."

"How old are you, the gentleman wants to know," I said sharply.

"Sixteen," Poppie whispered.

"The silly mutt is sixteen."

"Sweet sixteen and never been kissed."

"The gentleman says you're sweet sixteen and never been kissed."

Poppie's response to this was to bury her face in her hands and giggle. Presently she peeped out again and with her lower lip caught between her teeth shook her head vigorously.

"I think she means somebody kissed her sometime," I told Britt. "Probably she paid a forfeit when playing a game during Nachtmaal . . . Was it Hans Niman kissed you?" I said to Poppie. "Don't you want his letter?"

A remarkable change came over the girl: her shyness was overcome by rage.

"That filth," she said. I took out the letter and waved it in the air. "I wouldn't touch it," she hissed.

Britt said: "You're making her angry. Look here, Mannie, drop it. You're so used to the whores on the diggings that you forget how to treat a decent girl." He snatched the letter from me and tore it across.

"I want it," said Poppie.

She took the letter from Britt and hid it in her pocket.

"You know nix about girls," I said to him.

All through the midday meal Beneke talked about gold while his wife suppressed the four small boys. Food silenced Beneke and he dozed through the afternoon. The boys were made to lie down; Poppie was set to threading beads while Mevrouw Beneke supervised some Kaffir girls who were plucking the coir of an old mattress.

Poppie seemed to have got used to us. Once or twice she looked directly at Britt.

"She has taken a fancy to you," I said. "Shall I ask her if she would like to sit up with you tonight."

"I wouldn't mind."

"This fellow says can he come and sit up with you?"

The little velschoens scuffed one against the other. "He can't," she whispered at last. "I'm engaged to be married."

"Since when?"

"Since just now. Niman asked me in the letter."

"Your luck is out," I told Britt. "She is engaged to that rake Niman."

4

We travelled slowly now. The way to Baster's Pan lay through high, stony country where nothing grew except stunted grey bushes and a few aloes. We saw no white people except the son of a missionary who came running out of the mist one morning with a barrel of butter on his shoulder to sell to us: the place was so wild and lonely that

126

zebra and antelope and wildebeest grazed with the mission cattle on the grassy slopes running into the narrow valley far below where the station had been built.

We left this high ground and travelled through bush-veldt for ten miles or more to Baster's Pan where Halden had his camp. It was here that I got fever for the first time. While I was still sick, a runner came in from Vollantyne with the news that he had got the summonses against us withdrawn. We could return to Klipdrift. Halden decided not to come back with us but to go on to Grahamstown with samples of rock.

5

With fresh horses that we had bought from Beneke, we made good speed in spite of heavy rains and at the end of January we were on the long slopes of the diamond valley: Stokkies had been left to bring up the loaded waggon.

Long before we came within sight of the river we saw a cloud of dust.

"That means a new rush," said Britt. "Look, the dust is rising to the east of Klipdrift."

We urged our horses to a gallop.

Sunset had shattered the even blue of the sky. There was no afternoon peace but a steady, urgent sound as though a great animal were passing through the veldt. The sound came from a column of men and animals and vehicles that jammed the track leading away from the river. Men ran pushing wheelbarrows piled with their belongings. There were men on horseback and there were families of Boers in waggons; carts of every description with donkeys, mules, oxen and horses, from broken hacks to thoroughbreds, drawing them. A waggon rumbled by with a wood-and-iron store lashed perilously to it. Twenty soldiers in the tatters of their uniforms marched singing into the veldt.

"Where are you going?" I yelled at them.

"To Dutoits Pan . . ." "They struck it rich there . . ."

"Good luck," we cried but our voices were lost in the crashing of the store as it fell from the waggon.

"Dutoits Pan, where's that?" Britt asked a Boer whose waggon had been halted.

"Twenty miles inland."

Along the banks of the Vaal where thousands had worked there were now only a few hundred. I looked at my father's claim but it was derelict, filled with water. Nothing of his remained on it except an iron bucket without a bottom.

"My father must have followed the rush," I said.

Somebody was shouting and beckoning; it was an old digger named Tennessee Jones who had known my father.

He came to tell me that my father was dead. I went away by myself and cried out for my father, and rended my clothes.

Presently Tennessee found me and sat by me. He touched my shoulder. "Son, I been looking out for you. Your father . . . before your father crossed the great divide, it was the night before, he dreamt there was a whopper under a rock. He told me about it. But there was nothing under that rock except a big red earthworm." Tennessee groaned. "Lordy, how that man did work. Come and see the rock he tried to move. Dreamt there was a diamond

128

under it." The old man led me to the river bank and pointed out a great boulder. The top of the boulder had been rounded by weathering but the part that had been in the ground was sharp and pointed, with stones attached to root fibres and earth. "He moved that rock," Tennessee mused. "He shoved at it and prized it all day and at last he got it heaved up out of the earth, him and his two Shangaans. And all there was was an earthworm. I guarantee you that earthworm was every inch four feet. Come on, I'll show you where he is buried, son."

Britt joined me and we followed Tennessee to my father's stony grave. He had been buried beneath a thorn tree where weaver birds had built a nest. Somebody had inscribed on the trunk of the tree: Aaron Bernstein d. 2.10.70. R.I.P.

There he lay, the Talmudic scholar. I remembered his hands, the long hands once soft for the touching of paper, hands for gesturing during a discussion; hands for prayer.

I had not known the man who clawed at the rock to get a diamond. But now that he was dead I must accept him alongside the scholar and wish peace to him and name him too on each second of October.

"I put him there," said Tennessee, gesturing towards the grave with a thumb as hard as stone: he had mined in California and Australia. "When he lay dead, the diggers came swarming round and they promised his daughter the biggest durndest funeral you ever did see. But when the time came to bury him there was not one turned up except that singer they call Diamond Jo and a high-yaller girl and a old foreign type of hag and this big bastard Tungay. Because why? Because by then everybody was off to the dry diggings, the fools. They will have it they've found diamonds there. Twenty mile inland. There never was no diamonds except in the river. They'll come back. Yes sir-ree, they will all come back to the river again . . . There was no sense in any of them, glassy-eyed they were, like dogs after a coursing bitch . . .

"So I got his two Shangaans to dig a grave and I buried him. And there wasn't nobody came to the funeral except the girl Jo and Madame Whatsaname and this Tungay. All the rest was gone . . . and there was the high-yaller girl came . . ."

"Miri."

"It's hard. You know what it was like here, just one grand picnic and everybody your pal. Then to leave him like that, not caring if he was buried or the hyenas got him. The girl Jo was sure mad about it."

"My wife?"

Britt murmured: "I've asked him. She went with Jo Carr."

"Yes, she went with the singer and the foreign dame."

"Any man who has touched her I will kill, if he is Jew or Gentile, and I'll kill her too," I said weeping.

"Take it easy. She is a good woman . . ."

"Try your farm," Britt said. "She would have left a note for you. And she may not have gone with Uzzell's crowd. Tennessee may be mistaken."

"My Shangaan seen her riding in the waggon with them . . ."

"I'll go to the Reubens."

"Too late," said Tennessee with the ghost of a chuckle. "He was the first to leave. Upped his store on a waggon and off before anybody got wind of the strike. He was gone three days before your father passed on."

We rode to the farm. There was not even a Kaffir there. In this land of wood-and-iron buildings, a quick deterioration set in as soon as a house was left empty for any length of time. It was moonlight and I saw earthen runnels made by white ants. Weeds grew from cracks in the walls.

I called Leah.

There was a stirring in the old mealie lands next to the orchard. Archibald, my donkey, came trotting into the open, stopped and stared, then pulled back his lips in an ear-splitting bray. I tried to pat him but he was wild and galloped out of reach.

I lit a candle and we looked about the house. The furniture was still there. A book of music stood open on the piano. A few of Leah's things had been left behind; a scarf, a hat, a book.

Britt was standing by the piano now, softly playing the chords for the left hand of the piece on the stand.

"She would be glad to get away from here," I said. "She hated it here. Cards, talk, books . . . that's what she wanted. She is beautiful. She is the sort that looks you straight in the eye. She can talk like a man, clever . . ."

I wanted to stay in the house for beyond these walls would be vengeance and death.

"Here you are, here's the letter," said Britt. "She put it on the piano but it must have been blown down by the wind and fallen into the pages of this music . . ."

She had written to tell me of my father's death: she would go to the Reubens at Dutoits Pan.

We mounted again and rode inland. The moon was still shining when we saw the white blur of tents at Dutoits Pan. A township had already been outlined on the veldt, with a few roads leading off from a square. We rode slowly past the shadowed wood-and-iron offices of the diamond market, past the claims registration office, a bank and a marquee bearing the name of the Diamond Fields Hotel; the next place was Solly Reuben's store.

Solly answered my banging cautiously, from behind locked doors: "Vot yer vant?"

"It's Bernstein."

The door opened. He said in Yiddish: "Long life. Mannie, Mannie . . . Too late I heard . . ." He drew me into the store: Britt had remained in the shadows with the horses.

"Where's Leah?"

He stood before me, thin-shanked, in a nightshirt and cap, and he had a defenceless look like a child that is to be caned.

"My wife was sick at the time," he said, suddenly whispering.

"Answer me. Where is Leah?"

"We knew nothing about your father . . . peace to him . . . until a week later. We were already here. We have not seen Leah. I sent young Meier my nephew to the farm but nobody was there."

Mrs. Reuben came in. "You here at last, Mannie," she said.

"I came for Leah."

"She was not here at all," cried Mrs. Reuben. "Why should she stay away? Every day we expected her. Meier went to your place, he spoke to Tennessee Jones . . ."

"Then you know she went with Uzzell's girls?"

"I enquired there," said Reuben. "I enquired from the girl Jo and she said Leah has gone to Natal."

"Where is Uzzell's place?"

He took me outside and silently pointed. Uzzell's place was the grandest building we had seen on the diggings, a two-story structure made out of packing cases. It was well lit up although the time was close to four in the morning.

I put my revolver in my belt and with Britt behind me went up the ricketty steps into a darkened hall. The first door I opened led into a cosy bar with a red carpet and red wallpaper; it was empty though lamps were burning.

As we came into the hall again, a door opened at the back. Tungay entered.

"Looking for a game of cards like?" he jeered. "You got to have my permission, see. I'm doorkeeper and chief chucker-out here . . . Hey, what's the gun for?"

We went upstairs without answering. The staircase was flimsy and rattled beneath our boots. I threw a door open and we went into a large, well-lit room furnished with card tables. Jo, Uzzell and three diggers were immersed in a game of poker. They did not look up as we strode across to the table. The girl Bonnie, sprawled half-asleep, looked up in a friendly way, made her usual obscene gesture of greeting and subsided; but Sweet Jasmine, who had been playing solitaire, got up and fluttered round us.

"You dehling boys, we did miss ums . . ."

I said to Jo: "Where is she?"

Jo looked up. "She went to Durban with Madame Olpresci."

"The unfrocked governess," said Uzzell. "You knew about Madame Olpresci, Bernstein?" He had laid down his hand on the table and was collecting the chips due to him. He began to deal. "Madame Olpresci was a governess in a well-to-do family in her younger days but unfortunately one of the fathers unfrocked her. Madame is still a good teacher but she has changed the subjects . . ."

I pulled the trigger but my shot went wide for Tungay jumped me from behind. He knocked the revolver from my hand and held me. Britt flung himself awkwardly on

133

Tungay. I got away but Britt went down under a murderous kick.

"Out like a light," cried Jo.

She was up on a table, whirling a bottle round her head. Uzzell had picked up my revolver. I drove my fist into his face and he passed out. Then Tungay lit on me again. I boxed him all the way round the room, gliding from under his hand several times. But he caught me at last. We fell locked with a table splintering beneath us. Tungay's thumbs jabbed into my windpipe. I heard him whispering "the bitch Jewess . . ." and brought my knee up. He rolled off me. I got to my feet. There were flames in the room. Girls were screaming. Then Tungay was up again. He had picked up a bottle and he knocked me down into a welter of blood.

6

He would have left me to die in the flames but Jo came back into the building to help me. He ran in after her and she forced him to carry me down the stairs. I came round as I was bumped onto the ground.

"What have you done to him?" Jo said fiercely. "Here, how do you like it?" and she slashed Tungay's cheek with the bowie knife she had drawn from the sheath in the folds of her dress.

"Aw, Jo," said Tungay, shrinking in on his huge form.

Jo called Vollantyne to stitch my head where the bottle had caught me.

"Have you seen Tyzack?" I asked.

"Hell yes," said the doctor shortly. "Listen, Bernstein, you keep out of his way in future. You've brought nothing but trouble. I've taken Tyzack to my house." He stumped off to bandage another head.

"I must go after Leah," I said.

"She won't come to any harm," said Jo. "Madame is not really bad."

"I expected to find her at the Reubens'. Why didn't she stay there as she said she would."

"Tungay. I can make him do what I want him to but only while I'm there. You never told me she was beautiful. Even Tungay noticed it. He is lewd, damn dangerous unless you know how to handle him. I took him with me while Madame posted on to Natal with Leah. We had to foot slog part of the way . . . Uzzell had left a waggonette for us and that's what the other two travelled in."

"Lucky you were there."

"Madame had dysentery and I stayed to look after her while Uzzell joined the rush."

Uzzell's place was going up like a torch. Uzzell, with a bandage round his head, played to the crowd. He lifted his voice in a great laugh. It was a masterpiece, rueful but forgiving.

"He's a good sport," said a Coloured woman who was watching the fire with enjoyment; she had a handful of loose cooked mealies which she tossed one by one into her mouth.

"There's the Yid that caused the fire," roared Tungay, pointing at me.

A murmuring started. "Needs tarring and feathering . . ." "Run him off the diggings . . ."

"Fade away," Jo advised.

I dodged behind a shuttered canteen. I could hear the

crowd yelling. I put words to the bestial sound and ancient terrors rose in me. I slunk away in the shelter of the canteen wall.

Leah . . . in the keeping of an old whore. I must find her at once. The first thing was to get a fresh mount. My money had long since been used up in trading. I had only a few shillings left but I knew that Britt had ten pounds.

I went cautiously to the doctor's house, asking my way of a Coloured. Mrs. Vollantyne answered my knock.

"Aren't you Bernstein?"

"I want to see Britt Tyzack please."

"Out of the question," she said briskly. "He is not at all well. I don't wonder, getting mixed up in a brawl." She continued, without malice: "You know, in the hurly burly of life on the diggings, all sorts of people associate with each other. But blood will tell. Mr. Tyzack does not come of a class that can engage in brawls with impunity."

"But I must see him. I need money."

"Really. And I did at least give you credit for coming to enquire how he was."

"Please. Ask him to lend me his ten pounds, I know he has got it. I have to find my wife, she has gone off."

"I'm not surprised," said Mrs. Vollantyne who for some time had taken Jo to be my wife; but she did go inside, having first secured the door. She was back within a few seconds. "He's asleep. I can't disturb him now. Come back later if you must."

I went away. I was not able to stand up to such a woman; good-looking but hard and with contempt for anybody not of her class.

The Reubens had gone to watch the fire. I sent a passing Kaffir to fetch them and they came at once.

"Why, Mannie," cried Mrs. Reuben. Her lips formed a

rosebud of sadness. "Poor boy, poor boy. Come in. Take some nourishment. You look terrible. He looks terrible, Solly."

"He looks bad," Solly agreed.

We went into the room behind the store. Mrs. Reuben set about preparing a meal.

"I must go," I said but I sat down. Solly gave me brandy to drink.

"I cannot understand it," said Mrs. Reuben, hands in the air and eyes flashing. "Why did Leah not come here? Why not come to her friends?" The hands came down, the eyes dimmed. "Can it be? Something had already happened. She was ashamed perhaps?"

I was on my feet at once. Solly groaned.

"Such a fool, Becky, such a wide mouth. Sit, Mannie. Have some more brandy."

"I vos only toiking," said Mrs. Reuben, using English for some unknown reason. "Vot? Can't a poisson talk no more?"

"I want some money," I said. "I've got part of a waggonload of hides, ivory and honey as security . . ."

"No need for security," cried Mrs. Reuben but Solly murmured: "It's good security . . ."

There was a knock on the door. Somebody yelled: "We know you're in there, Bernstein. Open up."

"Let me go out."

Outside I was immediately in the centre of a crowd: Uzzell was there, Tungay, Jo, Bonnie . . . But the spokesman was Sharkey Williams, a shyster lawyer.

"Don't you move a step, Bernstein," he cried. "I've got a magistrate's order here and the police are on their way. Both you and Tyzack are up for damages."

"He's bluffing," said Jo.

"How much?"

"Three hundred," Sharkey said promptly.

"Shillinks?" Solly asked from behind me.

"Pounds. And that's only the beginning . . . What about the loss of business?"

"You must help him, Solly," said Mrs. Reuben, appearing with a little girl on each hip.

"I can put up a hundred pounds," said Solly. "That's all. I'm not exactly a millionaire."

"It's three hundred," said Sharkey. He read out an inventory of the damage; included was Uzzell's waggonette and oxen which Jo had borrowed for Leah.

"One hundred and then awready I'm ruint," said Solly.

"I've got to go tonight," I said. "My wife . . . I'm worried about my wife."

"He can do other men's wives but nobody must do his wife," Tungay spat.

"Shut up, you hound," said Jo.

I looked despairingly at the crowd. There were several Jews present but I knew them, battlers one and all.

I stripped off my watch and diamond ring.

"Take these as part security. And there's my property on the Vaal too."

Sharkey whipped out a glass and pushing his way into the Reubens' living room, examined the stone. Then he put my watch to his ear.

"It's going," he said.

Solly with trembling hands was writing out a cheque for a hundred pounds.

7

The diggers were at work as I rode away in the dawn and already a cloud of dust was rising on the still air; no water for washing the gravel here, it was dry sieving. From the north a dust cloud snaked across the plain, joining with the smudge of dust that was the diggings; vehicles making the last stage to the new fields. On foot came bands of Kaffirs, naked but for strips of hide or a tattered shirt; and lone Griquas and poor white men. And they looked with astonishment at me riding away from the El Dorado they were straining to reach.

I had gone about six miles when Jo came galloping after me, riding a big roan.

"Here, take him," she said, sliding out of the saddle. "I'll look after this poor old moke for you. I've just won the roan from Moss at the hotel. Shooting dice. And I brought you a revolver. There are highwaymen about these days."

I got down and stood beside her. In the harsh light I saw that her face was grimy, with dirt in the lines round mouth and eyes. This was one of her ugly moments but I kissed her and held her in my arms.

"You've been a good friend, Jo."

"They left your father, Mannie . . . It was rotten."

"Such is life."

"Even the Jews . . ."

"Solly turned up trumps last night."

"They always say Jews are so good to each other but they left your father when he was dead."

"We can't change the world."

"You shouldn't be travelling," she said tenderly. "Look at you. You're sick. And you'll be broke, cleaned out . . ."

"She mustn't be with that woman."

"Don't worry about Leah." She burst out laughing. "She is safe unless somebody rapes her and I was frightened of Tungay, I'll admit it. But otherwise . . . The first thing she did was to sew her surplus money into her corsets."

"What are you getting at?"

"She can look after herself. She's a good woman. She values herself. Perhaps she will reform Madame."

"I can see you don't like her."

"I've got to go back now. Uzzell will be having fits. He might think I've run off with you. Girls are scarcer than water. Fifi has made her fortune."

"Jo, look after yourself. Don't . . ."

She rode away. Suddenly she turned in the saddle and made one of Bonnie's vile gestures.

"That's for Leah," she yelled.

8

At the inn near van der Spuyt's old farm I had news of Leah and Madame Olpresci. Yes, a young girl like a white rose for beauty had passed that way; and with her were an old auntie, a Coloured maid, a Griqua and six queer animals said to be dogs. They were travelling in a waggonette.

The Dutch woman who told me this, the innkeeper's wife, went away and brought a pair of lace mittens and a bottle of cologne to show me.

"The young lady gave me these as a present." She drew the mittens on to her hands; she was a small woman with dimples in soft cheeks. "A girl like that brings back one's youth," she said. "I also was pretty."

"You still are," I said, bowing.

"What is she to you?"

"My wife."

"She seemed so young, so inexperienced . . . You should not let her go about with that old auntie."

"Was anything wrong?" I said, suddenly afraid.

"Not actually wrong. But a woman has an instinct about other women. And there are the Kaffirs . . . two women travelling alone. My husband rode on with them for twenty miles and from there, at Mullerskop, a friend of ours took them on another stage."

I went on, to the wreck of van der Spuyt's farm. All

around the yard and right up to the front stoep, there were craters and depressions made by the diamond diggers. The place was deserted. The sitting room wall had never been rebuilt. There were drifts of sand where once the red chair and rhinoceros foot had been. In the other rooms there were a few papers and old rags and the marks of fires that had been lit on the floors.

On my way to remount I picked up a handful of gravel. Shining there were garnets and the splinter of a diamond. I found an old sieve and all that day sieved and sorted; but there were no diamonds for me. That night I had to sleep in the deserted house.

Often during the journey I heard of Leah. I knew she had been safe at least until they reached the Darnalls' farm in Natal. Either the farmers themselves had seen her on her way or had sent a trusted servant with her.

Darnall's farmhouse stood at the head of a great valley in pasturelands of rolling hills. Here Leah and Madame had stayed for a week. Darnall had lent them his induna as guide, a Zulu of unimpeachable character.

A few days after they left, a tramp appeared at the kitchen door. Mrs. Darnall had been making bread that morning. She had put the loaves in the oven, closed the door and turned to find herself looking into the face of a big man, bearded and in filthy rags.

"Got some tobacco, lady?" he said. He was staring at her boldly; she was afraid. In the corner of the kitchen stood an old rifle that her son had cleaned and polished. She caught it up.

"What good is that?" said the tramp. He began to laugh; he had foul broken teeth. But still he was uncertain about the rifle: Mrs. Darnall pointed it at his stomach. "I'll let you have a bullet where it will hurt you most," she threat-

142

ened and presently he stopped laughing. But he stood there until he heard the children's shouts.

Her husband made light of her fears but she had often thought of the two women on the road and the tramp coming up with them. The induna had not yet returned but that in itself was not a cause for worry since he had been instructed to keep with the party until he could hand over to another responsible person.

Darnall exchanged the roan for a bay mare that was fast and a good stayer. Five days after I had acquired her I had news from some Zulus who were on their way to the diggings: two white women were stranded at a kraal ten miles away. The Zulus knew about the tramp too. He was not making for the coast but had gone into the Umkomaas valley and had taken up with a chief there. My relief at hearing this was so great that I shook. I wanted to weep. Every waking hour of those five days had been torment. My Leah and the tramp . . .

The valley had opened out to reveal a thousand bright hills. On the slopes were villages of grass huts and I toiled up to one after the other searching for Leah. At each place they told me they had heard of the white women; some claimed to have seen them. Guides took me to the places where they had lodged and in fact I gathered a retinue of twenty before I found Leah. I saw her from a hilltop.

She had heard that I was in the valley and had come with some naked Zulu girls to meet me. She was walking along a path beside a stream. In one hand she carried a sunshade and in the other held the poodles on leads. Her skirt kept getting caught onto thorn bushes and a good-natured girl would painstakingly free it.

"Leah, Leah."

She looked up. She sent the sunshade flying and let the

poodles go and ran to meet me. We hooked our fingers together and whirled like children; the poodles were barking and the girls cried shrilly.

We kissed. For me it was like tasting dew. Then we wept together for my father.

9

Leah and I sat on a rock overlooking the stream. The girls and boys who had been with us were skylarking on the bank, the poodles ran free.

"You should have waited at the Reubens'," I said to Leah.

"There was a man Tungay . . . I was afraid of him. One day in front of the others he tried to put his arms round me. Jo hit him on the head with the handle of her knife. Nobody could be bothered with me except Madame and Jo, everybody else was in the rush."

"I'm ruined by your going. I'm up for damages and I've involved Britt Tyzack too." I told her of the burning of Uzzell's place; and I was shy of her and did not look at her while I was telling her.

She said: "We can't go back to the diggings after what has happened. But you could trade in Durban, you could send goods to the Vaal . . ."

"Impossible. If I don't go back now, the door is closed to me forever. My name would be ruined."

"Our oxen are dead, all except one and that is very weak.

They are bringing some oxen to trade for my clothes. Let us at least go on to Durban until we can collect ourselves. The new team may never reach the diggings. They are small beasts."

I took her hand and held it against my cheek.

"There's no need any longer for you to make the plans. I'm here now." She nodded docilely. "Since I left the Darnalls' farm I've been in hell. A tramp frightened Mrs. Darnall and I thought he had caught up with you."

"We didn't see any tramps. The only awful thing has been that Madame got funny."

"Funny?"

"She drinks and then shouts for Günther. I don't know who he is. At the inns sometimes I sat up all night with my hands over her mouth. Even here she has to be watched, she gets beer from the old women. It's Miri's turn to watch today. Though Madame can be pleasant . . . we play cards when she is sober."

"You should have gone straight to the Reubens."

She sat quiet for a while and then began to make a pattern with the dog leads that she had bunched in her lap. She had, to shade her face, a wide Leghorn hat too heavy for the stalk of her neck and on her hands mittens of patterned mesh similar to those she had given the innkeeper's wife; so delicate her fingers were.

I said: "The diggings is no place for you."

"It is hateful," she said with hope flaring into her eyes. "Let us never go back. Truly, when we left, I looked around and I said: I will never set foot here again. I hate the place."

"A person would almost think you arranged deliberately to leave as soon as you got the chance."

"It was because of Tungay," she said sullenly.

"Well, I must go back. But I can see it's not possible for you to live there. The dry diggings are like an inferno. And Tungay is mad and dangerous . . . though I can deal with him. No, you must go to Durban. I'll return to the diggings and then join you as soon as I've paid off the debts and I've got a few hundred to make a start somewhere else. We'll live in England. That's what my father wished for you, peace to him."

"I'll go back with you, Mannie. What would my life be, alone in Durban?"

We went back to the kraal where Leah had been staying. Madame was reclining in the shade of a thorn tree that had heart-shaped shiny leaves. She sat up at once and pulled herself to rights.

"Monsieur!"

"We are going back to the diggings," Leah said.

"For that I thank God," said Madame. She turned to me. "Monsieur, the ennui!"

"How will I ever repay you?"

"Repay? Never speak of that. It was nothing I did," said Madame royally.

Leah was given room by the Reubens but there was no place for me. The living quarters at the back of the store, and even the store itself, were crammed at night with three hulking nephews and a brother of Solly's who had arrived from Poland; and there was the wife of Solly's eldest nephew. Leah had been given a share in the children's bed and she was kicked black and blue.

My home was in a piano case which I had bought for the sum of two pounds; it stood outside the Reubens' yard against a tin fence.

I tramped from claim to claim, picking up what stones were within my means to buy. Stokkies was working for Vollantyne who had a claim on the De Beers' farm; Miri had gone to live with Stokkies.

To avoid a scandal, Britt and I had settled the case with Uzzell out of court; it cost me every asset I had and left me owing Solly Reuben the hundred pounds I had borrowed, plus another two hundred that I felt was morally owing to Britt even if he had no legal claim. My friendship with him continued in spite of the trouble; but he was messing with some young men of his own kind and I did not often see him.

That debt of two hundred remains unsettled; he would never take the money though I offered to pay many times.

Even Archibald was sold. Jo bought him. She had a smart little turnout: Archibald in his straw hat, with crimson ribbons plaited into his mane; and a wicker chaise with satin cushions. The chaise was a low-slung vehicle seating one. Jo was to be seen in it on the roads, distributing cards. The cards were lettered in elegant gold type: DIAMOND JO THE DIGGERS' SWEETHEART EVERY EVENING AT UZZELL'S CRIMSON BAR SPECIALITY THE CITY OF DIAMONDS. Her name was on posters tacked to thorn trees or stuck on to corrugated iron walls: Uzzell was advertising the grand opening of his new place The Tickey Horse.

You could always be sure of seeing Jo near the diamond market when the diggers came up from their claims in the evening. I used to stop to pat Archibald and talk to her for a few minutes.

"How are you doing, Mannie?"

"No good."

"Uzzell has doubled my pay. And hell, I've been lucky at cards and at the horses these last few weeks. I've got a hundred quid! I'll lend it to you."

"I already owe Solly Reuben and Britt Tyzack. No thanks."

"Well, it's there any time you want it, provided I've still got it. You know me."

"Jo."

"Don't look at me like that," she said sharply. "I don't want to be caught here gazing into your eyes. I've got to get the cash customers in. I get a commission, Mannie. Every time a chap buys a bottle of champagne and he gives in one of my cards, I get a tickey from Uzzell. Here, take some cards and hand them around."

"When I crack it, I'll come in and buy the whole place out."

But Jo was not paying attention. A group of diggers had stopped nearby and she stood up in the chaise, showering them with cards.

The wicker chaises were popular with Uzzell's girls. A whole procession of them passed now: Bonnie, driving a spanking black mule, a new French girl screaming behind a team of trotting goats; and behind, a trippler drawing Madame Olpresci's chaise . . . she had her poodles with her, in caps and ruffs.

She stopped next to Jo, bowed elegantly to me and took from her reticule two letters which she gave to Jo.

"And these are for Madame Bernstein and the Reubens' children," she said to me and gave me three tickets for an

148

afternoon concert. "Tell her with Madame Olpresci's compliments." She drove on, proud as a duchess.

"Don't get them mixed up with my cards," said Jo maliciously. She read out the superscription on the envelope of one of her letters: "Diamond Jo, Dry Diggings, Cape . . . It's from New York." A banker's order fell out. "Bit of luck this. Smithers. I lent him ten quid but I never thought I'd see it again. Wow, Mannie, look at this . . . it's for a hundred nicker." She waved the draft above her head. "You know, he kept telling me his father was a millionaire in lil ole New York but I didn't believe him. Christ, he was unlucky, he was the unluckiest chap I ever saw."

"Unluckier than me?"

She looked at me contritely. "Mannie. Take this hundred. I'll only lose it. You can give me interest if you like."

"I won't take it. And Jo, you never used to say Christ like that . . ."

"All right. Get out of the pulpit. It's enough to make a cat laugh . . . a Jew sticking up for Christ." She tore the other letter open. "Here's a Valentine. I could get married, fancy that . . .

"Diamond Jo, say not no!
On my bended knee
I ask thee to be
My bride, my Jo!

"Isn't that nice? Diamond Jo, say not no! On my bended knee, I ask thee, to scrub my floors for me."

"Are you getting at me, Jo?"

She looked at me, startled. "What do you mean?"

"Oh nothing. But you be careful or you'll finish in the gutter."

"I'll have you for company," she retorted.

Scrubbing floors . . . One night when Leah was crammed into the piano case with me, I felt a roughness on her knees. Only then did I find out that she had been scrubbing the floor of the back room at the Reubens': the Kaffir girls had run away and Becky was sick . . . the floor had to be scrubbed.

"What about that other woman there?" I asked fiercely.

Then she explained to me that she felt awkward with Solly; never with Becky. She was one of the people crowding Solly out of his home, and a stranger; and there was the money we owed. He had never said anything unkind to her except to accuse her of being finicky but she felt that he disliked her. She had scrubbed the floor to propitiate him. But it wasn't necessary, he was a good man she said, weeping.

11

At night alone in the piano case I lay waiting for the tap tapping of the illicit sellers.

"Go away, damn you, come in the daylight."

"I got a diamond of diamonds for you, baas. Just have a look . . ." I would lie still. Sometimes a hand would grope for me over the top of the piano case, seeking my wrist to guide me to touch a diamond held in a palm. And sometimes the voice would change: "So you haven't fallen yet, Bernstein. Just remember, hey, I'm watching you."

That would be Thompson, the ace detective. I.D.B. Thompson, he was called, for the number of illicit diamond buyers he had hunted down. I feared him, a thin man with the piercing eyes of a predator.

It was the end of February, on a moonless night, that Stokkies brought the Griqua Moses to me. Stokkies woke me after midnight with an urgent tapping on the side of the case.

"Basie, it's me."

"What is it, Stokkies?"

"See what this Griqua has brought you."

I said: "I don't deal like that."

"Only look."

I sat up. Stokkies had hidden himself in the shadows of a thorn tree. The Griqua was a spear of darkness against the luminous sky. I saw the flash of the diamond in the starlight and put out my hand to touch it. The Griqua seized my wrist as my finger located it. I felt the size of the diamond with a tremor that reached to my bowels: four hundred carats. But flawed, that was certain.

"Get in here," I whispered.

The Griqua stepped into the case and crouched beside me. I lit a candle. He was holding out a dirty rag. In the middle of the rag lay a diamond.

"It's a schlenter," I whispered.

I held the diamond to the light. It was an octohedron, a white. I weighed it . . . three hundred and seventy carats, a fortune. I guessed that it was from the De Beers mine.

I wanted the diamond. Staring at it, I did not at first think of the money it would bring. From deep within me there spiralled a yearning for the gem itself. I saw it polished, the facets giving off blue fire, a pendant for Leah's throat. And I felt too a surge of hate against the Griqua

151

because he possessed it . . . the hate was like a desire to kill him. Only afterwards did I think of freeing Leah from the diggings with the money I would get for the diamond.

"How much?" I said: I kept my voice and my hands steady.

"A span of oxen, all red and white. An axe. A waggon eighteen feet long with a tent over it. A horse, sixteen hands, it must be a grey. Fifty sheep. A saddle. Twenty-five heifers . . ."

"Done."

"Ten sovereigns."

"Those also."

"I must have a coat."

"But nothing more." I blew out the candle. "Wait here. Quiet."

Stokkies drifted from beneath the tree as I got out of the piano case.

"You saw it, baas."

"I'd have to see it in the daylight, of course."

"I saw it by daylight. I know a diamond. You can get five thousand pounds for that diamond from a dealer in Christiana and no questions asked, my little old one. There's a slight feathering to one side. What Moses wants would cost not more than two hundred pounds. I want five hundred."

"I haven't got the money to buy it. I haven't got two hundred."

"How much you got? I got ten pounds, basie."

"I've got fifty-four pounds."

"Get the rest of the money," he said in a fierce whisper. "How often you think a chance like this comes along? Perhaps never again."

"Where will I get the money? I owe money already."

"Your friend Tyzack. Or try the moneylender Haase. And there is the nonnie Jo. Miri washes for her and she says she's got plenty money. Now listen. I'll take the Griqua away from here, I'll get him across the river. We'll meet you on the road to Christiana near the black rocks that are scratched over . . . you know the place."

"Yes."

"Then be there by midnight tomorrow."

"You're making a thief of me."

"You don't know where Moses got the diamond from, basie," Stokkies said placatingly. "You just don't know, my baas."

"He got it off Vollantyne's claim."

"How do you know that?"

"It's a De Beers diamond."

"You're only guessing."

He went to the piano case and whispered to the Griqua. The man climbed out and with a hand to his kerchiefed head, faded with Stokkies into the darkness.

I went to Solly Reuben as soon as it was light. He was already up and about when I reached the store. He stood sniffing the morning air while a Kaffir dragged bags of mealie meal onto the stoep. Inside I could see two of Solly's relatives like corpses laid out on the counter.

"Run out of skoff, Mannie?" Solly was amiable.

"No. I need two hundred pounds."

"From me again?" He was angry at once.

"I need it urgently. I'll pay you back within a week."

"Nuddink doink," he said. Then he spoke to me in Yiddish: "You get out, Bernstein. I would not give it to you if you went down on hands and knees. Am I a charity for Mannie Bernstein, am I a charity for the whole world?" He gestured towards the sleeping forms in the store. "I got mouths to feed, Bernstein . . . responsibilities . . . Get out. Don't look at me. I'm not a woman to fall for the big eyes."

I wasted no more time on him but hurried on to Britt's tent. Nobody was there except a Kaffir servant. Britt messed with four or five others; the servant told me that they were all duck-shooting at the Pan.

I knew that Halden was camped not far off in a waggon. He was drinking coffee but I waved aside the cup he poured for me.

"Can you lend me two hundred pounds?"

"Don't be a fool. I haven't got two hundred pence. I'm here to raise money to work my gold concession. But it's hopeless. I've struck a reef . . ."

Without waiting for him to finish, I left him sitting there. I went to Haase the moneylender. He slept in his office. I could hear him at his prayers. The moment they ended I burst in on him. I remember Haase. He was a spare man, bound within fine bones. A curved nose, smooth as ivory, was set above soft lips and a pointed beard.

"I want two hundred pounds at once," I said.

"And the security?"

"I'm a diamond buyer . . ."

"Your name?" he said courteously; but he moved to a table where a revolver lay.

"I'm Mannie Bernstein."

"A kopje walloper, isn't that the category? No office . . . just a few pounds capital and a scale. And now a big diamond has come your way. Is that it?"

"More or less."

"Well, I must have my security. What have you to offer?"

"My business," I stammered.

He smiled gently. "I have already enumerated your assets, my friend. I would rather have the diamond as security. Let me see the diamond and take particulars, perhaps even negotiate the sale for you."

"There is no diamond as yet," I said, suddenly fearing the bright rapacious eyes. "I was wanting the money so that I could expand. I get none of the good stones because I have no cash to pay."

"I see. So you come in here at six o'clock in the morning, aflame. No, Mr. Bernstein, there's a big diamond in the offing." He stood beside me with his hand uplifted to my shoulder. "What's the diamond like? Fiery, to set you on fire? Fit for a queen, hey, made for a beauty. Come, let me see it."

"There is no diamond," I said, moving away from him.

"Be careful Thompson doesn't hear of this nonexistent diamond," he said with a vicious smile. "We are great friends, you know. He calls on me to find out who is trying to borrow money suddenly and sometimes I tell him. Have you the diamond on you?"

I could have killed him where he stood. I looked at the revolver. He seemed to guess my thoughts for he picked the revolver up.

I went away, down the rough road. I wished I could rob him: there was a Gladstone bag which he must have used as a pillow for it stood at the top of his bed. That was full of money, I was sure.

I kept away from the store because I did not want to face Leah's questioning: Solly would be full of my attempt to borrow money. I went back to Britt's camp. Haase's servant followed me, skulking too far behind for me to catch him and hit him.

Britt had not returned to his camp nor was he to be found at the Pan or on his claim. There was a whisper going about that he and his friends were viewing a new prospect; he might be back at any moment. I sat under a tree to wait for him. I fell asleep there and when I awoke my mind was clear. The fever of desire had left me.

God of Israel: in my thoughts I had been a murderer and a thief.

The sun was in the west. Britt's camp still lay deserted. I could thank God that I had not asked him for money and so ruined our friendship.

An intense rage against Stokkies and the Griqua mounted in me. I knew that the diamond had been stolen from Vollantyne's claim; it only needed proof that the Griqua had worked for him. I would show them. There was Mrs. Vollantyne who had stuck it out through all the rigours of camping on the Vaal and on these more cruel diggings. The diamond was hers, to free her to live as a woman should. I was pierced by a memory of her when I had first known her. She was fresh out from England then and on the way to the Vaal. It was mud underfoot, waggons in mud to their axles and a fire lit under a stubborn ox to make him pull . . . She suffered for the ox and stood with her hands to her eyes.

I wanted to serve her now for I hated what I had seen in myself: murderousness and greed. Damnation to Stokkies, the source of evil . . . I hated the bastard. If I could prove that the Griqua Moses had worked on Vollantyne's claim, I'd tell the doctor where he could find his diamond . . .

I went to Vollantyne's house, still tagged by Haase's boy. The house was a cut-out, an ingenious affair that had been sent out from England to be assembled on the spot. It was made of wood-and-iron and there was white lattice work

156

on the dolly's verandah. No more incongruous residence could have been devised for the doctor and his wife; both were tall people with booming, authoritative voices and I had smarted many a time under Mrs. Vollantyne's gentility. But I had never ceased to admire her.

The door stood open and I walked straight into the sitting room which was crowded with men. Doctor Vollantyne leaned back in a chair, the dogs all over him and at his feet.

"Come in, Bernstein," he said cordially. "Gentlemen, you all know Mannie Bernstein. You can go on talking. Mannie is one of us, a true-blue Englishman."

"From the steppes via Whitechapel," drawled a young fellow seated astride a chair.

"Come now, be civil," the doctor chided. "Mannie was in the clash at the Vaal. Sit down, my boy." He made no effort to find me a chair and I stood there awkwardly. "Bernstein has been among the Zulus, he knows the new chief Cetewayo. Sit down, sit down, my boy. Tell them about the Zulus."

There was a general laugh. "Where the hell is he to sit, Voll?"

"On his backside of course," said the doctor. I edged towards the door. "Don't go without a drink, Bernstein. Get Bernstein a drink, Gisborne."

Gisborne poured a brandy for me. He was Vollantyne's overseer.

As I sipped the drink, I asked Gisborne if he had employed a Griqua named Moses.

"There's always a Griqua named Moses on the claim," he said. "Or a Bawenda named Moses, or a Xosa . . . I've got a fruit salad on the claim . . . Zulus, Basutos, even a few boys from Nyasaland. Find it keeps them honest to have different tribes . . . they fight among themselves . . .

157

Come to think of it, I did have a Griqua Moses who left last week. Why? Does he want a job with you?"

"No shop," said the youth sitting astride the chair.

Vollantyne said: "What can I do for you, Mannie?" and rose at last, dislodging the reluctant dogs.

"I wanted to see you privately."

"Anything serious? If it could wait until the morning . . ."

Mrs. Vollantyne, as though she had been listening at the door, swept into the room. The men stood up.

"Do I hear something about a patient, at this hour when the doctor is thinking of having a quiet chat with friends?"

"It's Bernstein," the doctor muttered.

"Oh be a sport, Bernstein," she cried. "What's wrong? Nothing broken, I hope. Can't it wait until the morning?" She sat down and allowed a bulldog to spring onto her lap; there he sat, panting and slobbering in the close room while she from time to time cooed over him.

Vollantyne forced me to sit in the chair he had vacated. There was a general movement among the younger fellows so that he should be seated; and a silence when after the shuffle round a fat important attorney was left standing.

I drank up hastily and left. The wish to retrieve the diamond for the Vollantynes had vanished; they had better take care of their own property, was the way I looked at it now. I would get on with my own business as if I had never heard of Moses and his diamond. My mood of righteousness had vanished completely.

Haase's Kaffir was waiting outside for me. I caught him this time for he had been dozing against the fence. I hit him on the jaw, turned him round as he was falling and kicked him down the road for about a hundred yards. He fled.

12

From there I went to the diamond market to dispose of a few small diamonds. Podbery, a Polish Jew I often dealt with, was the only dealer still at work.

"You're late today, Bernstein," he said. "What you got?"

I shook my diamonds out of the box onto the white paper fixed to his counter. He scarcely glanced at the stones. "Four pound ten the lot."

"Five pounds."

"Good," with a courteous smile.

He paid me. I pocketed the money and stepped out into the road. It was a cloudy afternoon. There had been a few spots of rain while I was in Podbery's office and the dust was marked with neat round spots and gave off a tang. I was considering the weather . . . no more than that was in my mind . . . when there came upon me again a craving for the diamond.

I looked about. Haase's boy had not returned so I couldn't send a message and Haase was not in his office, it was shuttered. Would old Podbery lend me money? He had closed his office and was walking along the road. I caught up with him.

"I'm looking for backing."

"No more business for today," he said cheerfully. "I'm off for supper and then a little game of poker at The Tickey Horse."

"I want to buy bigger."

"It's a good idea. Young feller like you, got to get ahead."

He clapped me on the back and hurried away to his supper. Some chaises were being driven on the road beyond to The Tickey Horse. I recognized Jo's and called out to her but she did not hear me. I caught her as she was going into The Tickey Horse.

"I've got to speak to you, Jo."

"I'm on in the Crimson Bar from six to seven . . . Come round later." She was about to hurry away but she turned back. "What is it, Mannie? Are you in trouble?"

"We can't talk here."

She followed me outside on to a patch of veldt next to the building.

"I came to borrow two hundred pounds from you."

"Haven't got it now. I told you to take it while I had it."

"I'd have given you interest. Fifty per cent and the principal back in a week's time."

"I lost every penny . . . Still, this might turn out to be good luck. You be careful, Mannie. What do you suddenly want two hundred pounds for? It's I.D.B. isn't it? They'll get you . . . seven years on the breakwater."

"I never said it was I.D.B."

She came close. "Is it a big diamond, Mannie?"

"I could get maybe five thousand for it."

"I might win some money tonight."

"It will be too late after ten tonight."

"If I can get it, I'll send it with Miri. Don't let her be seen handing the money to you. She can drop it in the piano case and walk on."

"Fifty per cent and your principal back within a week," I said.

She leaned forward and kissed me suddenly.

I went from there to the uproar of Solly's place to have my supper. Afterwards, Leah and I walked in the starlight. If Solly had told her that I wanted to borrow money, she had decided to say nothing about it to me; she was somewhat stiff with me, a little false these days in her efforts to avoid quarrelling.

"I'm going to the Vaal for a few weeks to see what I can pick up," I told her: I gave her a few sovereigns for her pocket.

"Shouldn't I give them to Solly?"

I put my arm round her and cuddled her and whispered maledictions against Solly in her ear. She was smiling when we said goodnight.

I hired a horse. I left him grazing on the outskirts of the camp and at half-past nine hid in the shadows of the tree with the piano case in view.

Miri came. She left two hundred golden sovereigns in the piano case.

13

It was a fortnight before we satisfied the Griqua. The span of oxen had to be matched in size and colour, the sheep had to be in prime condition, the waggon had to be painted blue and it must have a red kist.

"And now I'm going home," he said as we stood in the veldt with the waggon inspanned and the cattle ready to trek. He took the rag from his shirt, unfolded it and looked at the diamond. He gazed at it. "Diamond, good-bye. Little diamond, when I see my father I will tell him about you . . . Stone, shining stone." He saluted the diamond. "There, baas, it is yours."

He climbed onto his waggon; a servant drove the livestock and another helped with the oxen. They were going far, to the Maluti Mountains.

Stokkies and I watched. It was sunset. Earth and sky dissolved in a wash of gold; the waggon and the cattle and the thin whip and the men showed up in hard black lines as they moved further away from us.

"Aits, what will his father say to see him come home like a king?" cried Stokkies. "My baas, I am going to take my money and go home with Miri to my father in Coles-berg . . . No more waste, no more drink . . ."

"If my father could have seen this," I said, holding the diamond to the light.

Stokkies craned to look at it. "How it shines."

We doubled up and rode to Christiana. It was still hot, we were sweating. On the veldt there were drifts of red plumed grass, I remember.

"Christiana, basie," said Stokkies at last, pointing from behind me.

Christiana was a blur in the molten gold of the plain. I was sorry to see it. Soon the diamond would pass into a dealer's hands; thousands of other people through the ages would touch it. Would it be lost in a collection of jewels, outshone by larger gems? or be hung on some old woman's neck? I wished I could keep it for Leah, to be her solitary ornament.

Stokkies was jigging up and down in the saddle. "Christiana look out, here we come. Gits, we'll be rich . . ." He chanted: "Money money, geldt geldt, mali mali . . ."

It was dark when we rode down the single street of the hamlet. Stokkies had not been able to contain his joy and had slipped from the saddle. He pranced along beside the tired horse while he called out arrogantly the names of the diamond dealers.

"That's Paull's office and there is Goldstein's. You wait, basie, I know where you get the best deal. Shorty De Klerck is the one for us, he is a Belgian man and honest."

At the end of the street, he told me to dismount. We tethered the horse to a hitching rail. Stokkies knocked at the door of a shack. The top half of the door was flung open and a man leaned out.

"Stokkies Truter, where have you been hiding yourself, my boy? Come in." With a wink he included me in his affability.

"This is baas Bernstein from the dry diggings."

"Oho. From there?"

He pulled back the bolt and we entered a room furnished with a counter, two chairs and a bedstead. De Klerck seated himself behind the counter and motioned me to the other chair. Stokkies sat on the floor. There was silence.

De Klerck was a powerful, squat man with hair frothing at the open neck of his shirt which he wore unbuttoned to the navel and with the sleeves rolled up; body and arms were hairy but his head was bald. He had thick lips, red and wet, framed obscenely by the soft thin hair of a moustache and beard.

I placed the diamond on the paper in front of him. He examined it carefully, sighed and leaned back, stroking the hair round his mouth. Stokkies had risen to his feet, ready as a leopard.

"One thousand pounds," said De Klerck.

"Five thousand," cried Stokkies.

"Two months ago, even one month ago, yes. But the value of diamonds has tumbled. Go anywhere in Christiana . . . I'm telling you one thousand . . . guineas and that's my price."

"We'll go to Paull," said Stokkies. "Come, basie."

"Go," said De Klerck. "But remember this: when you come back here, my offer will be nine hundred."

Stokkies sat down again. "He is serious, basie."

"The market has fallen. I'm left holding a dozen big stones," said the Belgian.

"Make it two thousand," I said.

Shorty spread his hands. "Twelve hundred. And that is my last word."

14

From the deal I netted three hundred and forty pounds. I paid Stokkies ten per cent of the gross price: he had the cash next morning.

He went off on a spree that landed him in the jail; and had to pay his last three pounds to avoid lashes. A month later, he was working for Vollantyne again and was a married man. He never remembered marrying Miri but she had her lines to prove that he had.

I rode straight back to the diggings.

Madame Olpresci kept house for the girls in a wood-and-iron cottage near The Tickey Horse. I slipped in there to meet Jo, in a dusty parlour heavily curtained in green velvet. It was late afternoon and the girls were out driving. I sent the servant to find Jo.

She wore sprigged muslin and when she came in she brought with her a scent that had the sharp edge of geraniums to it.

"Got the money?" she asked eagerly.

"Not a fortune. He only paid twelve hundred."

"Damn."

"But you get seven-eighty."

"I don't get much of that. I acted for somebody else."

"Who?"

"Uzzell."

"Does he know it was for me?"

"Don't think so. Pay up. I must be off."

I said: "There's a blue velvet cloak in Solly's store, Jo. It's the colour of midnight. I thought of you when I saw it." I gave her five sovereigns.

She bit each coin, like an urchin.

"Now you've got a bit of cash, come and hear me sing in the Crimson Bar."

"What about Uzzell, though?"

"Chance it."

"I want to say thank you and thank you again, Jo."

She blew me a kiss and went out. Presently I heard her drive away.

The place was quiet. I sat on a plush chair and figured out how to spend the money. Sixty pounds to Leah for a new gown and bonnet and a pair of boots, all to be ordered from London; and something over to keep in her purse . . . To Reuben one hundred; that would sweeten the air round Leah until I could find somewhere for her to stay. Later, discreetly, I would buy a new outfit of clothes for myself. And there would still be money over to invest in a fair-sized diamond. I left a pound for Madame Olpresci and went down the street whistling.

I walked in on the chaos of a row at the Reubens' place. Leah had already packed and was sitting defiantly on our tin trunk. Becky ran in from the washing line with an armful of clothes which she hurled into a carpet bag. She was shrieking at her Polish niece-in-law, a sallow be-wigged woman now also packing to leave. Even the two little girls were stowing things in a bag. Solly stood helplessly in the doorway.

The niece did not answer Becky but hissed at Leah: "May your tongue rot and the marrow in your bones seep out . . ."

"Leave her alone," cried Becky.

"Take care of yourself, why worry about Leah?" bellowed Solly.

Leah had crept to my side. She was white; and thin to the touch beneath her print bodice. There was a sudden quiet in the room while I stood there with my arm round her.

"So you're back," said Solly.

Becky fell into a chair, threw her apron over her head and sobbed. Only smelling salts restored her.

"She is pregnant," said Solly, himself almost weeping. "Nobody knows what it has been like here for the past week with the women fighting." He took a bottle of brandy from a cupboard and we had a drink together.

Then Solly and I went over to the hotel and drank there. We found a solution. I offered to pay for a holiday for Becky and the children at Paynton's Rondavels, a resort on the Vaal; and Solly accepted. Leah was to accompany them. The niece was to be found somewhere else to live and of course this meant that Leah would not be given room either.

I spent a few days with Leah at Paynton's but though we were happy together, she still did not conceive.

15

Solly and I both went to the Crimson Bar one evening to hear Jo sing: I thought I might need Solly as a backstop if Uzzell or Tungay wanted to fight. But Uzzell was affable to me: he seemed to have Tungay in control.

"No hard feelings, Mannie," he said, shaking my hand. "As a matter of fact I've been hoping you would drop in. I've added to my collection of diamonds lately. I'll let you see them. I believe you're quite the buyer these days."

He led Solly and me into his office. It was no more than a cubbyhole under the stairs and contained a small table and a chair, and a safe, so newly installed that there were still wood shavings and lumps of plaster and stone left lying on the floor. Uzzell felt in his waistcoat pocket.

"Damn. I've left the combination at the house." He put his head through the door and yelled for Tungay. "Go and get the paper out of my red waistcoat on the end of the bed."

"You trust him," said Solly when Tungay had gone.

"How would he know what it is? He's got less brains than a Kaffir."

He did not trust us. When he opened the safe, he kept

his movements screened; and carefully put away the sheet of paper which had the combination written on it.

"I'll soon memorize it," he said. He emptied some diamonds from a chamois leather bag onto his desk. There were twenty and among them fancy stones; pinks, blues, yellows and one green.

"I won all of these playing cards. What do you think they are worth, Bernstein?"

"Hard to say. I'd want to have a look in the daylight."

"I'd like to sell. Come round tomorrow and look at them. Then see what sort of price you can get me."

The deal did not come off. I went round all the buyers with a list but I had no takers at ceiling price for the market continued depressed. Uzzell would not come down. Indeed I suspected him of not being serious: he liked to have buyers view the stones for the sake of showing them off. He hinted to me then that not all his diamonds were on view: some stones he had won were not registered.

It became a regular thing for me to call in at the Crimson Bar for snacks and a drink at the end of the day. Jo would sing and if we stood her enough champagne she would get up on the counter and dance for us.

We did not see each other alone until the night of Jo's trouble.

It was after midnight. She woke me by thumping on the piano case. I climbed out and drew her away to the shelter of the trees.

"Why have you come here?" I whispered. She was crying. "Quiet, somebody will hear you. I've got to think of my wife." She had sunk to the ground. I knelt beside her. "If you would only tell me what is wrong."

"I've killed Tungay." She sat up and leaned her head against my chest. "We were in the room upstairs playing

168

poker. The big game had broken up and Uzzell and I were playing a few hands. Tungay wasn't there, he went to bed: he acts as watchman, you know . . . he sleeps on the floor in Uzzell's office.

"And suddenly Uzzell set himself against me. You've seen him do it. But he has never done it to me . . . not like this, not testing me to the limit. He had won all my money from me and then he said: 'I'll play for you, Jo.' Righto, I said I don't mind Uzzell that way and Bonnie wasn't there . . . But it wasn't himself he meant.

"He said: 'Not for myself, for Tungay . . . how about it? . . . he's mad on you.' He knows how I feel about Tungay, all the girls feel like that . . . there's something terrible about him, he can never get a girl. But I said I'd play and it was a thrill. I lost. Uzzell went out laughing and shouted for Tungay to tell him the news.

"I sat there. Everybody went away. I heard the door bang.

"Tungay came in. I was thinking, I'll welsh, I'll do myself in first: I had my knife in my hand. I said to him: Leave me alone, and he caught my wrist and crushed it to make me give up the knife. When I dropped it, he threw me on my back and pulled my dress over my face. I found the knife on the floor. I stabbed him. I'll hang, they'll hang me, Mannie. I went and told Uzzell and he kicked me out. And Madame is drunk, no help there. So I came to you.

"Oh God, Uzzell . . . He used to care for me but now I've welshed, he is finished with me. I'm a welsher, Mannie. They'll hang me."

"I'll help you, Jo. Only we've got to be practical . . . I must think of Leah . . ."

"I'll go."

"No, don't. I'll have to get Britt Tyzack to defend you,

he's a lawyer. Will the police come here? Does anybody know you're here?"

"Miri. She sleeps in the yard behind Uzzell's. I told her I was coming to you."

"Sit tight. I'll go over to Uzzell's and see what is happening. Here, put on this. And here's a drop of brandy." I gave her a flannel shirt and the bottle.

"You are good, Mannie."

"Climb into the case and pull the lid down. You'll keep warm."

I lit a lantern and hurried to The Tickey Horse. There was a light on upstairs and I could hear the doctor's voice. Two of his bull terriers stood guard at the front door.

I went round to the back where a fire was blazing. Miri and Stokkies were warming themselves.

"Basie," said Stokkies with a helpless grin. He lay with his head in Miri's lap: she was holding a bottle of brandy to his lips and taking a sip for herself now and then.

"What's happening up there?" I asked.

"The doctor is looking after baas Tungay," said Miri.

"Nonnie Jo thought he was dead."

"Only wounded."

"Have they sent for the police?"

"No. They won't send for the police, baas Uzzell told me himself. He told us to keep our mouths shut. And I was so frightened that the nonnie Jo would hang or go to jail." Miri sprang up suddenly and let out a yell that the girls had learned from the American diggers. Round and round the yard she pranced, singing: "Tickey horse, horse horse . . . Tickey horse . . ." It was the refrain of one of Jo's songs.

I waited to see Uzzell. He came out with Vollantyne. The two stood chatting for a few minutes and then the doctor with his terriers at heel marched off to his house.

"Uzzell," I said.

"Did she go to you?"

"Yes."

"She is through here. I don't deal with welshers. Lucky for her Tungay is so stupid about her: he won't bring a charge. Lucky for her he didn't die. She owes me some money, Bernstein. Tell her I'll sell her donkey and her clothes and that will square us."

"Put your fists up. I'm going to teach you a lesson."

He folded his arms. "I'm not fighting. Goodnight," he said and turned his back on me and went into The Tickey Horse.

I returned to the piano case.

"Listen, Jo," I said. Faintly through the night came the sounds of Miri's rejoicing.

"What is it?"

"Miri . . . Tungay is alive and he won't bring a charge against you."

"Thank Jesus for that. Did you see Tungay?"

"No. I spoke to Uzzell."

"Is he still wild?"

"Yes. He says he will sell your clothes . . ."

"He'll put the finger on me," she said. "What am I going to do, Mannie? I haven't got a bean."

"I'll lend you some money."

"Tell you what . . . I've a claim. I won it from a chap who was down on his luck, Ponsonby. It's water-logged but if you will lend me fifty quid, I could get it working. How about it?"

"Of course, Jo. I don't forget how you helped me."

"They say a Jew never forgets a good turn," she said complacently.

16

Jo sat beneath an awning made by an old plaid rug thrown over two posts. She was combing gravel on the sorting table. Delicately, she picked out a diamond, then another and another. She held them out to me to examine. They were small stones, in all perhaps two carats.

"Skoff for the boys," she said.

She put the diamonds away in a matchbox. The matchbox was kept between her breasts for safety. She shook the flywhisk above her head and bent over the table again. Three hours later, when I returned from my rounds, she was still at it, raising her eyes only to glance towards the cradles in the hope that there would be a fresh load of gravel for the sorting table.

It was close to midday. Somewhere an iron was struck, and the labourers hearing the clang looked up hopefully at her. She nodded. The boys threw down their picks and shovels and climbed out of the hole. They did not eat now but only drank, in long desperate gulps from a small bucketful of water rationed to them.

Jo sighed. "It always seems to be time to stop." The subtle thrill of digging for diamonds had her on her claim from dawn to dark although she had made no big find.

She wiped some of the dust from her face, then took out the diamonds again to inspect them. For our meal there was cold coffee and some bread and venison. Jo snatched at the food, still looking at the diamonds. She had been digging for six weeks now. When she first started she was quiet for she thought that everybody on the diggings knew that she had welshed on a bet. When she found that the story had scarcely penetrated beyond the circle of Uzzell's company, she plucked up courage to swagger among the diggers; it was a joke that she wore a corduroy skirt, a boy's shirt, and velschoens, and a man's hat. She was noisy again and friendly to people but I knew her to be changed; weaker, I thought, and more like a woman in spite of the mannish clothes.

She was nearly always dirty for water was dear. A treat for her was to present her with a bottle of soda water for a wash. Freckles had spread all over her face. She had a looking-glass in her tent but she had hung a cloth over it.

With Leah still at Paynton's, Jo and I were living together in her tent, miles from Solly's store. On Fridays I would ride out to the Vaal to spend the Sabbath with Leah, and I stayed there until Monday.

Jo and I were losing money.

"I'm just one jump ahead of broke," she said gloomily to me that day.

"I'm two jumps ahead. Do you realize, there hasn't been a rise in diamonds for months. Bah, it's chancy. I heard that Britt Tyzack has got a lord in tow, Lord Alvers, and they are working on a scheme to get control of the output of the mines . . ."

"Trust him. He'd have us all down with a brass beak picking if it was left to him. Meanwhile I haven't got enough to hire a proper team of boys. I'm always short-handed."

The Kaffirs dropped back into the hole. Their picks flashed up . . . "blue ground and yellow ground, O

men . . ." and down again among the stones and earth . . .
". . . shining pebbles, men . . ." Up for the blue ground
and down for the shining pebbles: an old man chanted for
them. The picks were like silver in the white afternoon,
up and down to the faultless rhythm of the old man's voice
and the deep chorus of the workers. The men themselves
as they sweated were silvered over by the light.

"Stop dreaming, Mannie," Jo yelled. "Lend a hand
there."

Two men had begun to shovel up the stuff. I bent to
the sieve. The rattle of stones jarred across the chanting as
the cradle rocked steadily, slowly. I emptied the stuff into
the second cradle and the fine sieving began. Dust and
earth filtered away, and only gravel was left, spinning
against the mesh; green and white, shiny with garnets.

Jo was waiting to receive the new load of gravel. I spread
it on the sorting table. The triangle of the scraper shot out.

"Mannie," said Jo and her voice was deep in her throat.
She was holding out a diamond on the palm of her hand;
it was on the fifty-carat mark, I could see that. Suddenly
she yelled: "A whopper, I've picked out a whopper."

The boys scrambled up out of the hole and stood wiping
the sweat from their faces. Their laughter and Jo's shouts
brought old Herman Beyer from the next claim.

"Dot is a goot von, mein lieber kind." He thumped her
on the back.

"Steady on, sausage," Jo cried, staggering, but now she
was overwhelmed as several diggers arrived to congratulate
her.

"Good on y', Jo . . ." "Congratulations, Mrs. Jo . . ."
"Hoera for Diamond Jo . . ." and "You're a bloody marvel,
my girl . . ." She was kissed and shaken by the hand, pum-
melled and hugged.

When the first excitement had abated, the diggers still lingered, gazing into the pit where the picks and shovels lay tossed onto the yellow ground. Jo was emptying her pockets of loose change to give the boys for grog and meat.

"There's a party tonight at my tent," she cried to the diggers. "You all come. We'll make it champagne . . . but we won't forget the beer either, Herman."

17

At Solly's store, Jo leaned with her elbows on the counter.

"Sugar, Solly," she said. "I'll take a pocket of sugar. And I'll have that . . ." She pointed to a bottle of sugared fruit. "And Solly . . ."

"Vait," said Solly. "No more credit, Miss Jo. You haf credit to tree bounds, finish . . ."

Jo took out the matchbox and opened it. "Take a squint at that."

"De hull shob on credit." Solly shook hands with her.

"You must come to the party."

She bought a barrowload of groceries and three cases of champagne, and some beer; cigars and sweets; a blue silk dress and a blue velvet cloak like the one I had given her. She bought a white silk shirt for me and a silk dress for a Dutch child whose parents were out of luck. And as we were leaving the store, she snatched up two white trilby hats with blue ostrich feathers on them. Our old stained hats she sent spinning across the road to be pounced on by the horde of children who had gathered on hearing the news that a big diamond had been found. She set a hat on my head and with the other at a jaunty angle on the bird's nest of her hair, took my arm and made for the newspaper office to announce her find.

All the way along Eldorado Road Jo was scattering sweets and silver pennies for the children. They laughed and sang, forming a huge circle round us and the Kaffirs bearing Jo's purchases. "Sally go round the moon, Sally go round the stars, Sally go round the chimbley pots, on a Saturday afternoon . . . Whoops!" Round the other way they danced while idle Kaffirs clapped and screeched by the roadside.

"Look at that for a whopper," yelled Jo, bursting in on Charlton, the editor of the paper. She flung the diamond onto the table in front of him.

"Some diamond, Jo," he said, screwing a glass into his eye. "Just a spot in the centre. I'll roll the dice with you for it." He winked at me. I wanted to get between her and Charlton. I felt a rush of tenderness towards her for he was on the verge of making fun of her: she was a sight to see with her wild hair and earth-streaked face.

"Come on, Jo," I urged.

"Have you got it all down?" Jo said to Charlton who had been scribbling off the particulars of the diamond.

"Here it is," he said. "Miss Josephine Carr . . . correct? . . . our only lady digger, was in our office this afternoon displaying a diamond which almost outshone her own fair charms. The weight is fifty carats and the stone is of the purest water. How's that?"

"That's good," said Jo. "You can come to my party to-night, Mr. Charlton."

"Thank you, my dear."

We clattered down the stairs into the road again. The children had dispersed except for three or four small boys who kept with us until dark.

"Let's take the stone to Podbery," I said.

"Later. I want to keep it awhile. I'll have a bath first and put on my new dress . . ."

Although we hurried, it was sunset before we reached our camp. The water barrel was empty and it was too late to buy more water.

"I'll make do with champagne," said Jo.

She vanished into the tent and I heard the popping of a cork and Jo's little cries as the champagne fizzed over her.

"You too, Mannie," she cried.

A full blast of champagne hit me in the face as I entered. Jo was standing in a little tin bath and she held a bottle of champagne in each hand . . .

Jo, like a goddess in a fountain . . . I see her in the young girls I pass on the street, I hear her in women's voices.

She was the woman I loved.

18

Jo took the cloth from the looking-glass and stared at her reflection.

"Looks as if I had been sunburned through a colander," she mourned. Beneath her freckled face, her body was white; some drops of champagne still clung to the downy hair that covered her arms and legs.

177

In silk drawers and shift she sat in front of the looking-glass cleaning her hair with Fuller's earth. When she began to work the Fuller's earth out, I took the brush from her.

I was obsessed by the glittering swathe of her hair. I buried my face in it and held it in my fists and stroked it, so soft and rich. It was hair for diamonds. I thought of a small diamond circlet . . . silver leaves veined with diamonds and in the centre a white stone, a hundred carats, flawless, cut by Rudin . . .

Jo took the brush from me. "Off dreaming again, Mannie." With hard strokes she rid herself of the last of the white earth. She poured bay rum over her head. Her hair was dark now, in thick streaks on her neck; the smell of bay rum was masculine, quenching desire.

Her hair dried quickly. It crackled as she plaited it. She put on the silk dress. I watched her as she went round the tent, tidying up. Her hair now lay in a great shining coil on the nape of her neck.

She went outside and picked some leaves from a little bush. These she put in a jam jar on the table.

A dozen or more diggers were whooping outside. "Diamond Jo!" Jo seized my arm and ran to the entrance of the tent with me. "Here she comes, Diamond Jo . . ." "Mrs. Bernstein . . ."

The guests had brought their own mugs and cups with them, hooked to their belts or crammed into coat pockets. These were held out bashfully to be filled with champagne. Jo darted from one to the other with a foaming bottle, calling out to the boy to bring the tray of grilled mutton and bread.

I drank but waved the food away.

I remember plunging along the roads in the dark with

a crowd at my heels, Jo dancing beside me flourishing a bottle of champagne. We were making for the flaring lights and the music of the merry-go-round.

"Dabs I the green pony with the white spots," Jo was yelling.

I don't remember reaching the merry-go-round. My next flash of consciousness came when we were in the American Bowling Alley. Solly Reuben was with me.

"Where's Jo?" I asked.

"She went back to the merry-go-round," he said. He took my arm and we lurched towards the lights and music.

There was nobody on the merry-go-round except two tall Dutchmen. They sat with their feet thrust awkwardly into the stirrups of the wooden horses, shouting out in their enjoyment. When the merry-go-round stopped, they paid and went off for another turn. Solly folded his arms and gazed at the spectacle.

"Now I haf seen everyting. Mannie, I tought when I came to Africa, an elephant . . . it's vonderful. And a croc, vonderful too. Likevise a diamont in the grount. But ven I see these goyim . . . they spend their cash on vooden horses . . . Vy not on vimmen? . . ."

Solly, mysteriously, had some brandy with him. We drank, share and share, while we watched the Dutchmen on the merry-go-round. I remember no more of that night.

When I came to myself again, I was lying in a big bed in a strange room. Next to me was a woman, coarse and dark, and beyond her, Solly with his mouth open as he snorted and grunted in sleep.

I eased myself out of the bed and leaned over and touched Solly. He awoke instantly and stared up at me. I put my finger to my lips. Solly picked up his boots and tiptoed out after me. I saw with horror that I was still wearing my boots.

"I slept in my boots," I whispered to Solly in the passage, as he pulled his own boots on.

"It's a whore's house," he said. "They are Greeks. They come to the store."

We went outside. Some distance from the house we found a barrel of rain water and stole some to rinse our faces and hands.

"Becky will have to come home," said Solly, in Yiddish. "What a thing." He struck himself a blow on the chest. "What a vile thing. Becky . . . What a life she has with me. When our first child was born, I had nothing to bring her, Mannie. We were very poor then, in the Old Country. And I looked in my pockets and there was nothing. I went then and did some filthy work, cleaning out a place. And I had enough only to buy a small bottle of scent for her. I gave it to her and I knelt by the bed. I'll give you the world, Becky, I said, I'll give you jewels and fine furniture. But I am not even faithful to her. Damn you, Bernstein," he said, mournfully.

Jo was not in the tent or on her claim.

In the afternoon I saw Miri scouring a pot with sand outside the girls' house.

"Is nonnie Jo here?" I asked her.

"Yes. She went to The Tickey Horse last night, basie. She gambled away a big diamond. Uzzell has got it now. But he has given nonnie Jo her place back, she is going to sing tonight. He is short of girls."

She had gone on with her work while she talked to me and as I walked away she sang, a merry Cape jig.

19

Solly cleared all his relations out of his home and brought Becky and the children back from Paynton's. Leah and I lived in a tent near the store.

There was a sickness in me . . . I wanted Jo. Reason would not help me. I could say over and over to myself: She's your ruination . . . But the afternoon would find me watching for her chaise. On my way home I would call in at the Crimson Bar to stand her a glass of champagne.

Archibald had passed beyond our ken after Uzzell seized her goods. Her chaise was now drawn by a wild striped mule, a cross between a donkey and a zebra: the next girl who had it was kicked to death in the chaise.

I stopped to warn Jo about the mule one afternoon.

"That animal is not safe, Jo. Why don't you get an ordinary mule?"

"But isn't he pretty?"

The men were coming up from the claims. They came by in long lines, white men and black, and a hundred shades in between; but all were now uniformly covered with red dust. The dust was in the air too, glowing in the afternoon sun. Jo had stopped her chaise in the square, right across the way many of the diggers were taking. She handed out her cards.

"Gala night on Saturday. Something new . . . Uzzell's auctions. Great bargains at The Tickey Horse."

"How much for you?" said a digger.

"A diamond, a big 'un."

"If I strike it lucky, I'll be there on Saturday night."

I said: "What are you up to, Jo?" and took a card from her and read out: "Diamond Jo—Yours for a diamond as big as a star." I swore at her.

"It's nothing. Just a joke of Uzzell's. Who's going to bid a diamond for me?"

"I would, Jo."

"If you had it. I owe you money . . ."

"You don't. I'll pay Solly for you as well, later on."

"Later on."

She laughed in my face and drove off crazily.

A Dutch woman greeted me. She was sitting on a three-legged stool suckling her baby. I remembered her for I had once bought a small diamond from her husband.

"Mevrouw Pienaar," I said. "Are you leaving the diggings?" The waggon stood loaded on the square.

"Yes. The Lord has turned His back on us. Now we cannot even pay a Kaffir."

Pienaar came from behind the waggon and shook me by the hand. His wife had put the baby into a rough cradle beside her. She sat with her hands clenched in her lap; a wide woman but with no comfort in her.

"Misery," she said. "I think of our farm that we sold, Mr. Bernstein. There was a waterwheel and some old willows, I had a tame old secretary bird . . ."

"Be still," said her husband.

He was a big man, of tremendous bone. The tough hairy dark-brown skin was like the hide of a draught animal; his bones, like such an animal's would be hard . . . you see bones lying on the veldt for years without altering shape. The wide-brimmed hat and moleskin trousers and coat, the rough shoes cut from greenish hide were all he had ever thought to wear. Such a wild, uncouth figure he was, come to gather jewels. And she . . . broad of face and hip with the grained breast exposed, the nipple a plug in the mouth of the child. It was not sucking but lay there motionless except for a blinking of its eyes. The woman wore a dress of German print, a blue stuff printed over with white and too hard in texture to hang gracefully. Her bare feet were thrust into rough hide shoes, no different from her husband's except in size. Although the sun was setting she still wore a tucked bonnet of unbleached calico. She was an ugly woman: she had hard round little eyes set in a fringe of white eyelashes. But when she took her bonnet off at last I saw that her hair was pretty. It was golden, and fine like cobwebs.

A Cape cart was being driven onto the square, with men running on each side of it. A roar of delight went up from the passersby as a woman stepped out of the cart. She was wearing scarlet satin, even her boots were of scarlet satin.

"Well, I'm back, boys," she cried, "and broke again."

"Good ole Birdie . . ." "Hooray, now we're made . . ." "Come on, Birdie, I can't wait . . ."

Birdie quelled her admirers with a shriek: "What's the offers? For one night only, mind . . ."

"Ten bob."

"Get out."

The men began to bid for her. She went to a Greek for seven pounds. A Kaffir was summoned to carry her bag and she marched off arm-in-arm with her purchaser before the mules were outspanned.

Mevrouw Pienaar spat. "The ways of the Almighty are strange. You see Papanofolous, that Greek . . . he picked out four diamonds in one day, big diamonds. To spend on harlots . . . But we found nothing. Today we have not the money to buy a drop of water. To buy water. . . . Think of it. At Apie's Drift the water runs white past the door . . ."

"Mister, you have bought some good stones lately?" said Pienaar with a courteous gesture to draw me away from her whining. We stood chatting and I thought of ways to help without hurting the man's pride.

"I need a reliable messenger," I began.

"Your luck is in," smiled Pienaar. "Here is Klaas our eldest. I think you know him, mister. It's an old head on young shoulders."

His son came across the square. He was holding a lump of limestone and the last rays of the sun caught the shine of a diamond in it. Klaas put the stone in his mother's lap: the diamond was orange-coloured.

"I found him on our claim."

Children had followed him, singing and clapping as he crossed the square. They stood still now, all except a black boy who was jumping high in the air and clapping his hands beneath his heels.

"Mr. Bernstein, you can hire that little Kaffir for your messenger now," crowed Mevrouw Pienaar behind us. "Ag my treasure, let us buy some water at once."

"Show me the stone," I said.

I offered Pienaar three hundred pounds. He opened his mouth to accept but no words came, only a garbled sound. Suddenly he snatched up his rifle and fired a shot at the evening star.

"Aits the Boers!"

The children were dancing again. Dust, thick and bitter, set us all coughing.

20

On Saturday night the Crimson Bar was packed. I saw Halden leaning against the far wall and pushed my way through to him.

"Howdy. Thought I might see you here."

I said: "She's going to auction herself, you know. I suppose the silly ass is doing it for a bet. Anyhow, she doesn't expect any takers."

"There she is."

A shout went up. Jo had come into the bar and was sitting on the counter. She was downy and soft, with long dark lashes veiling her blue eyes. On the blue velvet cloak she had sewn a little lace collar such as children wear. And she was singing in a sweet girl's voice:

O City of Diamonds, O City so far,
Give me a bright diamond as big as a star . . .
O cry for him, diggers, he's lost all his geldt,
They've fetched him to bury him there on the veldt . . .

She had spotted Halden and me. She yelled and waved. Then suddenly she was on the counter dancing. I saw her long slim legs and dazzling body: she wore nothing beneath the blue cloak.

"Ah, you bitch," said Halden.

Somebody flipped a diamond up to her. She caught it and went through a pantomime of weighing it and examining it before she returned it.

"I'll take nothing less than five carats."

"Play the game, Jo, it's all I've got."

"Five carats."

Tungay had come in.

"Get out," said Jo.

"But I've got a diamond here, five carats."

"And I know who gave it to you. Hop it. I was only doing it for a lark anyway."

"A lark?" said Darnay, a French Jew; a most vicious man. "We don't stand for teasing, Jo." He had his gang with him, scum from every corner of the earth.

"Let's try and get her out," Halden whispered to me.

"Useless. We'll be kicked to pieces."

The Frenchman was up on the counter beside Jo.

"Any other bids?" he yelled.

Tungay was jerking himself backwards and forwards. With a savage gesture he tore his trousers open.

"We've got to help her," gasped Halden; I had him in an arm-lock.

"It's a put-up job . . ."

"God, if I had a diamond . . ."

"For this lovely young lady I'm offered a diamond of five carats," the Frenchman sang out. Jo looked towards us.

"I've got a diamond on me," I said. "You offer it, Halden . . . I'm a married man." I released him and slipped the diamond into his hand.

"Here's one of fifty carats," said Halden.

He got two or three other diggers and myself with him and we pushed our way to the counter.

Jo took the diamond. "You satisfied now?" she said to the Frenchman.

"It looks genuine," he sneered.

186

Halden spun Jo down. He slapped her hard, twice. Then with his fingers hooked into her hair, he pulled her out of the room.

I expected that Halden would explain to Jo that the orange diamond was in the nature of a loan from me to help her out of a tight corner. She did not return it. Two days passed and I heard nothing from either of them. I was anxious for my whole capital was invested in the diamond.

When I came to look for Halden, I found the waggon gone; he had trekked out and Jo had gone with him, a digger told me.

There was a letter given to me that day by Britt Tyzack; and a document he had drawn up conceding a half-share in Halden's gold mine to me. Halden wrote that he had not told Jo that the diamond belonged to me. She had decided to remain with him. He had meant to raise five hundred pounds on his mine and pay me for the diamond. Jo had gone to fetch her clothes and back pay from Uzzell and to say goodbye; but had got into a gambling game and lost the diamond to Uzzell. Halden had been out of luck too. He had been unable to raise the five hundred; hence the concession of a half-share in his mine.

Things went hard with Leah and me at this time. I had no money to buy stones legitimately so I dabbled in small stones brought to me by Stokkies.

The summer's heat passed. At night there was frost. The grass on the kopje was brown. We were cold in the morning but at midday on the claims we sweated; the sun shone day after day in a blue sky.

Summer had brought unpredictable changes in the sky and it was to the sky that we always looked for relief from the monotony of the endless grassy plain. There landscapes or the outlines of men and animals and edifices were formed by the clouds of summer. Darker clouds shook the earth with thunder and were split by lightnings; or shed hail from their greenish depths to bring out the diggers' ragged children, who darting for pebbles of ice to suck, cried out at the sting of the hail. On clear days the swallows made patterns on the sky and gave place in the evening to flights of bats, different from the swallows because they were not silent but flew clicking against the sky.

Now in May the sky was empty, soaring to infinity behind the sun or the stars. A change in it could be looked for at a certain hour and then it was only a change in colour at sunset or at sunrise; nothing varied the stillness of it.

On the claims the colour of the earth had changed. Yellow ground gave way to blue ground as the diggers mined deeper. When they reached the blue ground, they abandoned the claims, thinking that they had reached the end of the diamondiferous ground. Everywhere it was being said that it was only a matter of time before the dry diggings petered out.

But the men still came to The Tickey Horse in hundreds; Uzzell's auctions took place regularly now. We heard that Bonnie had been inveigled into offering herself and had been bought by a syndicate. A group of churchgoers picketed The Tickey Horse but they did not succeed in getting the place closed down.

21

Leah was crouched over a brazier. Her dress had withered on her body, her hair was lank and dusty. Fuel was now the great problem, a greater problem than water; many wells had been sunk on the diggings. But the veldt was bare of all vegetation except grass for the bushes had been cut down in a radius of twenty miles to supply wood for the diggers. In the past few weeks Leah had been selling her clothes for fuel: I had already sold my mother's ring.

"Where did you get the wood from?" I asked Leah; we had had only a few sticks for the morning fire.

"Stokkies brought it."

"Did he bring anything else?"

She looked at me steadily. "Yes. These." She gave me a matchbox. Inside the box were two small diamonds. "He says they come from a friend of his, a Malay digger. This digger is afraid of his creditors so he is selling them secretly." She held her hands over the blaze.

"It was decent of Stokkies to bring wood. How much did you pay him?"

"I had only a tickey. You'll do time on the breakwater."

"Oh, if you are suspicious of the stones, I'll give them back . . ."

A sudden bright flush burned her face. "You do go in for I.D.B., Mannie. But you would never tell me. I know Stokkies has stolen those diamonds. You trust him. You will have to trust me."

"If I did have anything to do with illicit stones, it would be better for you not to know."

"I would rather know. Trust me. I'm lonely," she whispered.

I was on my knees beside her. "Leah, whatever I do is for you. I've got to get you away. I can't stand to see you living like this."

"Try and get a job, Mannie."

"Then we'll never get away." There was a movement outside. "Who is there?" I called.

"Only the law."

"It's Thompson," I breathed. "I've got to get rid of these." I threw the box to the floor. Leah spread her skirts over it as Thompson came into the tent.

"Hand them over, Bernstein. We know you've got them. There was a boy here . . . we missed him. Who is it?"

"You can search me," I said.

"And your good lady."

"Not if I can stop you."

"Oh, I won't do it." He went to the door and whistled through his fingers. A dark woman came in; big-handed she was, and with a fringe of grey beard on the chin.

I led with my right to Thompson's jaw but he blocked me. He sent me sailing through the air and I landed with a thud that knocked the breath from me. As I attempted to get up, he hooked me under the jaw and put me soundly to sleep.

When I came round, Leah was bathing my temples with water.

"They've gone, Mannie."

"Whisper, they might be listening outside. Did they take the diamonds?"

"No."

"Where are they?" I whispered, pulling her head down to my mouth.

"In the fire. I threw them in, box and all, while Thompson was fighting with you. The woman was watching the fight."

"Have they been damaged at all?"

"I didn't look to see."

"I'll rake out the embers in a few minutes," I said. "It was clever of you."

She began to sob, heart-broken. If I touched her, she moved away. We quarrelled about that. Long afterwards she told me that the woman's fingers had been all over her and she could not be sure that Thompson was not watching. She was ashamed to tell me then.

The diamonds were unharmed by the fire.

22

It was clear to me that a trap had misfired. I decided to return the diamonds to Stokkies; it was too risky to try and sell them. It was easy enough to warn Stokkies. All I had to do was stop at Vollantyne's claim where he was working and drop a handkerchief: that was the signal that I wanted to see him. We used to meet in the backyard of The Tickey Horse where he shared a room with Miri.

"Doctor away?" I said to Gisborne at the claim.

"Yes," said Gisborne. "Called to a farm miles off—broken leg." He dropped his voice. "I've got a hunch

about that pea over there, the Coloured . . . good worker,
mind you. There's somebody getting away with diamonds
on this claim and it could be him. I haven't taken my eyes
off him for days. But he is too smart for me."

I dropped my handkerchief. Stokkies had noticed; the
rhythm of his pick broke momentarily.

"Oh look," groaned Gisborne. "Here comes the doctor's old lady. She wants to run the house, his practice, the
claim . . . and the whole diggings too. It's a pity the good
Lord didn't see fit to bless her with children. She'll jaw
and jaw . . ."

Mrs. Vollantyne, with her skirt sensibly in a holder,
strode down upon us. I left. When I looked back, I saw her
talking to Gisborne and stabbing the air with her umbrella.

Stokkies was not at The Tickey Horse when I reached
there at five o'clock. I told Miri to call me as soon as he
arrived. Then I went to the Crimson Bar for a drink.

The place was empty except for the barmaid and Madame Olpresci. Since Jo left, Madame had been the pianist
in the bar and she was strumming now, a little lively air;
she changed to Jo's song as a compliment to me.

"Give Monsieur Bernstein a drink on the house," she
called over her shoulder. "I'm in charge here. Monsieur
Uzzell has gone to Natal. Come here, I will tell you something." I carried my drink over to the piano. "Tungay
has gone, he left during the night and do you know where
I think he has gone? . . . to find Jo. The man is an ape
but he has a grand passion.

"But here is the mysterious thing. Uzzell has gone. He
left a note, telling me to look after everything. Between
you and me, monsieur, I think he was told to go by some
of the high-ups. Everybody knows what happened to that

192

child Bonnie . . . a disgrace. There will be no further auctions. They have threatened to tar and feather our friend Uzzell. He thinks it better to disappear for a while, no doubt . . ."

I stood there, listening to her playing. A few customers had come in.

I remember that room with its red walls and carpet, the gilt and the looking-glasses and the rosewood piano. I remember Madame's veined face; and I remember myself for the pride that was in me. My body, cooling in the shabby dusty clothes, was strong, loose-muscled; an instrument for my will. I thought I knew myself, that I could see into the well-spring of my being.

An Irishman I was acquainted with was saying: ". . . at the doc's place. They gave him castor oil in case he had swallowed one. Gisborne says the coon had the diamond in his mouth but he managed to hook it out. The doc's wife is sticking her nose in of course . . ."

I went outside. I would have to run for it. But then I thought: How do I know it is Stokkies they have caught? I went inside again to ask the Irishman who it was but my mouth was dry and my hands were trembling: I could not face him.

I drifted along with a crowd that was hurrying to the Vollantynes' cottage.

Stokkies was lying in the dust outside the cottage. Some men, cold as executioners, were kicking him.

Mrs. Vollantyne held up a hand to stop them. "Get back," she cried. "What is the good of knocking him unconscious? We must find the man he was going to deal with and we'll save hundreds of diamonds. Now, this is one time that we are not going to wait for the police to act. The chances are that his principal will never be caught unless we take matters into our own hands. It could be anybody. I say, Let this boy lead us to his principal . . . Is that agreed?"

A deep sound of agreement went up. She hung a sjambok in a thorn tree: some torches had been lit as the daylight faded. Stokkies had been hurt just enough to be made aware of the sjambok. He cried.

I thought, How old is Stokkies? I felt ashamed because I did not know. I played with guessing his age to keep at bay the terror that was rising in me. I was so still that my body ached: I dared not move for fear somebody would look at me.

But I planned to make a run for it as soon as Stokkies was hit; that would set the mob after me. I would run for the police or rescue Stokkies at the point of a gun. I saw myself twisting and dodging with the crowd behind me hopelessly foxed . . . Stokkies would free himself and hide.

Mrs. Vollantyne said: "He's looked at the sjambok long enough now. I understand this sort of person, cowards one and all. Just take it down and crack it on the ground next to the boy's ear, Gisborne."

"Why on the ground?" yelled a Dutchman. "Give it to him on the . . ."

But Gisborne had obeyed Mrs. Vollantyne and hit the ground near Stokkies. That stopped his crying. He lay still. His eyes were like a buck's eyes in the clayey mask of his face; there were tears on his cheeks. He had not seen me.

Gisborne said: "We're going to take every bit of skin off you if you don't tell us the name of the man you were going to sell that diamond to."

"There is nobody in particular," he said. "It's the first time I ever took a diamond, basie."

Gisborne and another man hoisted him up and tied him to the trunk of a camelthorn tree; Mrs. Vollantyne often sat in the shade of this camelthorn drinking tea in the heat of the afternoon.

Let them only touch him and I would come forward to save him . . .

A Dutch woman sprang out from among the crowd. "You hells, you've got your diamond. Now let him go."

"He's only a kid after all," said an Australian digger. "He could give you anybody's name. You can't rely on what he will say."

"Afraid he might say it is you?" Gisborne sneered.

"I am not afraid," said the Dutch woman. "I say, be merciful. Let him go." She was a dark, spare woman with a gentle mouth.

"We're not in church now," yelled one of her country-women. "Have you seen your children go without food while these people steal the diamonds from us? Lash him, get the name out of him . . ."

Stokkies turned his head and looked at Mrs. Vollantyne. "Missis," he pleaded.

"Hand him over to the law," cried the gentle Dutch woman.

"Has he been selling diamonds to your husband?" Mrs. Vollantyne asked coldly.

There was a threat here and the woman was silenced: she went away.

"If he is flogged, you stay and watch," the Australian said to Mrs. Vollantyne.

"I'll do that, never fear."

Gisborne lifted the sjambok. He smiled and struck. A white weal sprang up on Stokkies's back, another stroke and it was red, a third stroke and the blood came. I had

195

meant to go forward as soon as he was touched; but I stood watching like the others. I was too frightened to go away for I thought that would make me suspect. Yet the danger of remaining was greater for at any moment Stokkies might say my name.

Mrs. Vollantyne stood erect with the Australian by her side. When at last she turned her head away, a howl of derision came from some of the crowd. People were retching. It was safe to go now for many were leaving the writhing, bloodied thing that was Stokkies. The flogging went on.

He had not spoken except to cry for his mother.

Leah was in the tent, mending by lamplight. I sat down.

"Mannie?" She coughed nervously. "What is it, Mannie?"

"They are flogging Stokkies. They want the name of the person he deals with."

"You must hide." She began to cry. "Hide away quickly. Get across the river, Mannie."

"I should have confessed. I let them hit him. And he didn't tell."

"That doesn't matter now. Don't sit there like a fool. Go."

"Stokkies didn't tell them my name, Leah. And I just stood there. Do you see what I am?"

She stopped crying. She was calm suddenly.

"Listen. You listen to that, Mannie. He has talked now. Run."

It was the terrible music of an angry mob that we heard.

"Leah, go and fetch Britt Tyzack. He'll frighten them off. Or get the police if he is not there at his tent. It is only about fifteen minutes' walk . . . I showed you his place. I can keep them talking here, I won't let them touch me. But you go."

She ran into the darkness. I tossed the diamonds into the campfire outside and set a pick handy on top a tree stump behind me.

The mob came. Four men frog-marched Stokkies. Miri, with her clothes ripped in front, came on before all the others.

"Bernstein, Bernstein, Bernstein," she shrieked. She danced up to me, tearing her hair. "Bladdy fool, he wouldn't talk, he wouldn't tell them your name. Look what they've done to my man . . ."

Two fellows grabbed me while Gisborne went through my pockets.

"You've hidden the diamonds."

"I had none."

He hit me in the mouth. "You lying Jew."

"Gisborne, control yourself," cried Mrs. Vollantyne. "Now, Bernstein . . . It will be much better for you if you confess. We mean business. This fellow's wife has named you. But we want to be fair, we want the right man . . . Will you be quiet?" she stormed at Miri; somebody clapped a hand over Miri's mouth. "Now then, Bernstein, do you know this Coloured man?"

"Only slightly."

"He's lying," said Gisborne and slapped my face.

"Gisborne, I'll get the doctor to discharge you," Mrs. Vollantyne declared. "Pray be silent."

There was a momentary relaxation on my arms. I got loose, brought my knee up into a man's groin and landed a right to Gisborne's jaw. He staggered back among the crowd and I reached for the pick.

"Now, none of that, Bernstein," Mrs. Vollantyne was bleating. "You others behave yourselves . . ."

I might have had a chance if it had not been for Miri. Screaming with hate, she flung herself at me, and I lowered the pick so that I should not hurt her. The crowd swarmed forward. I was thrown across the stump. My jacket and shirt were torn off: my shirt was used to stuff my mouth. While I was being flogged, somebody set the tent alight with brands from the campfire.

23

They left me lying face downwards. I could feel the heat of flames on my back. Presently a hand reached out to me. Stokkies said hoarsely: "It was Miri told them, basie."

"I should have told them myself."

"Go and get water, bitch," Stokkies said to Miri. "And see if you can make a mixture of salt and water to throw over our backs. You hell."

"There is no water here," said Miri.

"Then go and get some, rubbish."

We heard her scuttling away. I could only think of the water she would bring.

But Stokkies said: "Did they get away with the diamonds?"

"No. I threw them in the fire."

He chuckled. "That's showing them. Basie, I would never have given them your name."

"Be careful. There's somebody coming."

Gisborne and Mrs. Vollantyne had come back. When a man has been flogged his need is for water. He will take water from the hands of the one who flogged him. I took water from Gisborne's hands, although I suspected that he was slyly looking at my back. Mrs. Vollantyne had brought a bucket of salt and water and she was splashing me.

"This will heal you."

"Put some on Stokkies. He is worse off than I am."

"He got what he richly deserved, the thief. Bernstein," she said more softly, "don't you think it would take a load off your mind to confess . . ."

"It might take a load off your mind," I said.

"That's lawyer's talk," she said, her voice still soft. "You know you've been buying stolen diamonds. Why would the Coloured woman pick on you? She wouldn't even know of your existence . . ."

"She used to work for my wife."

Mrs. Vollantyne brought her hand down, suddenly and hard, on my back. She sobbed a little as she wiped the blood from her hand on a tuft of grass.

"Better get home, Mrs. Vollantyne," said Gisborne. "Leave me to deal with this scum."

Mrs. Vollantyne poured some of the salt water over her hand to cleanse it.

"I shall remain here, Gisborne. You've had altogether too much to say for yourself."

Miri staggered in, carrying buckets of water. She was meek again.

"I looked all over for water and then I remembered the drum of salty water outside your house, nonna Vollantyne."

"I always keep a drum there for natives who have been flogged," said Mrs. Vollantyne. "But you needn't worry, Bernstein. This water I am using was specially mixed for you."

199

A light showed and there was the jingling of harness: Britt had brought Leah back in a surrey. I pulled myself up. I did not want Britt to see the pattern of weals on my back.

He handed Leah down from the surrey and strode into the firelight.

"My God, who was responsible for this, Mannie?"

Mrs. Vollantyne answered. "Oh dear, oh dear, I don't know what the doctor will have to say. The whole business got out of control . . ."

"Were you responsible then?"

"Dear dear, no . . . Well . . ."

"I flogged the two of them," said Gisborne.

"You mustn't admit guilt," cried Mrs. Vollantyne. "It's like this, Mr. Tyzack. The principals in the I.D.B. always get away, it's the underlings who are caught . . . it's costing us all thousands . . ."

"It was me who told, it was me," Miri cried, grovelling at Leah's feet. "I couldn't let them hit Stokkies like that and he wouldn't speak."

"He at least will be prosecuted," said Mrs. Vollantyne. "He was caught red-handed. He tried to swallow the diamond and Gisborne can prove it."

"Bernstein has a case for damages, serious damages," Britt said.

"Then we'll be ruined. Oh, what will the doctor say?"

"You should think of these things before you take the law into your own hands. . . ."

The voices went on inexorably, a duet between Mrs. Vollantyne and Britt. They were of the same class, you could tell that by their voices.

From Leah there had not been a word. She sat with head bowed, weighted by sorrows from immemorial times.

"Leah," I said.

"Yes."

"Do you remember the sparrow and the mules?"

"He's wandering," she said mournfully.

I was remembering my first meeting with Mrs. Vollantyne. The meeting took place during my journey to the Vaal; and it was not Leah who was with me, it was Jo.

We had come upon the Vollantynes' waggons in the Free State. There were two waggons, one used for transporting the household furniture and luggage, the other a huge two-tiered contraption used as living quarters. Jo, who had got a glimpse in, said that there were holders on the sides to take clothes and shoes; the beds were on the second tier and below were a table and some chairs.

I admired the waggon.

I admired Doctor Vollantyne. He was a compact square dark man who moved with velvety smoothness, an athlete. I admired Mrs. Vollantyne. She would often sit and stare across the veldt to the far horizon and though I had never seen her with a book, I made sure that she would be a reader. I thought we might discuss Shakespeare.

Jo became jealous of the Vollantynes and their possessions, I remember.

The waggons moved ponderously over the plain and for two or three days we kept pace with them. Then we fell behind and only came up with them again because of another rainy spell. The big waggon had bogged in the mud.

Mrs. Vollantyne crouched beneath a tarpaulin thrown across some thorny bushes, with puppies in her lap; the doctor's bulldog had whelped some days before. Jo and I were allowed to handle the puppies: Mrs. Vollantyne called Jo Mrs. Bernstein although we had not claimed to be married.

Doctor Vollantyne had nothing to do with mundane affairs and his waggons were in the sole charge of a towering Dutchman named Coetzee. Coetzee had had everything removed from the waggon but it was still stuck fast, its wheels invisible in the mud. One of the oxen chose this time to lie down. He was a big black ox that I had noticed giving trouble before. Mrs. Vollantyne glanced uneasily at her husband and he shook his head in warning.

"Don't interfere with Coetzee, my love, he's in charge."

Already the Coloured driver under Coetzee's orders was smashing at the ox with doubled whip. The ox lay motionless. It seemed to feel no pain; not in its horns nor on the ridge of its back, nor in its tail which a Kaffir was bending over and biting.

"Get a fire going," Coetzee shouted.

"What did he say?" Mrs. Vollantyne asked.

"He said: Light a fire," I explained, pleased to demonstrate my knowledge of the Taal.

"Oh, curse you for a smart Alec," the doctor said. "Now you've set Mrs. Vollantyne off."

"Light a fire? Not . . . He can't mean to light a fire under the ox," shrieked Mrs. Vollantyne. "I'm going to faint, I know I shall."

"Look out for the puppies," said the doctor; Mrs. Vollantyne had jumped up, spilling the puppies from her skirt. The doctor restored them to their dam and then gave Mrs. Vollantyne some smelling salts. He led her firmly away, across the veldt to a little kopje. She stopped to look back.

"Lot's wife," I said to Jo.

"She shouldn't give way like that. It hasn't helped the ox."

"You can't expect a lady to stand by and watch them light a fire under an ox."

"You don't have to be a lady to feel sick about that," said Jo. "I'm clearing off too, lady or no lady."

"Sorry, Jo. Come behind the kopje."

We came up with the Vollantynes. Mrs. Vollantyne stood in the veldt and bowed her head and brought her clenched fists up to her forehead in a gesture of pain. Reverently the doctor touched the air above his wife's head.

"I know it is terrible for you, my darling, but what is to be done? We'll never get to the Vaal without Coetzee."

"Doesn't she play the clinging vine?" Jo muttered. She looked back. The ox was standing. "You can look now, Mrs. Voll." Mrs. Vollantyne still stood in that pose of despair. I said: "Madam, don't take on about the ox. It's better for him if they get him to move. Do you know what will happen to the ox if he won't work? He will be butchered."

The lady took her hands from her face and looked proudly at me. Then she walked on with her husband towards the waggons. We kept close behind.

Presently Mrs. Vollantyne picked up a dead sparrow on the side of the Kaffir path. She dug a hole with a stone and laid the bird to rest in the earth. Vollantyne's eyes met mine: we shared a tender, mocking smile.

"See how he fits in, how his little head is pillowed on the earth," she said.

It was true, the sparrow looked as if it had fallen asleep on the kind breast of the earth. Jo flared into a temper.

She shouted at Mrs. Vollantyne: "Look over there and there," and pointed to the carcasses of some mules that had fallen on the trek to the diggings and had been torn by vultures. The vultures drifted on still wings beyond the dead mules, waiting for us to go away, some close enough for their colour and shape to be seen, others dwindling into the sky, mere specks against that vast emptiness. With Jo's pointing, death became again an ugly thing; I saw maggots churning in the eyeballs of a black mule, black now only in patches of dulled hide, and red and purple where the vultures had feasted.

"Would you bury the mules if you could?" Jo said. "If you had the power, would you bury the mules too?"

Mrs. Vollantyne answered: "My good girl, the vultures are there to deal with the mules. God put them there for that purpose, to clean the land. They are God's undertakers." With a victorious smile she drew away from us.

Jo stood there watching the vultures. She had crossed her arms so delicately that she had not moved the stuff of her gown. There were harsh lines on her face.

"I could cut my throat," she said. "I feel sick of life . . ."

24

I wanted to be alone on the face of the earth. I wanted silence. But the camp was still noisy. The braying of donkeys dominated the singing and yelling of the white diggers and the beat of African voices. The screaming of a pig, fusillades of shots, barking, shrieks . . . these came and went but the roaring of the donkeys continued unabated.

Leah and I were under a canvas awning that Britt had procured for us. Miri had got Stokkies away in a scotch cart; she was taking him to a Mission station across the border. Miri had wept over Stokkies but Leah was silent. She was a sphere of quiet in that uncouth landscape. From my own affliction I felt a rush of pity for her. Her husband flogged for being a Jew . . . that might be a matter for resignation, even pride . . . but her husband flogged for being a thief . . . Was she quiet because she hated me?

I wanted to finish with everybody who knew about me. I had told Miri to hide Stokkies in the Malay camp for the night and to come back in the morning to search in the debris for his diamonds. I had said to Stokkies: "If I do not bring a case of damages against them, they will leave you alone. They will be afraid to stir anything up. But hide away for a while."

Now I said to Leah: "I've got a half-share in a gold mine in the Transvaal, Halden's mine at Alidasrust. The paper is burned but Halden will honour it."

She stirred. "You won't die, Mannie."

"You hate me."

"No."

"I will disappear, pretend to be dead. You will be free. You can sell that half-share in the mine."

"That isn't necessary," she said. "Mr. Tyzack has said he will help us. You'll receive a thousand pounds in damages and we can get away from here."

"And it's the breakwater for Stokkies."

She had nothing to say to that. I got up and went outside. Leah followed me and held onto my arm.

"Where are you going?"

"To Reuben. He will lend me transport and take you in."

"Listen to reason, Mannie. Mr. Tyzack will help us . . ."

I pushed her off but she plodded on behind me. I

knocked at the door of Solly Reuben's place. When he opened up and saw me, he tore his beard and wept.

"Will you give me a waggon and oxen?"

"My waggon is at the coast. There is only the scotch cart . . ."

"Miri borrowed that, I suppose. She took Stokkies away in a scotch cart."

"What happened?" he asked in fear.

"They flogged me for I.D.B."

"If he stays, he can get damages, take them to court. Mr. Tyzack is on our side," said Leah in a flat voice.

"Of course, of course. You talk foolishness, Mannie. Come inside. But come into the store. I don't want the children to see you like that, and Becky . . . you know how it is with Becky . . . only two months to go . . ."

From the darkness of the living room Becky called out: "What is it?"

"Stay there, my girl . . ."

But Solly could not keep her out. She lit a candle and with a pencil lifted the latch of the inner door and came in.

At the sight of me she wailed and drew Leah into her arms. The children, on the other side of the door which Becky had secured again, stamped and cried to be let in. And Leah now added her voice to the confusion in a long, primitive wail.

"I've got to go, Solly," I said.

Becky broke away from Leah. "You need to eat, you need nourishment . . . I'll go and cook."

"Quiet," Solly roared. "Now, Mannie, tell us what happened."

"I asked you for transport," I said in the sudden silence.

"You want to go away? But the damages?" Then understanding came to him: he knew I felt ashamed. "Well, take the scotch cart when Miri returns it. Nu, take whatever you want. There is a waggon . . . I remember it this minute."

"Is it something criminal?" said Becky. "Are you running away from the law?"

"He can get damages," Leah began. Then she said: "Becky, give me one or two old dresses. All our stuff was burnt."

Solly went out to load us some provisions on the waggon. The dawn was breaking, there was greyish light in the store. I put my hand on Leah's soft cheek.

"Even now you are beautiful. You mustn't come with me. I want you to make another life, you understand."

"I'll come with you."

"After what I did to Stokkies?"

She said: "It was not only yourself you were thinking of. You thought of me too."

Solly Reuben was hurrying to and from the waggon, putting on everything that we might need. Becky insisted on cooking a meal; and she would rush out now and then, with a pack of cards, a roll of tape, even with such absurdities as a bunch of artificial flowers and a lace tablecloth.

At last she embraced Leah and gave her hand to me; we kissed the children. Solly shook hands and stood gnawing his lower lip, perhaps already regretting his generosity. Leah and I climbed onto the waggon.

The Barolong driver cracked the whip and shouted to the oxen: "Blauwman, Rooiland . . ." and we rolled away across the veldt. The sound of the whip on the oxen's hides was a torment but I hid my feelings from Leah.

"We will go to Alidasrust," I said to her, taking her hand. "There is a nice family there, not Jewish, but good people, the Benekes. And we have a ready-made business. Gold mining. You'll be rich yet, and happy. You'll live in London, wear jewels and go to the Opera . . ."

She gave herself to the rocking of the waggon and listened to me with a sad smile.

"You will have to buy another book of Shakespeare," she said.

"One day. In the meantime, I can remember . . ." and I recited to her as the waggon broke out of the pallid dawn into brilliant light.

25

Van der Spuyt came riding to meet us as we skirted the boundary of his farm. From a hundred yards away he let out a bellow of greeting that was jocular yet carried a hint of menace.

"So it's you again, Bernstein." He spurred his horse, swung down from the saddle and gave me a clasp of the hand that brought a grunt from me. "I heard you had been this way last year . . . I hope you are not going to bring the Philistines in hordes upon us again."

"This is my wife," I said.

Van der Spuyt bowed. "Mevrouw Bernstein." Then to me: "I compliment you, Bernstein . . . a lily, a rose of Sharon." He sat down and took a cup of coffee from Leah. "It is like that other time when they found the diamonds. People, people . . . Beneke and his concession, he has got the Government behind him, that's the trouble. But the Lord is taking a hand now. This man Halden got mauled by a lion. He will die." Van der Spuyt slammed his coffee mug down, wiped his mouth with a red cotton handkerchief and stood up. "Thank you, mevrouw. Nice coffee. Bernstein!"

"Yes?"

"No digging round here. Leave us in peace."

"I'm not after diamonds."

"Gold, it is now."

I was worried about what would happen to us without Halden on the mine. "Is Halden so bad then?"

"Well, perhaps I exaggerated. He is at the Mission station. I was there when it happened, you know." Van der Spuyt sat down again. "Niman was killed, Hans Niman, my nephew.

"It was in the evening. I had met Halden by chance, he was after elephant but I persuaded him to come along with us. The lions round here . . . in tens and twenties, still, man. I had shot six. You know how it is when your luck is in. But Hans had nothing but bad luck. And he wanted to bag a lion. He was unpleasant; jealous, you know. He kept accusing me of stealing the shots. Well, it happened he went into the reeds after this wounded lion, you understand. Mad. But he went in there. The lion got on top of him. Gits, I heard a horrible sound . . . to my dying day . . . But I'm not a fool. Hans is finished, I said to Halden. But he wouldn't listen to me. He went into the reeds. Presently I heard him say: Van der Spuyt, come and get this thing off me.

"The lion was dead. Hans was dead. But Halden was still alive. He had drawn his hunting knife and got the lion in the throat. I took him to the Mission station. One arm was useless and you should have seen the face . . . a rake from the corner of the eye to the mouth."

"He is a friend of mine," I said.

Van der Spuyt got up again. "Well, just remember what happened to him, Bernstein. Don't go digging for gold or diamonds, do you hear? Remember I'm watching you. I've got my Kaffirs watching all the time. Turn one spade of earth, wash one pan of gravel . . . I'll know."

I followed him to his horse. "Halden's wife was with him when he left the diggings."

"She is at the Mission now."

"Perhaps I'll leave my wife with the Benekes and go on to the Mission."

"You'll have to take her with you. Beneke and his family have gone away to Pretoria." Van der Spuyt mounted but he did not ride away at once. "The girl Poppie looked as if she would die of a broken heart," he said. "It seems that she considered herself to be engaged to my nephew Hans but I never heard anything of it."

"I took a letter to her from him."

"So there was something between them? I must tell my wife." He gave such a bellow of laughter that his pony sprang away, almost unseating him.

We had only one view of the farmhouse as we turned southwest towards Beneke's farm. Everything round the place was still. I thought of her there, Mevrouw of the soft big breasts and tender lips; I remembered her caresses.

26

I had no desire to examine the shaft that Halden had dug nor to travel on and see Halden. Sufficient unto the day is the evil thereof . . . We made a camp on Beneke's farm. The house was locked up and we did not even think of breaking in and establishing ourselves there. For hour after hour I would sit without speaking until Leah brought me the Book to read: Solly had given it to us that night. I read aloud. And I prayed.

If Leah had not been with me, I should have travelled on, neither praying nor reading; and I might have gone on foot for I had the idea that if I could be alone, and no animal even near, on some high bare mountain perhaps and there could be stars above me, I would come to the truth which would be a single fact.

I had found within myself the coward I had always dreaded; and something else for in spite of everything there had been a certain relish in watching Stokkies's skin break open beneath the sjambok. What am I then? I asked the nameless force of creation.

Yet I was grateful to Leah for keeping me on the familiar paths of religion. Our Sabbaths are still wonderfully clear in my memory. Becky Reuben had seen to it that we had two brass candlesticks and a linen cloth. Our food was of the best. We had chickens from the Benekes' yard, eggs, and good bread that Leah baked in a Dutch oven, hollowed out from an antheap.

The flesh on my back healed. Here and there I could feel lumps where the skin had been torn and had grown together imperfectly. I was ashamed. It was like a leprosy to me.

For the first time now I understood the purpose of marriage. Leah had been without reproaches through the bitter days and had made a home for me in the covered waggon. I trusted her whereas before this I had suspected her of studying her own comfort, of desiring my success for what it would bring her.

It was for Leah's sake that I decided to go back to the diggings and fight Gisborne. I would smash him. I began having daydreams of the fight which always took place before a huge crowd. After it, I was carried on the shoulders of my followers while Gisborne lay abandoned, a bloodied pulp. And Leah I saw in velvet and satin with a fur muff and diamonds, walking past Mrs. Vollantyne who was in rags . . .

There was another daydream, that still comes to me in an idle moment. In it I rescue Stokkies from being flogged.

27

One afternoon the Barolong come running to tell us that a waggon was approaching from the north. We watched until sunset and then we saw the waggon materialize out of the glowing veldt, a black dot that grew to the outlines of a heavy buckboard and sixteen trotting oxen. On the blue waggon box sat Jo and Halden.

"Get into the waggon," I said to Leah. "You see who it is."

"But I've spoken to her before," Leah protested.

"It's different now. She wasn't living with a man then."

"Very well," said Leah.

She hid herself and I went to meet the waggon. When Jo recognized me, she leapt down though the oxen were still moving.

"Look at that, Mannie," she said, extending her left fist. She had on a wedding ring.

"When did you get married?"

"Last month. The missionary's wife turned nasty. It was after Halden was mauled. She wouldn't allow me in to see him because he had let on that we weren't married. I think she frightened him with hellfire. Hellfire! I'd have frozen out there on the veldt so we got married. They have these rings to marry their converts with. And they gave us a wedding present. We've got a Symphonium, wait until I play it for you . . . Lovely hymns . . .

> "When you get to Heaven you must look for me,
> For I'll be there, I'll be there,
> Yes, I'll be there . . ."

Halden had got down from the waggon and was walking slowly up to us. His arm had healed but there was a deep scar cutting his left cheek.

"Hear you had an argument with a lion," I said. "Van der Spuyt told me."

"I hope he hasn't been interfering with you . . . that concession is watertight."

"I haven't been doing any work. But he has got spies round all the time."

"I am going to take an option on the farm," Halden

213

said. "Old Van der Spuyt doesn't know this yet. I don't think the Benekes want to come back here."

"My wife and I are camped beyond the old mealie-lands."

"Why didn't you go into the house?" Jo asked wonderingly.

"It was locked up. We didn't like to break in."

"Blow that." Jo was already on her way to the house. Presently I heard the sound of tinkling glass as she broke a window to get in. The waggon was unloaded.

I went with Halden to inspect the mine shaft. The frail, unearthly notes of the Symphonium followed us, but were soon drowned out by Jo's voice:

> Row for the shore, sailor, row for the shore,
> Leave your sins behind you and row for the shore . . .

"The hymns are to keep us on the straight and narrow," said Halden. "Jo knows every one of them and there are twenty."

"I'll come over for a sing-song."

"We've got a demijohn of peach brandy. Say, you could bring your wife. We're respectable now . . ."

"There's something I have to tell you," I said. "I was in trouble at the diggings. I was . . . flogged because they suspected me of I.D.B. I'm going back soon to get the fellow who did it. Gisborne . . ."

"You can count on me for a second. I don't think it's a good idea if the ladies meet though . . . Jo still lets out the occasional swearword . . ." We grinned.

There was no question of keeping Jo and Leah apart. They were soon visiting each other every day. Leah taught Jo to bake good bread: every afternoon the two of them sat down to a game of cribbage.

214

And they talked for hours on end. Leah told Jo about everything that had happened to her, even about my being flogged. They wept together.

28

In the middle of the month, van der Spuyt called on us to hunt lions with him. Two old lions had taken a cow from his kraal. Halden and I were required to cover a portion of the Alida River which was dry at this season.

We were unsuccessful in driving the lions from cover on the first day and camped that night in a bywoner's ruined house on the veldt. There was a bitter wind blowing. We had no fire because van der Spuyt did not want to frighten off the lions. By dawn in the bitter cold, I was shivering with an attack of fever.

Halden and van der Spuyt remained on the Alida and detailed four Kaffirs to carry me back to Beneke's farm. We had fifteen miles to go. I have only a vague memory of the journey but I know I was carried over a man's shoulder for the last part of it.

I was put in the Benekes' double bed. Outside on the veldt a bird was calling. It had only one note, a clear sound that I thought became solid as soon as it left the bird's throat. The sounds then took on the shape of cigars and were of a dull metallic substance. They floated just clear of the long, tawny grass. Leah ran outside to find the bird and to seize the cigar-shaped sounds . . . then she was back in the room, sponging me down with vinegar and water.

And Jo was there. It was night time now and the bird had ceased calling. Jo wore her bowie knife strapped to her hip.

"What about Mevrouw van der Spuyt?" I said. "She must be afraid to be alone in the house all night."

"So you've come round. Van der Spuyt is back home. They have scared the lions off. But Don has heard of some elephants further north. He won't be back for a month, I daresay."

Tungay came. I heard him say: "I've come for you, Jo. I've travelled three hundred miles looking for you, my girl."

"You keep your hands to yourself or I'll run you through again."

Tungay was laughing. "You're a good plucked 'un. Bah, you're not one of these milksops, can't stand up for their-selves . . ."

"I'm warning you. Leave her alone."

Throughout my delirium there was a corner of my mind weighing and appraising what was happening. The bird's notes were unreal, I knew. Tungay was real, gaunt like a man who has travelled far.

I know he said to Leah: "There's a shrub grows on the veldt round about here. If you boil the leaves, it cures fever."

"Tell me where it is," Leah said.

PART
3

1

We left Alidasrust while I was still delirious. Jo sent a runner to Halden with a message: she wrote to him that we were going back to the diggings where I could be treated by a competent doctor. We travelled swiftly. Jo did not give the oxen a good rest until we had crossed the Vaal into the Cape. She had used Solly's light waggon but Halden's oxen, a crack span.

"Where is Tungay?" I asked one night.

"Don't you remember?" said Jo. "He died of apoplexy, just fell down dead. Oh, it was horrible. He went purple in the face, then pitch black and he fell down dead."

"I remember now that he died," I said and indeed I could recall Leah's dreadful weeping.

When we reached the diggings, Jo would often sit and recount the story of Tungay's death; but never once did Leah speak of it. I felt helpless because of Leah. She had grown thin and she was lazy now, Leah who had always been a great worker: she would sit for hours crouched over the fire. Jo did most of the work. We were encamped near a pan and Jo often took in bottles of water labelled Jo's Spring Water which she sold on the square for a shilling a bottle.

Uzzell's company had scattered. Madame Olpresci now ran The Tickey Horse as a boarding house and canteen. She had money to spare and Jo borrowed from her to buy a claim. Jo moved to the diggings but she used to send out the medicines prescribed by the doctor for me, and such delicacies as she and Madame could obtain.

After a fortnight the fever left me and I recovered my strength quickly. Leah was able to leave me alone now and she went one day to the Jewish women's bath house.

The bushy vegetation round our camping site had been hacked down to provide wood for the diggers' fires. We were near a kopje which blotted out part of the great encampment but we could still hear the noise beating against the silence of the veldt. I watched the familiar pageant. Hour after hour there were vehicles appearing on the road as more and more men came to the diggings; there were bands of natives coming from all over the country; and lone horsemen and walkers, grim-faced as they made their final dash to the Fields.

The thought that possessed me was how to get away.

A trap drawn by a white horse bowled across the veldt towards me. Jo was in it. As she got down, I saw that she was wearing red woollen stockings: the weather was cold, threatening snow.

"I've something here might interest you, Mannie," she said. She untied her bonnet and blew on her cold fingers, then took a matchbox from between her breasts and threw it across to me. Inside was a diamond of about forty carats, of a pinkish hue.

"Nice stone," I said.

"I thought so too. I want you to sell it for me, you know the values. I found it on my claim."

"You're a blessing, Jo. I was wondering how to start, where to turn to . . ."

"I knew you would be worried. Come in now and sell it. I need some cash. There's something else . . . that mine of Don's. Give me an option on it."

"All right. Twenty pounds?"

"I can manage that nicely."

We got five hundred and seventy pounds for the diamond. Jo paid me out on the spot, fifty-seven pounds commission and twenty for the option. I was in the diamond buying business again. I bought a diamond that very day and made ten pounds on it.

Stokkies soon found me. He was working on the diggings openly for no charges had been brought against him; Gisborne had left after a hint from the authorities, Britt had told me.

It was a Sunday afternoon and I had been visiting Britt. I was on my way back to the waggon when Stokkies called out: "Day, my basie."

I waited for him to come up to me and we walked on together.

"You heard I was in the business again?"

"I heard, my baas. How about it? There have been one or two chances lately . . ."

"Not for me, never again."

"Never is a long time, my baas."

We had come to the kopje where a Coloured man was working on a prospect pit.

"I know him," said Stokkies. "You think I'm a nuisance. My baas. That one, he is drunk every second day. He comes from round Colesberg, same place as me, only he is here with his baas he grew up with . . . Baas Rawstorne, he's in the Red Cap Company from Colesberg." He called out to the Coloured: "How goes it, Damon?"

"I'm in trouble again, man," Damon said, grinning. "Fleet said to me: You get off home. But I asked for one more chance. I'll never drink again, I promised him. All right, he said, you can stay but keep clear of the camp. He said, You go and prospect the kopje and don't you come back until you've found some diamonds." He sorted through some gravel. "Plenty rubies," he said. "Maybe some diamonds, too, hey?"

We watched him at work, long after the sun had gone down; he kindled a fire and worked in the small circle of its light. The moon rose. Shadows were black and bushes and trees too were black against the silvered sky. In the tents the lights were golden and we could see men playing cards or yarning.

Stokkies remained with Damon but I left for it was growing late. From our waggon when I looked back I could see the fire on the kopje; and the grass with frost on it shining in the moonlight.

2

"Where have you been?" Leah said, weeping. "I get so frightened here alone."

"There's nothing to be afraid of. There are camps within call."

"I get so frightened," she repeated.

"I was on the kopje watching a Coloured prospecting . . ."

She had been in bed when I arrived. Now she got up to give me some food. By the light of the lantern I saw that her face was strained. She was so thin as to be ugly . . . Leah. She wore an old red flannel shirt of mine with a rent in one arm. Her hair was a thick, furred rope . . .

"Leah." I sat next to her and stroked the rough hair. She sobbed helplessly. I took her in my arms. "Leah, my poor Leah, I'll look after you. I didn't mean to stay away so long."

"You must have your food," she said, freeing herself. She began to put on a jersey. I took it away from her and made her lie down again.

"I can get it for myself. Did you have something?"

"I wasn't hungry."

There was some stew simmering on the fire. I sat with Leah and fed her from my plate.

"I'll get a house for us," I said. "You can grow a few flowers and you will have some new dresses. I feel lucky."

"Oh, be careful, Mannie."

"Don't nag. Am I never to be allowed to forget that I made a mistake?"

"I'm sorry."

I blew out the lantern and took her in my arms.

The grass grew round the wheels of the waggon, she cooked over an open fire. I thought with horror of what she endured.

"Tomorrow you must buy yourself a flannel nightgown," I said. "You mustn't sleep in my old shirt, Leah."

She did not answer but only sighed.

3

Somebody was calling outside the waggon.

"Who is it?" I cried.

"It's Stokkies, basie."

"Tell him to go away," said Leah. "They'll get you again." She raised her voice. "Go away from here . . . voetsak." She twined her arms round me: she was shaking.

I called out: "You'd better go, Stokkies."

"Basie, I came to tell you they are pegging claims. Damon found diamonds at ten last night." I sprang out of the waggon onto the frosted grass so that I could dress more quickly. Stokkies went on: "Damon took the diamonds in his hand and went to his baas's tent. Fleet, he said, Look what I've got here. Baas Rawstorne was sitting there playing cards and he said, Let's see. And Damon

224

went in and showed him the diamonds. They pegged claims in the moonlight and wouldn't let me go until just now. Come on, basie, the rush has started. I've brought stakes for you. I've already got a claim and Damon is looking after it for me . . ."

In the grey light there were figures to be seen on the kopje and rushing towards it from the encampment a straggling line of men. I grabbed the stakes and began to run, Stokkies beside me.

"Go for the claims as close to Damon's pit as possible. That's where the pipe is . . ."

He dropped behind. I was among a crowd of men rushing the kopje. An ox had broken loose and was charging the runners. He came for me, head down. I swerved and he sent a man near me sprawling. On I ran. I remember that I tripped over a man lying unconscious with a rivulet of blood flowing from him: he had fallen onto the point of an iron stake.

The light was stronger now and I saw the faces of men I knew in a nightmare of movement and noise. I fought my way to a point some hundred yards distant from Damon's pit. The Red Cap Company stood embattled nearby, fighting off claim jumpers. I got three claims staked, only to have the pegs kicked out by a gang of desperadoes. Stokkies joined me in driving them off.

Presently things eased round us; the rush was extending right on to the plain. I sat on a rock, ready to defend my claims with fists and feet and a pickaxe that Britt Tyzack had given me. Britt had got a claim on the kopje, so had Vollantyne and Solly Reuben. Solly was still wearing a nightcap.

"You've got a son," Vollantyne yelled at him. "Had to

use the forceps, but both of them are all right." His shirt-sleeve was streaked with blood.

"Have you hurt yourself?" Solly asked him.

"Not my blood. I had to deliver three babies before I could get here," said the doctor. He yelled and rushed forward with a pick handle to do battle with a claim jumper who had knocked out some of his stakes.

4

Claims were staked for miles across the plain. The Government surveyor had marked off our claims and given us temporary registration certificates and we were working the claims within the week: the name given to the mine was New Rush. Jo at Old De Beers had been finding diamonds; a pink one worth four hundred and a yellow stone worth one hundred. From these two transactions I had an extra fifty pounds which I used to work my claims.

I had a team of thirty boys to remove the grass and overburden of red soil. I had promised Leah that I would sell the claims and take her back to Durban: she was staying with Becky Reuben again. What I got for the claims would depend on whether I struck reef or not. If I did not strike reef, I could count on a hundred-and-fifty apiece.

My luck was in. The claims went down to a depth of fifty feet of yellow ground. I offered them to Britt Tyzack for three hundred pounds. He was to inspect my claims one morning in October. I arrived there at dawn for at

226

this time there were bands of diggers roving about ready to jump claims; they were men who had pegged outside the pipe and struck reef. We used to go armed for scarcely a day passed without a fight taking place on the kopje. That morning fights broke out as soon as it was light. I found myself fending off something like a dozen men single-handed; I had to shoot. They left me but that was not the end of it. The fights spread like a grassfire. I ran from place to place helping my friends and then rushing back to stand my ground on my own claim.

It was while I was taking a breather that I saw Gisborne. He had come back, unable to resist this new strike. He had been engaged in fighting a sailor and had laid the man low: he put the boot in.

"Gisborne," I yelled.

We hurtled towards each other. I saw his fist coming for my face, ducked, and gave him one in the solar plexus. He was a powerful, hard man with fists like iron. He landed some wicked blows to the sides of my head. But I connected over and over again: he had a habit of dropping his guard just as he took a swing at you. They were the sweetest punches I ever got in. I dropped him to his knees and then I let him have the boot, right in his mouth.

The police had arrived in force. I had to leave Gisborne for a trooper was riding straight at me. When he saw that I had stopped fighting, he swerved and made for some men who were fighting and clawing in a heap.

"Well, it's over and done with," lisped Gisborne, spitting blood and teeth. He staggered over to me and held out his hand. We shook hands.

"My, that's good boys," cried a trooper, riding past.

Some semblance of order had been restored. I saw that Britt was approaching and I sat down on an overturned bucket to wait for him. The ground had been churned up during the fight. It was my lucky day. I saw a diamond lying on the surface. I picked it up. It was a small white of a quarter of a carat or so. I put it into my pocket.

There were pebbles beneath my foot. I rolled them as I watched Britt picking his way over the broken ground. I bent down and felt in the gravel. In the handful of gravel that I picked up there were two big garnets and a diamond of the first water, about two carats.

"You've been in trouble again, Mannie," Britt observed.

"You want to see Gisborne." I held out the diamond. "I've just found this," I said. "Sorry, Britt, I'm not selling. I'm starting work here tomorrow."

5

I did not find another diamond, in six months. My money evaporated for I had installed Leah in a house of her own with a servant. Labourers were hard to get at a reasonable wage although they were pouring in from all over the country; the population on the diggings swelled to something like sixty thousand; men were coming from all over the world to New Rush.

Jo remained at Old De Beers. Commission on the fancy diamonds from her claim kept me going; there was a red that brought me in seventy pounds. And Halden took up the option on the gold mine, paying me five hundred pounds. I bought in claims with this windfall.

On the claim next to these and on the one beyond, the diggers struck bonanzas. For me there were only a few splinters. As my cash dwindled, I had to do more and more of the manual work myself. There were times when I could scarcely put one foot in front of the other for tiredness as I walked home.

Leah and I lived in a two-roomed house near the store. She had got some marigolds to grow in a border at the fence and she had some parsley and herbs growing near the tank. In her neat, shabby clothes she might have been mistaken for a schoolmistress: she was wearing her hair pulled back into a tight bun beneath a shapeless black cap. She could never be still, I remember. She helped Becky Reuben in the housekeeping for Becky had not fully recovered from the birth of her son and the boy himself was a weakling. At home Leah sewed or knitted, or worked in the tiny garden; and if by chance a moment came when she had nothing to do or if she had to listen to anybody talking then her hands were constantly moving; clenching, rubbing, even pinching the flesh at her wrists. I would shout at her to be still.

Kisses from her at that time were feverish, insincere; when we made love she smelled of wine. And besides the wine, she was forever drinking concoctions to hasten pregnancy. Becky had known a miracle-worker in the Old Country who had handed on some recipes to her. Occasionally, I was made to swallow some vile brew on the pretext that it would clear the fever out of my blood; but I knew that she suspected me of sterility.

I remember one night when Leah tore herself from my

embrace and rushed away to drink a glassful of wine. When she came back to me, I felt no desire for her.

She began to sob, it was terrible to listen to her. I tried to console her.

"I must have a child," she said.

I began to fear her. To be shut in with her was to be constantly nagged. One day it would be: Let us go from this place, it's a dry arid place . . . the next, Give up your claims, I know you can get a thousand pounds for them . . .

"It's your tiredness stops us from having a child," she shrieked at me. "What's a Jew doing blistering his hands? Like your father . . . but peace on him . . ."

She was thin, almost gaunt, and at night she cried out in horror at her dreams.

6

The money ran out. We were living on credit. Now Leah had to come down to the claims and work at the sorting table for I was down in the hole every day doing pick and shovel work. She sneered at me: by then I could have demanded three hundred each for the claims.

We quarrelled bitterly and she refused to come to work. I worked alone. She used to send a Dutch child to me with a pail of dinner.

"The auntie says come home."

"Tell the auntie to voetsak."

For the first time in months I was finding a few diamonds though nothing more than a quarter of a carat. Yet the Dutchman on the claim next to mine had found diamonds to the value of thirty thousand pounds. And Stokkies Truter was driving his own trap and pair . . . he had found a diamond worth a thousand.

Leah took the attitude of not speaking to me for days on end. Exhausted after work, I would fall asleep against the blank wall of her silence. Rain brought out fever in me; I was sick for three days. On the morning that I returned to the claims, I found a diamond weighing an eighth of a carat. In a rage I threw it back and stamped it into the earth.

"What are you up to?"

Jo was standing on the rim of the crater. She was dressed in a white muslin dress and a bonnet of purple flowers. The diggers lifted their hats and cheered.

"Come up here, Mannie," she called.

The slope was hard going for me and the exertion brought on the shakes. Jo pulled me up the last few yards.

"Fever again?"

"Yes."

"I want to talk to you. But not here."

She had come in a polished carriage drawn by a pair of fine bays. She made me get in and told her Coloured driver to take us to her tent. She lived like a lady at Old De Beers in a partitioned baize-lined tent with flooring and rugs. Mrs. Halden . . . probably none of the families living round about knew anything of her past.

"I saw Leah in Reuben's store yesterday," she said. "She serves there sometimes, did you know? That time Madame Olpresci took her down to Natal, it wasn't only because of Tungay. Leah told us she detested the thought of living with the Reubens and working in the shop. Both Madame and I understood her."

"It's life."

There was a table standing in a shaft of sunlight and Jo put some white paper on this. Then from a chamois leather bag she poured out a heap of diamonds, of many colours. At a glance I estimated them to be worth fifty thousand pounds.

"Sit down," she said. "I want you to negotiate the sale for me, Mannie . . . appraise them now. We have at least two hours. Don is on the Vaal taking leave of old Tennessee Jones. They were shipmates, you know. We're going to Europe on the *Miranda* at the end of the month."

"It's a mistake to put so many diamonds on the market at the same time."

"I realize that. I've been holding them back. But the *Miranda* sails on the twenty-eighth . . . we must be on her. I want you to share in my luck else I would take them over with me and sell them on the Continent."

"You've been a good friend, Jo."

I began to list the diamonds. The first one I recognized was Pienaar's orange diamond.

"Where did you get this from, Jo?" I laid the diamond between us with the sunshine on it.

"Found it on my claim, same as the others."

"This is the stone Halden bought you with that night at the auction."

She went white. "You lying Yid. I found it on my claim."

"I know diamonds, Jo. I can tell a river stone from one found on the dry diggings. And I can tell more or less what mine a stone comes from. I know a lot about diamonds, Jo. This is the stone Halden paid for you."

"You cast-iron Jew, I'm trying to do you a favour. I need not have brought the stones to you. I was trying to help that miserable-looking wife of yours."

"Be quiet a moment."

She drank some brandy, neat from the bottle, and sat down opposite me, holding the bottle by the neck. I was ready for her if she made the slightest movement; for even before I made a tally I knew that these were Uzzell's diamonds. I thought back to the diamonds I had bought from her previously . . . they had all been in Uzzell's parcel.

Jo moved and I tensed; but she had put down the bottle. She touched the orange stone with her fingertip.

"How did you know this diamond, Mannie?"

"A Dutchman's son found it on Old De Beers. I bought it for three hundred pounds."

"You were broke after the auction and you should have had plenty of money. Leah told me how poor you were and I couldn't understand it."

I looked at her warily. The sun shining in on her burnished the down on her upper lip; her face was beautiful, kindling with some thought.

"You gave the diamond to Don. But didn't you want me for yourself anymore?"

"It wasn't possible. And afterwards Don gave me a share in his gold mine."

"You're square, both you and Don. Bonnie wasn't lucky enough to have friends . . . I knew you were square the moment I saw you walking along with Archibald. It only comes once, I think, it's like being lit from inside . . . to love somebody . . . Did you feel like that?"

"Yes, I did."

She sat there quietly, washed through and through with joy, and her flesh took on a glow as it fused with her spirit.

233

We had forgotten Leah and Halden. She reached across the table and put her hand on mine. Words came hard to her. As she struggled to express herself, the power of feeling in her swept over me; we were united like lovers. It was over in a flash.

Presently Jo said: "I took the diamonds from Tungay's body after he was dead. Don doesn't know."

"Tungay must have killed Uzzell."

"Oh yes," she said. "He led Uzzell on a wild goose chase, so he told me, first into Natal. Then he said he shook him off, doubled back and came to Alidasrust to ask me to go away with him. He thought I wouldn't be able to resist the diamonds and he showed them to me, the whole great heap of them."

"And now you tempt me with them."

"How was I to know you gave the diamond to Don? Sell them, Mannie. Who will ever know? I've got certificates to prove I found the diamonds on my claim. Sell them to separate dealers, why make one parcel of them? Tell you what, I'll give you a week to do it."

"Very well. But I can't guarantee the best price."

7

The diamonds brought in twenty thousand pounds and my commission was two thousand. I took a chance and sold them to Britt Tyzack for Southern Mining; he offered a shade better than other dealers, for his Company was buying in and was said to hold gems valued at a quarter of a million.

Once I had done it, I was uneasy for the thought of Uzzell persisted: I was sure he had been murdered and the diamonds were evidence of a sort.

One night I dreamed of Uzzell's corpse on the veldt, picked at by the vultures. I awoke sweating.

Suddenly I needed Leah.

I whispered: "Leah, are you asleep?"

"No, Mannie."

She had this habit of lying awake in the darkness.

"We're going to have a bit of money. You must get yourself a dress and bonnet. Have they got anything at the store?"

"Becky showed me some foulard. I can make it up from a pattern she has. Mannie, you haven't done anything . . . silly?"

"Do you want to start quarrelling again?"

"It was only that I saw Miri the other day and she told me that Stokkies still takes chances although he has made money honestly out of his claim."

"Well, if you want to know, I bought from Jo Halden. She let me have a parcel of diamonds from her claim."

"She deserves her luck," said Leah warmly.

"Leah, we won't stay here for long. I promise you. Let me work the claims for another month, just for mazzol. Then win or lose, I'll take you away from the diggings."

This time there was no running for wine, no tautness or clenching of teeth. It was that night, I think, that she conceived.

She gave some flowers to Jo, in a posy with a blue ribbon tied to it. Jo carried the posy when she left. I had to fight my way through the crowd that had come to wave her goodbye. They were drinking champagne and roaring out some of Jo's old songs. The members of the old company were there in force; and Madame Olpresci.

Jo reached out her hand to me and drew me alongside the coach. She held her glass of champagne to my lips: the coachman was on the box already, the crowd was singing *Auld Lang Syne*. The coach moved. I held on to Jo's fingers and ran alongside for a few paces before she was whirled from me in the enveloping cloud of dust.

I went home.

Our rooms smelled of the stew that could be kept warm for the next day which was the Sabbath. There was too a smell of fresh bread and the loaves were on the table beneath their red velvet cloth.

Leah had on a new dress, so hastily made that here and there you could see the basting threads. She had on a new cap too, prettier than those she usually wore.

When I had bathed, I carried the water outside and carefully ran it over the flower borders: I noticed that our flowers had been picked and I remembered the posy Jo had been carrying.

I felt ashamed and uneasy as I always did when Leah and Jo had anything to do with each other.

I watched the Kaffir children dancing on a roadway between the claims; all were naked except for one boy who had on a ragged shirt. One of the children was playing a reed pipe: I could hear the slight, lilting melody. Such a desolate scene it was, the dust-reddened children and the piles of debris and tailings beneath a clouded sky.

I went inside and hung the bath on its hook. Leah had been waiting to light the candles. There was a prayer on her breath, and suddenly peace in the home.

8

We worked in a frenzy: I employed an old Dutchman at five pounds a week. His name was Snyman. The Kaffirs worked well for him.

We were finding diamonds though only one or two a week. But on Road Seven, where my claims stood, every other digger was rich. I felt that my turn must come.

I grudged the time for eating and sleeping, for walking to and from the claim. I would get up in the middle of the night, to be ready for the first streaks of dawn. Leah often forced me back to bed after promising to keep watch herself. So I was never later than the second crowing of the cocks. For all that I never once beat old Snyman to it: I suspected him of sleeping on the claim.

He worked before the Kaffirs arrived, singing a chant of sweat and labour.

"Morning, Mr. Bernstein."

"At it already. I'll get here first one day, see if I don't."

Some rain had fallen during that night, I remember, just enough to pit the earth. But the dust had been laid and the claims looked tidy. At that time there was an orderly criss-crossing of numbered roads between the claims so that the debris could be carted away. The perimeter of the mine was clearly marked by black shale and basalt: the mine stretched far, over more than two hundred acres.

We were the only people to be seen for it was so early that occasionally a cock crowed. I got into the pit and began to shovel into buckets the gravel that Snyman had loosened; and I saw a shining pebble rolling over and over. I seized it and looked at it in the light of the rising sun. It was a fifty-carat diamond of the purest water.

"A big old one," I said to Snyman.

He nodded. A grin of delight split his heavy features. "I was wanting you to find something too. Here." He had plunged his hand into his pocket. He held out to me ten diamonds, all white. They were larger than the one I had picked out, ranging from one-hundred-and-six carats to ninety-four carats, I found. The old man went through his pockets systematically: he brought out more diamonds. He had found seventeen diamonds that morning.

"We'll have a drink later, hey?" he said. "No use celebrating now. Let's keep the boys at it. We needn't even let them know what we've found. At the end of the day, give them a beano. And at the end of the month, a bonus. But keep your pistol handy, mijnheer."

I put the diamonds into a tobacco bag. I acted calmly although within me there was a shuddering of excitement.

The boys came. At first I stood vigilantly on the edge of the pit but after the first sieving and sorting, I gave that up for I found another twenty diamonds. We sent for one of Solly's relatives to come and keep watch.

That day we found diamonds on all the claims; six hundred stones. At four o'clock I put the diamonds in the bottom of a bucket. Then I threw some money onto the table for the boys to buy grog and meat. Snyman I invited to drink with me at the hotel that night.

I picked up the bucket and ran to Leah. She was at the table peeling vegetables.

"Hold out your apron," I said and rattled the diamonds in the bucket.

She laughed at me, she thought I was teasing her.

I poured the diamonds into her lap. She put her hands through them and felt them before she believed in them.

Within three months I was worth fifty thousand pounds and my income was steadily rising as I invested. Yet the core of our lives was not yet wealth. We had been poor too long for that. After the first few days of elation, both Leah and I became anxious: we feared that we would die before we had had time to enjoy the money.

We lived much as before except that we had a carpet and an ice-chest, a new mattress and new clothes. But I was conscious of the money. I heard the chinking of it wherever I was.

"We are rich, Leah," I would say into the darkness when we had gone to bed; and beside me she quivered.

"If the bank should fail . . . We must take care of our health . . . I've been constipated for days . . ."

"We'll go round the world, Leah."

"Think of it, Mannie, I can buy clothes in Paris."

"You can have a diamond necklace, rings, bracelet, a tiara, earrings . . ."

"At the Opera. I understand music . . . You can study in Europe . . ."

We lay hand-in-hand like sweethearts. Once or twice we cried together because of our riches.

Presents of money we sent immediately to our relatives in Whitechapel and the Warsaw Ghetto. I who had been able to give only one pound to the synagogue building fund was able to clear the whole debt. My father's remains were brought to the cemetery.

The horn was pressed down and running over: Leah had missed twice. By the third month we were sure. Well, there was no need for her to endure the diggings: in spite of our prosperity, she still cried out at night with crude sounds of fear.

9

In this fine house of ours Mordecai our son was born, on 6th December 1874. By then Leah had regained her beauty and I no longer heard the night cries that had plagued me in Africa. So it was a new life for us, an unfolding. Leah became fanatical in her orthodoxy but I would not have had it otherwise; the boy must learn, before he could read, something of what it is to be a Jew. He was young, only three years old, and he looked for the lighting of the Sabbath candles and soon afterwards knew what the anniversary of my father's death meant to me. We have had other children in the fullness of our lives but we were easier with them: Mordecai was our glory. I was teaching him to play cricket and to box when he was a year old!

My interest in diamonds at this time was restricted to dealings in an office in Haddon Garden and to reports I received from Britt and Snyman who were managing my affairs at New Rush. I was known as an expert and offered many fine gems, even the Verdoucq diamond when the old marquis died. I was in Paris to view the diamond and one afternoon went out to the races with a colleague.

I saw Jo sitting by herself on a bench. She was wearing a dress of blue shot taffeta and a toque with a tall gold feather on it. Jo was busy. From between her breasts she pulled out a bundle of notes and tickets, she emptied her gloves of small change and gold and more tickets and even felt in her shoe for a wad of notes she had inserted there. She then began to smooth out the money and sat there feverishly counting, and sorting the tickets. I excused myself and went close to her but she did not look up.

"Jo," I said.

"Hm." She did not remember my voice.

"It's Mannie Bernstein."

She got up, scattering money and tickets, and kissed me on each cheek.

"You're beautiful," I said. I picked up her stuff.

"I haven't got any freckles."

I caught the scent of her, sharp as geraniums.

"Where's your husband?"

"Gone back to Africa. He wants to work the mine. I'm

to go back soon if . . ." She took my arm and we strolled to the railings to watch the horses going down to the start.

"What's the if, Jo?"

She looked at me sidelong. "If Uzzell hasn't turned up. He is still missing. He must be dead."

"Don't ever worry about those diamonds if he does turn up some day. I'll reimburse him. You'll be quite safe."

"Would you really do that for me?"

She turned to me and there was again that look which had ravished even Tungay.

"Leah . . ." she was saying.

"We have a son."

"What's his name?"

"Mordecai."

"Golly."

"He is like Leah, good-looking. Dark curly hair, big brown eyes . . . Well, I'll admit it. People say he looks like me." We stood there laughing.

We became lovers again. I remember an evening in spring, going up to Jo's apartment in the Rue Tronchet. I had in my pocket a present for her, a shooting star pin, designed by Drotz . . . there were tiered rows of marquise diamonds, white and yellow, and trails of baguettes flaring upwards in a crescent; the falling star was of white diamonds mined at De Beers on my claims.

One had to be careful for the concierge was greedy, a woman known to have blackmailed a French minister. I knocked on the door discreetly.

"Come in," Jo cried.

She had bathed in a tub before the fire in her bedroom and now she sat in a low easy chair, naked and with her hair down. She was sewing a buckle on her shoe. The bath tub stood in a ring of water and in a heap on the floor were some of her jewels; a diamond necklace, earrings and two rings. I examined them all. They were genuine. Sometimes Jo gambled away her diamonds and wore paste replicas for fear her creditors would close in on her if she were seen without jewels.

"You've been lucky, I notice."

"I can't go wrong," she said smugly.

"Look at this, Jo."

I opened the case. She gave a flat-lipped grin like an urchin and held the pin between the tips of her forefingers, against her shoulder.

Afterwards in the darkness we remembered that champagne bath in the tent at Dutoitspan.

"You gave me a baby that day," she said.

"Jo."

"Yes. The only time it ever happened to me. I drank laudanum. I wanted to die. That half-zebra, you remember it. I took an awful spill . . . and that was that. I got over it."

"I knew you were different, more reckless . . ."

"But I was frightened underneath it. Uzzell had turned on me. He turned on Bonnie. You remember Bonnie."

"Yes, she was the prettiest of the lot of you."

"I like that. But it's true. Uzzell picked her up at a Boer farm near the Drakensberg. He taught her low tricks within a week. She took to drink straightaway. And when her father caught up with us, it was too late. Anyhow, Uzzell said he had married her before a travelling parson. Her father pretended to believe that. Do you think he believed it? He was simple . . ."

"He had to save his face."

"I get letters from Madame Olpresci. She wrote that

Miri the Coloured girl found Bonnie in the Malay camp. Bonnie had the horrors from drink. I saw her get the horrors once. She thought things were turning into crocodiles . . . we had to tie her up in the end." There was a silence. I was beginning to fall asleep. "She gouged her own eyes out," Jo was saying. "She lives with Miri now. She was never lucky like me, I had good friends . . ."

10

Out there a great game was being played. It was to end in Rhodes and Barnato facing each other but at that time many others were sitting in. Individual diggers were being squeezed out as company after company was floated.

New Rush was now known as Kimberley. Where the kopje had stood there was a hole hundreds of feet deep; the diamondiferous stuff was brought to the surface by means of windlasses for the system of roads had long since collapsed. One of my claims had been lost; twenty Kaffirs were buried beneath the earth.

Britt Tyzack was still in the game. He had raised solid backing and the Southern Mining Company shares stood at 160s. He had a new and wider interest, in a general trading company, the Cape and Cairo Investment Company of which Lord Alvers was Chairman. Halden was on the Board; his gold mine had been swallowed up in Cape and Cairo.

I fought shy of buying Cape and Cairo. I knew that Britt

and Halden were ready to risk every penny from the diamond fields in the gold mines of the Transvaal and of those further north. Diamonds had been good to me. Gold was an unknown quantity.

Britt introduced us to his cousin Lady Beulah who had married Alvers. That was an education for Leah, a woman like Lady Beulah. She was hard and clever . . . and what a card player! I'd like to have seen her matched against Uzzell. Leah often played cards with her but she was no match for that cool brain.

The woman gained influence over Leah and I think it was because she was an absolute materialist: Leah felt safe in her orthodoxy. I was intimidated by Lady Beulah. But Leah admired the strength of her and the cold hard lines of her beauty.

We were to be used in some scheme, I was sure of that. And it was not long before Britt's letters and Lady Beulah's conversation all tended towards one subject: the desirability of my returning to Kimberley to support Britt. It went without saying that I would be appointed to the Board of Southern Mining: I would run for the Legislative Assembly. The Cape and Cairo Investment Company was dangled before me . . . after all, Lord Alvers was an old man and the Company would be needing a new Chairman . . .

I was beginning to be attracted but Leah shied away from the prospect of going back to Africa. The tactics were changed. I was given a London directorship in Southern Mining. Lady Beulah pushed us in Society. We became well-known. My philanthropies were recognized and in 1876 I was knighted. Obviously I was to be made use of in London. It suited me.

Lady Beulah took herself off to Kimberley. Our days were rich in peace.

What I remember about that time are the concerts. Leah was obsessed with music and it seems to me now that we went to a thousand concerts in a year.

It was after a concert that I came home to find Britt's letter about the Cape and Cairo shares. We had been in Buckinghamshire for a week and some clerk had brought down the post with documents that it was necessary for me to sign.

We were having tea and Leah spoke about music. She could talk with authority for she had studied since we came to England. When I listen to music, I see visions. There are times when I feel I will come face to face with something infinitely beautiful, in a solid form . . . But Leah is one to note arrangements and technique. Beside her in this matter I often felt myself to be foolish: it was as though in this she had the man's mind and I the woman's.

She moved about the room quietly, filling my cup from the samovar, slitting open my letters . . .

"There is a letter from Mr. Tyzack," she said.

She left me to read it while she went upstairs to peep at Mordecai. I still have Britt's letter. It foreshadows the realization of all his dreams; by then he knew Rhodes well and was fanatical in his adherence to him. He wrote that the annexation of the Transvaal was only a matter of time and that the Zulu war was a foregone conclusion. The Zulus were arming; on Saturday afternoons the young men paraded in Kimberley with the guns they had bought out of their pay . . . good. Let them arm. The British Government would soon be forced to take action . . . Tucked into the letter was the information that disturbed me. Britt had taken five thousand pounds of mine to invest in the Cape and Cairo Investment Company. He apologized for not getting my permission first: any delay would have meant the loss of the shares on a rising market.

When Leah came back into the room I said: "Look at this, Tyzack has put five thousand of mine into Cape and Cairos without so much as by your leave. I've got a good mind to cable him and ask what he is up to."

"Beulah says in her last letter that they are aiming at a merger between Southern Mining and Cape and Cairos. Cape and Cairos have gone up to five pounds."

"So now you are an expert on business as well as music."

"Perhaps I do talk too much," said Leah, flushing.

"Why doesn't Tyzack say something about a merger? The man has my power of attorney, what's he going to let me in for?"

"You trust him, don't you?"

"I'm not afraid that he will rob me in the vulgar sense of the word. What I'm afraid of is that I'll become their puppet, manipulated by him and Lady Alvers. This five thousand pounds . . . brazenly taken from my funds . . . might be the thin end of the wedge. I might find myself in a position where I can't even protest. He could have cabled."

"Perhaps he didn't cable because of the smallness of the amount," said Leah and we both burst out laughing.

"Five thousand pounds is a small amount?" I cried.

"I was thinking of the huge sums you deal in."

"It's the principle. Today five thousand, tomorrow fifty thousand. And he doesn't give his reasons for buying into Cape and Cairos. I've to take your word for it that there is to be a merger. Then they can say, You knew through Leah . . .

"I am going to Kimberley."

Leah was silent. I glanced across at her. She was not wearing diamonds that night but a collar and cuffs of pearls, to set off a low-cut dark red dress. This temperate climate had brought her to the flood tide of her beauty. In Africa she had been pale but here her cheeks were pink. From childhood she had been beautiful; motherhood and the glory of our wealth had touched off a spark in her.

"I'm not leaving you behind here. You will come out with me and stay in Cape Town."

"I don't want to go back to Africa."

I went round to where she sat and bent over her. Her hair with intricate patterns of curls and waves was built up high and twisted into a loop on the nape of her neck. I put my hands into it and felt the hardness of her small round skull.

"Cape Town will do Mordecai good. It's a healthy climate."

"You want to go there and fight."

"Yes. I want to fight. No man is going to do as he likes with my money."

She got up from under my hands and turned to look at me, leaning against the table.

"It is not enough then?" she said. "We always thought you would go back to studying . . . But have you ever opened a book? Are you a better Jew today? What use is money if you go on struggling?"

"Now you start to criticize."

"Please, Mannie. We have everything . . . Mordecai . . . all this here, so lovely. Must we give it up?"

"We don't give it up. It will not be for more than a year and we're back again. There are some splendid houses

248

in Cape Town. I'll build if you like. You will take your maid and nurse. Why, you'll be better off in Africa. Lady Bernstein . . . they'll fall over themselves to know you . . ."

She shivered and took up the cloak she had thrown over a chair. I helped arrange it over her shoulders and stood with my arms round her.

"It will be different in Africa this time," I said.

"Yes."

Late that night while I was still writing to Britt Tyzack, she came downstairs and stood at the window with her back to me.

"I've been lying awake thinking of New Rush . . . Kimberley. I can't get to sleep. Tell me, Mannie, what happened to that woman Jo Halden?"

"She left Africa," I said cautiously.

"I know. But didn't she ever return to Kimberley?" I did not answer. "I'll write and ask Becky Reuben. She knows everybody there."

She sat down. She was quiet for such a long time that I thought she had fallen asleep. I looked at her. She met my eyes in a long, intent stare that had something inhuman in it. Suddenly I was reminded of the way she had cried out at night years ago before Mordecai was born.

We went upstairs without touching each other. When I slipped into Mordecai's room to look at him asleep, she came in with me and picked him up and brought him into our room, to sleep in our bed.

11

In the end Leah came to Kimberley with me. We had a house standing behind trees. It had been built by the millionaire Pauw on the site of an old farmhouse. Pauw had committed suicide but not in the house . . . overseas on the Riviera. He had been a dealer in illicit diamonds and had married a Coloured woman to prevent her from giving evidence against him.

I kept this story from Leah and when she did hear it from someone or other it seemed to make no impression on her. By then I suppose she had grown used to the house. It was me whom Pauw haunted.

The house was single-storied, built with wings to enclose on two sides a courtyard where there was a fountain. The sight of this fountain playing was the wonder of all Kimberley and passersby used to stare in from the road to see the jet of water mount in a silver parabola against the sky. At first I used to like walking there in the evenings to smoke a cigar but then I grew afraid of Pauw for a while. I used to ask people about him: Britt had known him. He told me that Pauw's widow lived in poverty in the Malay camp. In his will Pauw left everything to his sisters and brothers.

Never a Coloured woman passed and looked in but I wondered if she were the widow. From Britt I knew that the Pauws had been ostracized in Kimberley and he had afterwards fallen in love with a young English girl, an earl's daughter. But he and his Coloured wife were condemned to live in this house with nobody else to see the furnishings for which he had paid thousands.

This phase passed and I forgot Pauw: the house belonged above all to Mordecai. That little rascal was to be found in the garden, the drawing room, the native quarters, wherever his fancy led him. And wherever I saw him, he was still a wonder to me, my son.

The canvas townships of the dry diggings had been largely replaced by wood-and-iron buildings. The Tickey Horse had blown over one September during the windy season and on the site there was now a bar and supper room of wood-and-iron. Madame Olpresci presided over these. All her poodles except Toto de Fropps were dead. Few of the original members of Uzzell's Entertainers were in Kimberley . . . Sweet Jasmine was there, married to a diamond millionaire and every inch a lady. And Bonnie was there, living with Miri and Stokkies in a cottage that Stokkies had bought. He had prospered to such an extent that he had fifteen of his relatives living with him as well. Miri had borne him two children, a girl and a boy.

Snyman had left the diamond mines. He saw the landslide that had killed my labourers as a warning from God. Gisborne had gone too; I was told he kept a shop in Cape Town.

The Vollantynes and their pack of dogs occupied a brick house on the outskirts of the town. The doctor himself had thickened though he was still something of an athlete; he shone at the sports days and mammoth picnics that were now the vogue. A fortune in diamonds had eluded him but he had a good practice. Not many knew about his Rush babies. Old-timers could point out the three palsied children he had dragged from their mothers' wombs on the day of the rush to Colesberg Kopje. His wife had grown stout and hectoring. Her manner to me was polite but I knew she was keeping a watchful eye on me, knowing I must make a mistake.

And the mine . . . I remember going with Britt to view it soon after our arrival in Kimberley. I was easy with Britt again since I had control of my affairs and I did not quarrel over the five thousand pounds.

At first sight the mine looked chaotic but I discerned that the claims in the centre were served by whims on an upper tier and claims on the outer edge by whims on a lower tier. Buckets of blue diamondiferous ground were being rattled constantly to the surface, to be pulverized and sorted.

Britt, shouting above the noise, pointed with his stick to the claims where Cape and Cairo had an interest, and to the Southern Mining blocks. He showed me too the slope where my claim had slid away. A deep cavity had been formed there and had filled with water.

Down in the mine, one of the foremen raised his hat to us.

Dust was everywhere, on our shoulders and hats, on our boots: I could taste grit. But even in the haze there could have been no doubting our affluence: a tattered man came running after us to beg for a job. Britt dashed off a note to the foreman down below.

My house was not far off and Britt accompanied me home. In the garden some boys were watering the plants. Plump smooth leaves shone with water. Leah had brought shrubs in tins from the Cape and already these were flowering in twenty colours; the lawns were bright green. A little smile touched Britt's lips and he pressed my arm.

We passed through the hall into the cool glitter of the drawing room. Leah and Lady Beulah were there. Leah rose to her feet and came towards us, her reflection blurring into shining boards: she was wearing a white dress.

"I'm expecting the Reubens," Leah said.

Britt and Lady Beulah exchanged glances.

"I think I shall go, Britt," Lady Beulah said.

"I'll see you home."

I realized now that Leah had come to me in distress.

"What's the matter?" I said.

"Oh, Leah will explain," said Lady Beulah, gathering up her gloves and drawing them on to her long fine hands. "It is simply that I don't want to meet Mrs. Reuben socially . . ."

"Why?"

". . . at the moment. But if it offends you, I would remain of course."

"No, don't do that. I shouldn't like them to meet you under duress."

Lady Beulah kissed Leah's cheek. She offered her hand gingerly to me.

"There is no sinister reason for my not meeting your Becky and Solly. But all in good time . . ."

When we were alone, I said to Leah: "That woman . . . what was she getting at?"

Leah was trembling a little. "Beulah explained. She doesn't object to Becky and Solly in themselves . . . you know what she is like, everybody is the same to her. But they are thinking of this amalgamation business. They will want Solly on their side eventually, I am sure. But they don't need him yet. Everything is going into the merger between Southern Diamonds and Cape and Cairos. When that is through, they'll go after Solly. They are waiting for the right moment. You know Solly is anxious to get on, in the same way as we have got on. Only he can't get into the Club and people don't call on Becky . . ."

"Was she expecting to meet Beulah today?"

"Yes. I more or less promised."

"From what I can make out, they will bribe the Reubens when they are ready to take over Solly's claims."

"Mannie, it's business."

"I hope somebody else gets at him in the meantime."

"I promised Beulah I'd watch out for that."

"You . . . Well, it's a big game you're sitting in on, Leah."

She put her hand on my arm. She was taut.

"You know you're going to be given the seat in the Legislative Assembly. Beulah said so today."

"I wouldn't mind that."

She smiled at me tenderly.

The Reubens had come. They drove up in a carriage painted black with gold and red stripes at window level. Four creamy hackney prancers completed the outfit. From this equipage I assisted Becky to descend. She was ablaze in yellow satin and diamonds. Solly carried his son Benjamin who could not walk; one of Vollantyne's Rush babies. The little girls I had known were now young madams of fourteen or so, making eyes at you without even knowing they were doing it. Becky's last baby, a girl, was being carried in by a white maid. Following all was a bull terrier pup which had been given to the crippled child by Doctor Vollantyne.

Mordecai came shouting to meet our guests. And Becky's love spilled over onto him and she took his hand and made him walk beside her; but Solly could not look at my boy.

254

Sipping brandy, he ranged the drawing room: this was the Reubens' first visit since our furniture was installed. He stroked a Kashan carpet and beckoned his wife over. She had been given Benjamin to hold and she in turn dumped him on Leah's knee . . . he was beautifully dressed in green velvet and lace. The carpet inspected, Solly put down the brandy glass and stood chewing a cigar. With thumbs hooked in the armholes of his waistcoat, he assessed item by item the cost of our furnishings.

"It must have gost you . . . lemme see . . . one tousand bounds to furnish this room."

"Solly, you're right almost to a penny," Leah cried. "Only you would never guess how the money was spent. I bet I catch you on that. The curtains for instance cost more than that chair."

"I don't belief it."

"It's true. The chair we bought on a sale. The curtains are new. I got them made in London, the agent sent the measurements over as soon as we bought the house. They cost one-hundred-and-three pounds landed."

Solly approached the curtains, stared at them respectfully and then picked up a corner. Becky, the child in her arms again, came to look too.

"Vhy so dear?" she asked.

"It's a special stuff. But I do ask myself why they were so dear. What have the makers done? . . . put a few tucks here and there . . . it looks simple. Mind you. I have them only in this room," Leah added apologetically. "I tried for the same effect in the dining room but I had the curtains made here. Come and look, it's not the same."

We all trooped into the dining room.

"No, it's not the same," said Becky.

"You should haf had the lot made in Lunnon. Nu, for vhy you saf money now, Leah?" cried Solly and dealt me a blow in the ribs: the brandy and cigar had mellowed him.

"It's a habit," said Leah gaily.

On our return to the drawing room, we found the puppy sniffing at the expensive curtains.

"Oh, be careful," cried Leah. "Mind he doesn't wet them."

"It's a she, not to vorry," said Becky.

Now Solly must needs recite *The Peeing Pup*. Mordecai listened carefully; he had been good all afternoon. Lines sprang up on either side of Leah's mouth.

"Don't say that in front of Mordecai," said Leah. "Please. He's so quick he picks a thing up after hearing it only once and he will be saying it in front of our visitors."

Solly was annoyed. "Vot harm if he does? But it's the grand vons you vorry about, the lords and ladies. Vhere are they? I don't see them. Do you see any lords and ladies, Becky?"

"Lady Beulah . . . she was here earlier but she couldn't stay," said Leah, ashamed. "I wanted you to meet her."

"Like hell," said Solly.

"Papa! Brandy alvice makes him gross," said Becky. "Better ve're goink now. I vos enchoyink myself." She sent her maid round the room to pick up a toy and a handkerchief and to wipe up a puddle the baby had made. The girls got up obediently at a nod from her and followed her out. Solly stumped along with Benjamin in his arms.

"Imborted gurtains yet," he said, and with a malevolent glance at me: "And ve haf artists from Paris too. There are bosters for Diamond Jo in the town . . ."

He made me feel I had no right to my luck. I put my arm round Leah and called Mordecai to me. Suddenly I was afraid of an accident.

12

The posters Solly had been talking about were to announce Jo's arrival in Kimberley: COMING NOVEMBER THE ONE AND ONLY DIAMOND JO . . . I saw them plastered onto corrugated iron fences and on frames attached to light poles. The posters had been put up as a joke by Miri: it was Bonnie's idea. Halden had them all torn down again. He had taken a house for Jo on Bonanza Road. It was a large red-brick suburban house and furnished with good solid Cape furniture. Miri took me in there while Halden was in Cape Town where he had gone to meet Jo.

I looked round the place and tried to think of Jo moving through the rooms, a respectable matron. Miri must have been thinking on the same lines for she said: "Can you see the nonna Jo here?"

We had entered a bedroom curtained with dark blue velvet. Sunlight was pouring into the room. Bonnie was asleep on the bed. Compassionately, Miri drew across Bonnie's face a chiffon veil that had slipped off but not before I had a glimpse of shrivelled eyelids and pockmarks.

I retreated to the front door.

"You shouldn't have brought her here," I said to Miri.

"She wanted to feel nonna Jo's furniture so I got the key from the caretaker, old Norris, and brought her here. There's not much she can have as a treat these days. She and the nonna were friends . . ."

"I suppose the nonna Jo will live like an ordinary married person now," I said.

Miri looked unblinkingly at me. "Basie means she won't want to know my nonnie anymore? I think you are wrong. You wait and see, she'll be kind like she always was. People don't change, basie."

Miri was right. Any hope Halden might have entertained that Kimberley would accept Jo was blighted by her loving kindness to Bonnie. She took Bonnie to live with her. And who can blame her? . . . they had been friends.

But I think that without Bonnie she might have settled down; there were many women in Kimberley who had lived fast lives but were now respectably married. They were accepted in that rough-and-ready mining community.

Jo made a real effort for Halden's sake. She swore off gambling at first.

Bonnie was lewd, an obscenity in our midst. It was felt that she should be banished where decent people could not see her. If she knew that Jo had visitors she would stumble into the room and do a travesty of a dance; it was vile among married people bringing up families. Jo looked on with horror and pity; nothing was too much to do for Bonnie. Bonnie might have killed herself one night while she was drunk. She fell down the mine and broke her arm. After that Jo was always with her, to make sure that she kept sober: she rationed Bonnie's drink. She marked cards so that Bonnie could play, she took Bonnie for drives and picnics, read the newspaper to her . . . Often when you passed the house you heard Jo singing the old songs: *The Alabama, The City of Diamonds, A Diggers' Lament* . . .

Halden was away in the Transvaal. He was making a report for the compiling of prospectuses for companies

258

which Britt was floating. Jo must have been lonely for she began to gamble again. Leah had called on her once or twice but she did not come to us.

She and I seldom met. I was a candidate for the Legislative Assembly and my time went in electioneering. The times were exhilarating for the Transvaal had been annexed and the development of the gold mines was in sight. I was caught up in the great events that were shaping. Britt had offered me the next vacancy on the Board of the Cape and Cairo Investment Company which was committed to financing gold mines at Barberton. It was an honour, for this Company was to be the vehicle for consolidating trading throughout the continent.

13

Jo asked me to come and see her. I had been at a dinner and an election meeting and it was after one in the morning when I received the note from the hall porter: Miri had given it to him soon after I went in to dinner. I read the note with a sense of foreboding.

Bonanza Road lay only a few hundred yards off and I walked there. The lights were still on. Miri answered my knock.

"The nonna has gone out," she said. "I'm here looking after the poor little nonnie. But nonna Jo wanted to see you. She was so anxious she nearly went mad. She said you must wait."

"Isn't baas Halden here then?"

"No. He is at the gold mine."

I waited outside in the moonlight. It was nearly dawn when Jo came home. She came in a cab and when she got out, she took the diamond clip from her hair to pay the driver.

"Mannie. You did come. I thought you weren't coming."

"The porter didn't give me the note until after the meeting."

"I see. I might have known you wouldn't let me down."

She took my arm and walked a little way along the road with me. We sat on the low stone wall surrounding the house. From here we could see into the mine. The claims were cut out in squares and oblongs far below, or towering like columns in a ruin, with long ladders at their sides for the diggers to reach their crazy height. Buckets and cradles caught the radiance of the moonlight and overhead were the bright humming wires of the windlasses.

Jo said: "Uzzell is alive."

"Is it money you need, for the diamonds? Where is he?"

"In jail, in Mozambique. The police were making enquiries, it's just a whisper. Madame Olpresci told me. They'll soon come round to me, I suppose."

"Well, I'll stand by you, Jo. I'll make the diamonds good."

"Find out what's going on if you can."

"Yes, I will. It shouldn't be hard."

The moonlight was fading into the rising sun. A window in the corner house was thrown open. A Dutch girl was nursemaid there, a big placid thing with corn-coloured hair.

"Good morning," Jo said.

The girl smiled, looking at Jo's diamonds. Jo grinned back. She wore a low-cut bodice. Her breasts gleamed white, a field of lilies to run wild in.

"Hey, you there," she cried, "have you been behaving yourself?"

The girl laughed aloud. A hand plucked her away and the blind came down with a snap.

Some diggers on their way to the mine smiled to see Jo in the sunlight and me beside her still dressed for the evening.

"You'll get a bad name and you can't afford it," she said. She stood up. "I felt afraid when you didn't come, Mannie. I went and gambled. It rests me. Some people drink." She smiled wryly. "Promise you won't tell anybody about the diamonds. That's the important thing. Never let anybody know I took them."

"Why should I? We might have to reimburse Uzzell."

"No. Give me your promise."

"Very well."

"I trust you, Mannie. But last night I was afraid. I thought, If they come for me I'll kill myself. But I'm not afraid anymore.

"Perhaps I'll go back to France . . . Let me know if you hear anything."

That evening while Leah was at the theatre I called on Britt to sound him out on the subject of Uzzell: little happened in Kimberley that he did not hear of. He lived in his office where he had a truckle bed and washstand behind a partition. I found him washing the dust off his feet. He was sitting with his trousers rolled up and his feet in a basinful of hot soapy water. He was sipping brandy.

"Help yourself to a drink. Why aren't you at the theatre? They'd expect to see you there."

"Leah went. She is with a party. I'm to call for her after the performance. I've got the carriage outside."

Britt dried his feet and drew on a pair of socks. "Dinda," he roared. A Kaffir in skins crept in and removed the basin.

"The way you live," I commented.

He laughed. "I've got used to roughing it. As long as the brandy is drinkable. And there is always the Club to fall back on for a civilized meal."

"Have you heard that Uzzell is alive?"

"Yes." Dinda had brought in a stew of venison and onions. Britt said: "Have some? No? You don't mind if I eat . . . haven't had a bite since five this morning. You're doing well, you'll get in, you know . . ." He began to wolf the stew.

"What did you hear about Uzzell?"

"The consul is making enquiries from Portuguese East Africa, very discreet as yet. Uzzell got caught gun-running, that seems to be definite . . . Look here, I want you to have a look at this report. Halden got in today. He's been in Barberton."

Britt kept me until eleven and I had to tell the driver to gallop the horses to the theatre. I saw at once that something unusual had happened: people were standing about in excited groups. Lord Alvers hurried up to me as I got out of the carriage.

"Damme, Bernstein, I can't understand a thing like this happening. Let's get your wife into the carriage as quickly as possible. Some prostitute slapped her face."

Leah had been standing out of sight round the corner of the building. Lady Beulah hurried her along now and I ran to meet her. She had her cloak drawn up to her face.

"Thank you, thank you," she said to Lady Beulah.

"Shall I come with you? We have such a long drive out and it is late . . ."

"Please, no."

"Have a good stiff brandy like a sensible girl," said Lord Alvers, "the moment you get home. Nothing like a good stiff brandy. And believe me, we'll catch whoever is responsible . . ."

"Let the girl go," snapped Lady Beulah. She patted Leah's hand but I detected a wariness in her manner. "I'll try and stop the fuss. I know how you feel, my dear."

We drove away quickly. Leah sat without saying a word. Once a campfire momentarily illumined the interior of the carriage and I saw her face; she was afraid.

I said gently: "Leah, who did it?"

"I don't know."

"It must have been a Jew-hater. Or a prostitute, they get vicious."

"I suppose so."

14

We lay side by side in the fourposter, her head on my shoulder. A shaft of moonlight fell through the long windows.

"She must have been jealous," I said to Leah. "You looked lovely tonight."

"They clapped me when I came in . . . That vieux rose was always my best colour."

She got out of bed and crossed the room into the moon-light. She opened the french windows: the night was hot. A bat flew in.

"Brr . . . ugh . . ." She covered her hair with her hands and raced for the bed and dived under the pillows. We were laughing as I chased the bat out and closed the windows again.

I drew her close. She gave herself to me with a calculation that left me restless and suspicious; it was as though she lay in the embrace of a stranger whom she was anxious to please.

I awoke long before dawn with a plunge of the heart. The room was filled with moonlight now. I thought of Jo lying next to Halden. I turned restlessly and faced Leah. She was awake, staring at the ceiling from the black pools of her eyes. I watched her. She lay still. I might as well not be here, I thought. But she turned her head suddenly and spoke to me.

"Mannie, look after me."

"Haven't you slept at all?"

"No."

I held her in my arms until she slept. I watched the moonlight give way to a clear dawn. In her sleep Leah was crying out with a terrible sound.

Then I slept, far into the morning. When I awoke Leah was not with me. Mordecai was prizing my eyelids open.

I had my breakfast with him sitting on my knee. The maid told me that Leah had gone out: I remembered that she was to attend a luncheon and sewing bee at Mrs. Vollantyne's house, in aid of hospital funds. I was free until that evening when I would have to address the Diggers' Committee at Klipdrift. I need not set out until four o'clock. Mordecai and I went to the stables, to look at the

264

racehorse Lelie that I had bought during the week; and then we played cricket.

Afterwards he fell asleep in my arms and I gave him to his nurse to put to bed. I strolled over to Jo's place. Miri and Bonnie were in the road outside.

Miri said: "Something is happening in the house. Nonna Jo is like a mad woman. The nonna Leah was there. She was saying nonna Jo smacked her face. Wah, they quarrelled. I should be at home looking after my own but nonna Jo asked me to stay on last night. And lucky I did. My poor girl gets frightened of so much noise and fighting . . . in the dark. Foei tog."

"But where is baas Halden?"

"Gone off on business."

I hurried into the house. A frightened maid crouched on the stoep. The other servants had fled: I walked through the rooms without encountering anybody. I was guided to Jo by the sound of a crash.

Leah was not there. Jo was in the bedroom. On the beds, on chairs and on tables were billowing gowns, shoes, hats, jewels. As I came in Jo was lifting an alabaster lamp; she let it go with a crash.

"I'm packing," she said.

"Miri told me Leah had been here."

"Leah?" Jo sat on top of a heap of silks and velvet piled on the bed. "Why would Leah come here?"

"I don't know. Why should you slap Leah's face?"

"Me slap Leah's face? Did Miri tell you that?"

"Yes."

"She's a bigger liar than Tom Pepper. Leah did call in, all dressed up. She was on her way to the luncheon at Ma Vollantyne's."

Jo was in a wrapper of white lace that I remembered

from Paris. Her hair had been loosened from its night plait but had not yet been bound up; it hung to her waist in shining coils. I came close to her and touched it. She pulled me down to sit next to her and began to wrestle with me like some great hobbledehoy of a girl. Then she pushed me from her.

"No, Leah came about some sewing I'd promised. She told me about somebody slapping her face. Miri got it all wrong."

"Are you leaving soon?"

"Yes. Halden's making arrangements for a Cape cart. We'll travel fast. But dammit, Mannie, I wanted to stay. Our whole life is here. God knows what will happen to me or to poor old Bonnie . . ."

When I last saw Jo that afternoon she was picking up a glass bell clock and hurling it at the wall.

15

I made no speech that night. As I was riding to Klipdrift I was overtaken by one of our stablehands who was up on the racehorse Lelie. My thoughts were immediately for Mordecai.

"Is it my son?" I said to the boy.

"No, baas, nothing serious. Only a letter." He gave me the letter. "Lelie can go like the devil, basie. Man, if he doesn't win in a month's time . . ." He chatted on as I read the note.

It was from Britt: "Come at once to Halden's place. Hurry."

I sent the boy on to Klipdrift with a message and rode Lelie back to Kimberley. It was dark when I galloped onto Bonanza Road.

Leah was in Jo's drawing room. Britt had placed his chair so that he sat between her and the other people present: she was sitting upright but had her face hidden by a hand held across her eyes. In the room were Jo, Halden and a stranger; and Proctor, the chief of police.

"Your wife sent for me," said Britt. "Shall I remain?"

"Of course."

"We won't beat about the bush, Mannie," said Proctor. "Here's the trouble. You remember Tungay . . . Mrs. Halden in June 1871 described his death by apoplexy to any number of people. Now we find that Tungay did not die of natural causes. He was murdered, stabbed in the back.

"I think Mr. de Villiers had better sum up for you. This is Mr. de Villiers, a magistrate from the Alidasrust district."

The Dutchman was a small, lively fellow with the air of one anxious to please. He got up and shook hands. His English was good.

"I've come on an unpleasant duty, Sir Emmanuel . . ."

"Sit down, Mannie," said Jo. "That is, if I can ask somebody to sit down in my own house."

"That attitude will get you nowhere, Mrs. . . . ah . . . Halden," said Proctor; there was a hint of brutality in his voice.

"Watch yourself, Proctor," Halden said passionately. Britt vacated his chair for me but drew up another so that we sat side by side in front of Leah.

De Villiers was saying: "On the thirtieth of June 1871,

Uzzell appeared in the Alidasrust district . . . poking about, looking at stones . . . you know how it is with prospectors. Van der Spuyt, a farmer there, reported him . . . he thought the man was prospecting and that was breaking the law according to him . . . Van der Spuyt is a bit of a fanatic . . ." De Villiers smiled, the man of the world. "There is no law that says a man may not look at stones . . . To get a conviction we should have to prove that the man was prospecting without a license and I myself have always been one for opening up the country . . . but we must not digress into politics. Van der Spuyt had a Kaffir watching Uzzell. Uzzell had consulted a witch doctor and as a result he found and entered a shaft that had been dug by Mr. Halden here while he was mining on Beneke's farm. The Kaffir sent for van der Spuyt.

"Uzzell wasn't after gold, he was after diamonds which he thought would be in his employee's pocket . . . Tungay was the man's name. So Uzzell said. But there were no diamonds on the body and none in Uzzell's possession. I took Uzzell for a murderer. I've seen it before, a man returning to the scene of the crime, and I thought he wanted to get back his knife . . . I had him arrested.

"It happened that we had arrested ten freebooters caught gun-running. The lot were under guard awaiting trial. They got away, wounding two of the guards, and crossed into Portuguese East Africa with a commando on their heels. From Portuguese East we heard that they had started trading in guns with the Zulus. We lost track of them. But this year an appeal was made to the British consul in Lourenço Marques by Uzzell who is a convict in a penal settlement. He had been arrested by the Portuguese in August 1871 but was not charged until two years later. By then all his comrades had been killed or had disappeared. He claims that he was forced to go along with the freebooters and intended to escape at the first opportunity. His appeals to his consul were not passed on until a few months ago. The consul ordered an investigation into Uzzell. That investigation eventually led to me." He laid a bowie knife on the table.

"Biddy," said Jo. "You remember, Mannie."

"I still had this knife in my possession," de Villiers went on. "It was found in Tungay's corpse, in the back. As the lady remarks, it has Biddy carved on it.

"Colonel Proctor asked me to come here tonight and interview this lady, Mrs. Halden. He wants, as I do, to prevent a scandal if possible."

"Uzzell made a statement to the consul," said Proctor. "It came into my hands only this afternoon though there had been some enquiries last week about Uzzell. Uzzell claims that Tungay stole a parcel of diamonds from him and he had been after him for weeks . . . Tungay had headed for Natal but had doubled back into the Transvaal.

"It is obvious to all of us here that Uzzell could not have murdered Tungay. We have Mrs. Halden's description on record. I have already sent in a report to the consul in Lourenço Marques and he will no doubt work for Uzzell's release."

Jo said: "You know that is my knife, Mannie. But I didn't kill him. Leah killed him with my knife. He had attacked me . . ."

Bruce Proctor said harshly: "Lady Bernstein denies this. And I've pointed out to Mrs. Halden that Lady Bernstein must have been fully aware of her reputation, as I am. Mrs. Halden had been friendly with Tungay for years . . . She is trying now to say that she fought Tungay off and her screams brought Lady Bernstein to her aid. Yet we know from other sources that Tungay has been an admirer of hers for years."

"Tell him, Mannie," Jo cried. "Tell him how I hated Tungay."

"It is true," I said. "She stabbed Tungay once. Doctor Vollantyne attended him and will remember. Jo would have resisted Tungay. That part is true, Bruce . . ."

"Then you think that Lady Bernstein stabbed him, in spite of her denials?"

"Of course I believe my wife. I was simply stating that Mrs. Halden would have resisted Tungay."

"I did not kill him," said Leah, taking her hand from her face. "She must have murdered him to get the diamonds. I did not know that he had diamonds on him until Mr. de Villiers told us."

"You bitch you . . . You lying bitch . . ." Jo yelled and sprang across the room with fists clenched. We stood up to protect Leah. "You dirty, lying bitch. All right, I'll tell the truth now. I killed Tungay. Yes. But not for the diamonds. I killed him because of her." She pointed at Leah. "He raped her. That's the truth of it. I stabbed him in the back while he was raping her."

"I'll kill you, Jo," I said.

"For trying to save her? She behaved like a fool with Tungay. She knew what he was like but she wouldn't take proper care. Ask her husband, Proctor, ask him how I kept Tungay from her once before . . . Madame Olpresci knows. She will tell you when she is sober. I got Tungay to come with me while Madame took her to Natal."

"That's true, Madame Olpresci did take Lady Bernstein to Natal," said Britt.

"I sent for Madame but she is drunk," said Jo. "What I

270

am telling you now is true. The boys had taken the oxen to water. Mannie was delirious. We thought he was going to die that day.

"Tungay caught Leah. He told her that he would show her a shrub on the veldt that would cure fever. And she went away from the house alone with him. I was looking after Mannie and she was supposed to be resting.

"It was still in sight of the house, near that old shaft in broad daylight. I heard her crying and I ran to help her. I got there too late to stop him and I stuck my knife in his back while he was helpless.

"We got a piece of canvas and some skins and sewed him in. By the time the boys came back, the knife in his back was hidden and they saw no blood. I told two of them to dig a grave and we trekked that afternoon. But they must have thrown him into the shaft as soon as my back was turned. It was no use sacking any of the boys, they were all from the diggings, so when we got here I told everybody he dropped dead from apoplexy.

"You tell them, Lady bloody Bernstein, you tell them the truth."

Leah had hidden her face again. "It isn't true. You told me he died of apoplexy. I did not see his body."

I said: "Gentlemen, you must believe my wife. Tungay was killed for those diamonds he stole from Uzzell. I bought the diamonds from Mrs. Halden. I have the whole transaction recorded. She told me the diamonds came from her claim and I recognized them only in the final stages of the deal. Britt Tyzack and other dealers can identify part of the collection . . ."

"Give me a list, Mannie, and we'll compare it with a list by Uzzell, that's the simplest way out of it," said Proctor.

I heard Jo say: "Don, give me some brandy," and she

271

went back to her chair and sat down. We were all quiet. She drew in her breath sobbingly as though she were crying without tears.

"You got her on the raw there," whispered Proctor jubilantly. I knew him well, a fine slow bowler. We were due to play in the same team against the River Diggers at the end of the month: he and I had often sparred together in the early days. I saw now for the first time the touch of brutality in his good-humoured face.

He said: "We are to assume that Mrs. . . . ah . . . Halden . . ."

Halden said: "Look here, Proctor, she is not Mrs. . . . ah . . . Halden. She is Mrs. Halden and we are legally married. So watch it."

Proctor smiled indulgently. "We are to assume that Mrs. Halden took the diamonds off Tungay's body. There is just one question I want to ask you, Mannie. When you discovered that the diamonds were Uzzell's, why did you not hand Mrs. Halden over?"

"She told me that she had won them from Uzzell at cards," I improvised.

"And you never suspected until now that she had killed Tungay to get the diamonds?" Halden asked sneeringly.

"Did you, Halden?" Bruce Proctor asked.

Halden stood up. "I knew that Tungay's body had been found with a knife in the back and that Uzzell had been arrested for murder. When Tungay died, I was hunting elephant. I received a note by runner from my wife telling me she was taking Bernstein to a doctor on the diggings. I bypassed Alidasrust and took a short cut to the diggings to sell my ivory. My wife then told me how Tungay died. Some months later when I was at the mine, I heard from van der Spuyt that Uzzell had been arrested and had escaped. I returned at once to the diggings and we left Africa . . ."

"You mean you were anxious to get away with the diamonds," Proctor snapped.

"Steady on," said Britt.

"Don did not know about the diamonds until this evening," said Jo. "Only Mannie Bernstein and I knew. Don always thought I found the diamonds on my claim."

"I was in a difficult position," I said to Proctor. "I had already bought some of Uzzell's diamonds . . ."

"It was that orange diamond he recognized," Jo muttered.

"That one . . . I know it too," said Halden. "It is the diamond I bought my wife with, Proctor. Afterwards she lost it playing cards with Uzzell."

"Ah, you swines," said Jo. "Tell them everything."

"So you can identify this orange diamond?" Proctor asked Halden.

"Yes. I had it from Mannie Bernstein," he drawled. Coolly and appraisingly, he looked across at Leah. He leaned forward so that he addressed her directly. "On the night that my wife offered herself for sale on a bar counter, Tungay made the highest bid for her. Both Mannie Bernstein and I knew that she hated Tungay. Mannie gave me the orange diamond to save her from Tungay. He couldn't bid for her himself, you see, because he is married."

Proctor said: "It's a rotten business but we have no way out. I shall have to get a warrant for Mrs. Halden's arrest. Please remain here with Mrs. Halden, Mr. de Villiers. You others may leave."

When he had gone, Halden spoke to Leah again: "Lady

Bernstein, you believe me? You believe that Mannie gave me that diamond to save Jo from Tungay?"

"Yes. If you are trying to say . . . he must have loved her . . . I believe that too . . . for I went without, I went cold that winter."

"Leah," I said.

Halden silenced me with a stern and terrible look. "Go on, Lady Bernstein."

"There's nothing more to say."

Halden said: "Then you've lied, Jo. You've lied. Jo, tell the truth. What really happened? Tell the truth and we can help you." He spoke to her as if they were alone.

Jo stood there considering. The room at first was still but suddenly there invaded it a thin sound; Bonnie's nails on the door as it turned out . . . Halden got up and opened the door.

"Jo?" Bonnie said, standing feeling the air round her.

"I'm here, Bonnie."

"It's time for my drink. You've damn well forgotten my drink."

"I'll get it for you. There are people here now, dearie . . ."

"Why didn't you tell me? Are you trying to make a monkey out of me?" I sprang before Leah as Bonnie lifted her skirt above her naked thighs and stumbled into the room. "Look then if you want to, you bastards, have a good look."

"Here's your brandy," said Jo.

Bonnie took the bottle which had a few inches of brandy in it. She shook it next to her ear. "I thought you were going to go off without giving it to me."

"You've been listening at the door. You knew there were people here, Bonnie."

"I heard. Jesus, you stuck a knife in Tungay. You get yourself a good lawyer, Jo."

Miri came in. "Now, nonnie. She got away from me . . ."

Bonnie suddenly began to whimper. "What about my game of cards?"

"Don't cry. I'll come and play with you for a while. Miri will have to learn how to mark the cards. Bonnie depends on a game of cards in the evening," Jo said, looking round the room.

Bonnie said: "I don't cry. I can't. Something happened to my tears . . ."

She went out with Jo and Miri. The small sounds of their going scratched against the silence.

"She has pricked holes in the cards so that Bonnie can read them," said Halden.

16

At home, Leah would not go to the bedroom to lie down. She sat in my study. She was icy cold although it was a warm evening. I lit a fire. I rubbed her hands and brought her mulled wine.

"Drink."

She took the wine.

She said: "I don't think she fully understood what Halden tried to do for her when he told me about the orange diamond. She was confused. She thought he had turned against her. But he did it to test me."

"He certainly didn't believe her lies in the end."

"That diamond . . ." She began to walk about the room, touching ornaments and smoothing fabrics. "When did you give it to her?"

"I gave it to Halden, not her. He paid me for it with a half-share in his mine."

"It must have been just before they flogged you." Her voice took on a wailing tone. "We were poor then, Mannie. I had to sell my clothes for firewood. There was your mother's ring . . . And you had given her that diamond. Remember the red flannel shirt I wore. And that policewoman searched me, she scraped at me and I don't know if the man wasn't watching. And it wasn't necessary, all that suffering. You gave her our diamond."

"She had often helped me. She used to lend me money when I needed it."

"You saved her from Tungay. You loved her, you still love her."

"Leah . . . Please don't . . . You are tearing us to pieces . . ."

"She isn't a whore to you, nor to Halden. You both see more in her than that." She stood with her arms on the mantelpiece, her back to me.

"I'll tell you the truth. I have loved her. Men love in different ways."

"What did you love her for? She isn't better-looking than me. I wasn't cold . . ."

"My dear, my dear."

"Perhaps she was more generous. Yes. That was it. She doesn't seem to think of herself. I suppose she is like that when she makes love."

"You must not do this, Leah."

"She didn't lie tonight," said Leah.

276

"What are you saying?"

"That Tungay raped me."

I took her by the shoulders and swung her round. In that first fury I would have choked the life from her but in an access of terror she screamed once piercingly and I heard the watchman coming; at the other end of the house, Mordecai began to whimper.

I went outside to tell the watchman that it was nothing, the missus had seen a spider. Leah had gone to the nursery.

I walked about outside in the moonlight. My mind had become acute. I could easily believe that Tungay had raped her. I remembered the changes in her after that journey to the north. I remembered how she had submitted to me with clenched teeth, wanting a child; no: needing a child to restore her . . . a finger of pity touched me.

I found her sitting like a stranger in the hall.

"Why did you never tell me?" I said.

"She and I decided that it would only hurt you. I always thought she did it partly for your sake: I believed she loved you. I didn't know about the diamonds.

"Last night she called me as I came out of the theatre and I followed her to the side of the building. Then she told me that people were making enquiries and she said she had taken the diamonds from Tungay's body. If Uzzell accused her of stealing them at any time and if there was any question about the way Tungay died, then I must say I killed him. I said: I will never brand my son like that, that he should think his mother a murderess. As soon as she told me, I knew she had killed him not for your sake or mine but for the diamonds. I said that to her and she hit me. I was frightened.

"But I went to see her this morning. She had already

decided that she would make a bolt for it. She realized, you see, that now the Transvaal is under British rule, she could be arrested here. I said to her that if she were caught I'd stand by her and say I killed Tungay to save her. But I did not mean to do that. I wasn't going to ruin our lives for a murderess and a thief. But what I hoped for was that she would go and we would be free of her."

I said: "Halden is clever. He played a trump card. He knew you must crack if he told you about that orange diamond."

"I should have kept this to myself. But I can't face it alone, Mannie. Wait . . . is that Mordecai crying?"

We listened. All was quiet. The town was still for a few moments. Then some dogs barked, on and on: a donkey brayed.

"I'll make tea," said Leah.

I followed her to the dining room where the samovar was.

"They will hang her," I said.

"She did kill him. She did take the diamonds."

"Yes."

"You think she did it for your sake because of what he was doing to me?" She put the table between us as though to defend herself.

"I know her. Most likely she did it for your sake. She hated Tungay. She wouldn't let him touch her, she would understand your feelings . . ."

"Diamond Jo they call her. She loves diamonds. She sold herself for the orange diamond. You know her. But I know her too. She killed him to get those diamonds."

"That is what a jury will say."

"What are you asking me to do?" she whispered. "Must I tell them what happened? Must I say it out loud in front of everybody . . . and Mordecai know . . . Why should I profane the name?"

She had turned her back, facing the wall. Now she swung round fearlessly.

"I know she killed him for the diamonds. But you will see me disgraced because you love her."

"Leah . . . wife . . ."

"*She* is your wife. You saved her from Tungay, not me.

"For my part I will not tell. I will deny it with my last breath. Because she is using me, using an accident that happened to me, to save her own life.

"I did trust him but only because he loved her. He seemed to me no more than a faithful dog at that time. He was her slave, he was tender. He would work for her and sit and watch her face." Her voice rose to a scream: "How was I to know that he was dangerous? He only spoke to me once, to tell me about the shrub . . .

"I am a woman. I know her. What does it matter to her that Tungay raped me? Nothing. That's a thing could be forgotten, wiped out. Even I have wiped it out, it's nothing to me personally . . . I was forced. Oh, I've heard women talk and they were decent married women, not dance-hall prostitutes . . . and they wouldn't kill for another woman's sake or even their own. So why should she care, a girl like her, a prostitute?"

17

Later that night we were once again sitting in the study, the samovar still yielding tea: Leah would glide away to refill our cups.

She said: "You want me to tell them?"

"No."

"I will do as you say."

"Are you being vindictive, to make me choose?" I cried.

"You are the man." Her gown was stained with earth for we had walked and walked in the garden. There was blood on her wrist where her nails had scored the flesh. Now she sat, calm again, and leaned her chin on her hand. "I have thought it out. I have never been one to ask: Why does a person do this or that? With me it has always been the act that counts. Your father, peace on him, used to say that it was wrong to unravel a kind act and look for a motive.

"So I must believe she killed Tungay to save me from him. And if you want it, I shall tell that to the court."

She sat still, hour after hour. I forgot her presence.

I was in hell. I decided one way and then the other, a thousand times that night.

It seemed to me that Leah's evidence would be disbelieved now and even if it was believed, Jo would be imprisoned for stealing the diamonds. I should have held my tongue. It would be useless to speak out now: I had betrayed Jo beyond all remedying.

Now if we spoke, could I not be accused too and even Leah dragged in as an accomplice? I thought of the disgrace to Leah's body and to my manhood; of our son who must some day know . . . poor chaste Leah; of my ruination in business and politics . . . I would not survive this scandal.

Trifles weighed with me: Mrs. Vollantyne's justification; Lady Beulah's friendship for Leah . . . she would drop Leah; and Britt . . . he had suffered a broken head for Leah, he had treated her always as if she were a great lady; Solly Reuben . . . he had not Becky's vast compassion and would he not feel perhaps one flash of triumph when he heard of Leah's fall?

I thought of Jo. It was true what Leah had said. I loved Jo. They would hang her.

A deep anger against her burned in me. She was a fool . . . worse, a sort of animal, trusting like an animal. Does a beast on the veldt that has been hand-reared by the farmer's wife know that it is destined for slaughter? Men must eat. The fool she was to have trusted me. She could have covered her tracks by selling to a dozen different buyers or taken the diamonds overseas; but Leah and I had to be helped. And she must kill Tungay, the one human being who loved her without question.

I washed and prayed; it was another day although sunrise was an hour off.

Leah had gone to the bedroom. I found her lying beside Mordecai. She had been writing, page after page; but she had destroyed most of what she had written. There were torn pages on the floor and ashes crisp in the grate.

I spoke without knowing what I would say: "We are

thinking on the same lines. Have you written down what happened? I will take it to Britt and he can let Proctor have it as soon as we are safely away. You get ready. Pack what you can. We'll go at once . . .

"But you will say I chose her."

"It is so but I will not say it."

"If Mordecai has to know, he will realize that it was harder for us to speak than to keep silence."

"I thought of that."

I read through the brief account that she had written, put the page into an envelope and addressed it to Britt.

I went to the stables and saddled a horse but as I led him out, I saw Britt riding through the gateway. He came up to me and leaned from the saddle.

"I knew you would be anxious and I came to tell you: they got away. It appears that Halden had his Flemish stallions inspanned and waiting at Stokkies's place soon after Proctor and the magistrate arrived; he used Miri as the go-between, I suppose. I should think he will make for the Portuguese East coast, they'll get a ship or a dhow there. You are rid of her at last, Mannie."

Leah . . . there was no need now to tell the truth. But that was not my first thought. I thought of Jo with Halden, looking to him for what she might have found in me.

"I wish I could have spoken to her just once more," I cried.

I mounted and rode beside Britt for I had no inclination to go into the house. Dawn and the moonlight were again in the sky: the town beneath emerged shining. There were splashes of darkness against the light, made by vultures. They did not settle but drifted on still wings above the town and the crater until somebody fired a shot at them. Then they were gone, mysteriously.

282